Dead Drop

D.A. Brown

This is a **work of fiction**. Names, characters, businesses, places, events and incidents are either the products of the author's imagination or used in a fictitious manner. Any resemblance to actual persons, living or dead, or actual events is purely coincidental.

ISBN-13: 978-0-9985995-0-2

For Deborah Brooks: Your loyalty, love and encouragement makes life a joy.

Author's Note

This book took so long, I'm undoubtedly going to forget to thank someone. If I leave you out, you have my sincerest apologies.

I'm old enough to know that I'm incredibly lucky to still have both my parents in my life. Thank you, Ray and Yvonne Brown, for allowing me to nurture an imagination from a very young age and encourage me to indulge in the arts. And a special thanks to my Mom for enduring an amazingly horrible first draft that shouldn't have been foisted on my worst enemy. You're a trooper.

To my brother Steve who did it before me when he published a biography of his mother-in-law many years ago. My sister-in-law, Alison doggedly scouted locations for me in the Bay area, reporting back with photos and geo-tags. Thank you for making the locations believable.

Kate Cronon also read a crappy first draft and gave me wonderful insights and suggestions. Thank you.

To my beta readers, James Forkner and

Marissa Brooks, thank you for your great suggestions and kind words.

John Hough, Jr., you are an editor extraordinaire and tireless cheerleader.

Melissa Fenno, your photos were amazeballs. And it was fun pretending to be a supermodel for a few hours.

Alex Tibeo, thank you for a cover that won over even the harshest critics.

For encouraging me from the beginning and selflessly providing tips, thank you Mary Buckham.

Deb, thanks for putting up with the craziness that accompanies the writer's life.

And last but not least, I'd like to thank the women and men of the Seattle Police Department. I know what you do everyday, what you give up and what you endure. Be safe always.

For more information and to join my mailing list at www.writerdabrown.com

CHAPTER ONE

August 2000

She will never forget her first dead body. To be precise, there were two - a mother and her teenage daughter. In her third field rotation, student officer Sophia Benedetti arrived with her field training officer shortly before the homicide detectives, but after the district car had already been dispatched on a welfare check, when the mother hadn't reported for work that afternoon. Just as they rolled up to the meticulously landscaped Tudor, an officer bolted out the front door and vomited on the lawn.

Her FTO was a twenty-year veteran with a less than stellar attitude about the job but an impeccable record as a trainer. Dead bodies were considered good teaching moments for new officers, especially rookies still on probation and fumbling through field training straight out of the academy. He'd volunteered Sophia for the call.

"Maybe we should let one of the other guys handle this one."

"I'm good," she said and marched through the front door.

Soft rock hummed on the stereo. Magazines and catalogues, sorted and dog-eared, were littered across a coffee table.

Wadded up on the corner of a couch was a cashmere throw, a paperback nearby. Everything looked as ordinary as you would expect in a family home.

Sophia stepped around the corner and into the kitchen. A wine glass and a tumbler sat on a built-in breakfast nook next to an empty bottle of Zinfandel. Family pictures covered the front of the refrigerator. A couple of dishes in the sink; a few more on the kitchen counter.

Sophia followed the staccato sound of cops moving around upstairs while her radio chirped with requests for supervisors, a public information officer, CSI, all coming from the rooms above her. Patrol was always the first to arrive, and their job was to secure the scene and get the right people there to take over the investigation. But human nature being the curious beast that it was, brought with it every rubbernecker not already on the call. The house was filling quickly with officers and commanders.

She climbed the stairs slowly.

"What kind of fucking animal does this? And to a kid? Jesus Christ."

"My wife wants one of these beds. Wait until I tell her about what happened on this one…"

Four medics passed her in the hall. They all nodded as they squeezed by with their gear.

Another couple of medics came out of a bedroom at the top of the stairs.

"I didn't sign up for this shit," a female medic said to her partner as she met Sophia's eyes.

Sophia looked past the woman and saw the first body, lying on a pastel bedspread. The girl couldn't have been much older than fifteen. Her face was slack and her eyes still open. Blood covered the front of her night gown and pooled onto the floor.

Sophia's FTO tried to pull her away.

"Don't go in there. You'll piss off homicide."

Sophia stood in the doorway surveying the bedroom. Stuffed animals with black, button eyes stared down from a dresser. The walls were covered with posters and photos of smiling boy bands and track and field ribbons. On a built-in desk was an open laptop displaying a screensaver of several young girls, their faces frozen in unguarded and unabashed glee.

The master bedroom was at the end of the hall. Four officers stood around something on the floor. Sophia peered into the room. What she thought had been a bedspread was the body of an adult female, presumably the girl's mother. Her blond hair was matted with blood as it swirled against the carpet. Embedded in her throat was a large screwdriver. When she told the story later, Sophia would marvel at how she could still see the black and orange handle with the bold 'Craftsman' lettering glowing in the dim room.

"Sweet Jesus."

"This is a bad one." An officer she didn't recognize held her gaze and then looked away.

The scene was surreal. That's how she'd choose to remember it.

Sophia walked to a large window at the end of the hall and looked out at Lake Washington. Her reflection signaled back that she'd forgotten she had cut off most of her dark brown hair and the hairstyle was still foreign to her. Her kevlar vest and uniform gave her lean frame some bulk, etching an oddly androgynous image. At a distance, she'd easily be mistaken for a man.

"Hey rookie, don't go walking through a bunch of blood and shit and tracking it all over the place."

The cop looked older than her grandfather. He stood in the corner, an unlit cigarette dangling from his mouth. Sophia strained to read his name tag.

"It's Miller." He didn't move forward, didn't make any pretense of a proper introduction.

"Benedetti." Sophia held her ground. "How'd you know?"

"Cuz, boot rookies still polish their shoes and their gun belt. And they don't have these." He pointed to a poorly sewn patch over his uniform shirt where his holster had rubbed a hole. "Also, your FTO is my old partner. Stig Hansen is good people. You got lucky."

"I did."

"Like I said, just watch and learn. Stig's a little soft but he's a good cop."

Sophia scanned the hallway for Hansen before returning to the window and the scene below.

The full moon bathed the back yard in an eerie shade of pale gray, reflecting in a lap pool below her. Adirondack chairs surrounded a small fire pit on a terraced ledge framed by lavender. Sophia imagined a late summer afternoon of laughter and cold drinks, quick dips in the lake after a strenuous round of touch football.

Her eyes drifted over the long, narrow dock behind the terrace where a twenty-seven foot Sea Ray Sundancer bobbed softly in the water below. Something glinted near the boat's bow. Sophia ran past Miller and down the stairs. She sprinted through the kitchen and out the back door.

"Where the hell is she going?"

"Probably gonna lose her dinner,"

Her FTO followed, breathing heavily despite the downhill slope.

"Benedetti, hold up."

"There's someone out there."

She ran down the grassy slope to the water, the beam from her flashlight jumping with each stride. She drew her gun, married it to her flashlight and scanned the dock.

"What the fuck, Benedetti?" A tall squad mate named Jack came up behind her with Hansen.

"I saw something down here."

"What?" Hansen's breathing was labored. He leaned over

with his hands on his knees to catch his breath.

"I don't know. Something moved. I saw it from upstairs." She walked slowly down the dock, keeping the beam of her flashlight as steady as the adrenaline would allow, shifting her attention from the SeaRay below to a fiberglass shed at the end of the pier.

"I can't see shit," Jack whispered.

Sophia paused and listened to the voices filter down from the house. Water lapped against the shore. The boat rocked in rhythm with the current.

He lunged from behind the shed, crashing violently into Sophia and lifting her off of her feet, forcing all of the air out of her lungs. She twisted out of his grasp as the two fell to the dock, his right arm cocking back with a large butcher knife pointed at her chest. The vest wasn't going to stop it nor was she going to win against his strength and gravity.

Officers would later testify that she told him to drop the knife, but she had no recollection of saying a thing. He was on her so fast that the muzzle of her gun buried itself in his chest as the round from her Glock exploded through his heart. But the bullet didn't stop the momentum of the knife's path into her shoulder.

When the lab came back with the results from the weapon, her DNA profile was mixed with the mother and daughter. She later learned that the suspect was someone the mother had picked up at a local bar and brought home for a night cap.

As the medics rolled her on a stretcher to the Medic One rig, Hansen grabbed her hand.

"Thanks for the paperwork, Benedetti."

He leaned in and whispered, "Welcome to the club."

CHAPTER TWO

Present Day

Sophia's drive into work from West Seattle was predictably slow. It was raining sideways again, the drops flying from light gray to dark gray, propelled by wind from the southwest. It was day five of unrelenting rain and grayness, turning Seattle into a caricature of itself. Even the weather forecasters were glum, having lost any interest in sugarcoating the news. It was going to be one of those winters.

The inside of her five year-old Jeep looked like a cross between a locker room and a doggy daycare. Old running shoes she'd meant to stash in the dumpster at work, filled the footwell of the backseat behind her. And fur from Bodhi, her Labrador Retriever, swirled inside the cabin, buoyed by an ever present draft. Two gym bags occupied most of the cargo hold, their contents long forgotten. A white exterior had been a perfect choice for the truck, but a black interior had to be the single worst color for someone who did not excel at cleanliness.

Sophia dialed her voicemail. She had two calls; one from her mother asking if she was going to make it to California for Christmas and the other, from her friend Robin.

She called Robin first.

"When am I going to see you?" Robin said.

"I'm a shitty friend."

"You are and yet, I still want to see you."

"How about drinks next week? I'm slammed the next few days." Sophia tapped her brakes and reflexively looked into her rear-view mirror.

"I will hold you to it and I will make you pay for all the frickin' martinis I'm going to drink. You cops make too much money as it is."

"Thanks, counselor. I'm sure you could find a way to write off your alcohol habit onto one of your dirtbag clients. By all means, let a public servant support TiniBigs martini bar. I'll call you later and set up a time."

Robin was Sophia's last best friend. She was the only one who hadn't married a lawyer or an accountant and moved out to the suburbs. She had a successful law practice defending the same people Sophia arrested. The two of them had both survived horrible men and it bonded them like sisters.

Sophia skipped the call to her mother, who was just angling to smooth things out between Sophia and her father. It was going to take more than a quick visit to Tiburon to mend the mess she and her father had left behind. Four years later, he still couldn't forgive her for leaving California to become a cop, a profession he held in low regard. Every conversation between the two ended in a vicious argument. She'd inherited her relentless stubbornness from him.

Seattle Police Headquarters was one half of the Justice Center, sharing the block-long building with the municipal court. A largely uninspired stone and glass exterior housed several detective units including homicide, robbery, sexual assault, domestic violence and gangs. The remaining floors were crammed with records management, information technology, fiscal and human resources. The eighth floor was largely reserved for the Chief and his inner circle of assistant chiefs and civilian managers.

Sophia dodged an incoming Crown Vic as she traversed the parking garage, swiped her access card and entered Headquarters from the back side. She descended the stairs to the sixth floor and quickly rounded the corner to her cubicle. A couple of guys were already in, evidenced by the soft tapping of computer keyboards.

Her partner, Tommy Stinson had already assumed his morning position; chair tipped back, feet up on the desk and a newspaper opened wide but at a strategic distance from his gleaming and pressed white dress shirt. They shared the space between standard issue cubicles made of pegboard wood and fabric borders.

"You're playing with fire allowing newsprint within fifty feet of your fancy Nordstrom suit, aren't you?"

"I like to live on the edge."

At sixty, Tommy was seven years past retirement eligibility but he still loved the job. He was a dead ringer for a slightly younger Harrison Ford, minus the facial scar and movie star money. Blue eyes, the color of robin's eggs, softened the edge of his graying hair.

He rubbed his chin. "I'm thinking of growing a beard, what do you think?"

"Don't like 'em."

"On anyone or just me?"

"Anyone. It's not fair that men can change their look so drastically." Sophia said.

"Someday, you'll have a beard. Maybe you'll change your mind."

"Jesus, Tommy." Sophia laughed, picked up the file on her desk and swatted him with it. She looked at the memo affixed to the front of the folder. A large, red 'Confidential' was stamped on the white space below the narrative. The victim, Grace Halifax, was five years-old and in a special learning program at a local private school for children with autism.

Sophia's unit didn't get many cases from private schools. Most of those students came from families with enough money and influence to keep child abuse off of their resumes.

The memo was confusing. Her sergeant, Randy Pierson, had used terminology that was completely foreign to her. 'Avatar, MMO, Furries.' There was no way he came up with those terms on his own. Someone had dictated this to him.

Sophia pulled her chair up and flipped up the top sheet and scanned the second page.

"What the hell is a 'furry'?"

Stinson chuckled. "As I understand it, furries are perverts who get off on having sex with people dressed up like animals. Like mascots. You know, someone who gets wood over say, the Mariner Moose."

"Jesus. I thought I'd heard everything."

"Why are you asking?" Stinson looked at Sophia over the top of his glasses.

"Well, this referral talks about furries and avatars and all sorts of crap that sounds like a foreign language." She lowered her voice. "This one came in anonymously with a thirty minute post-report follow up call from an assistant chief."

Stinson frowned.

"And it involves a five year-old austic girl."

"That'd be a first for me. I've heard about these assholes but I've never caught a case on one of them."

"Looks like the kid's older brother found pictures of her on some website." Sophia ran her finger along the text of the report. "On some site called New World. It's not very detailed." She laid the file down on her desk. "Of course, it sort of begs the question as to why the brother was on a website that contained child porn."

Stinson had gone back to reading the paper.

Jimmy Paulson walked over and planted his crossed arms on one side of Sophia's cubical. His blond crewcut was so tight, he looked bald. "New World isn't a child porn site. It's a virtual world."

"You don't say, Jimmy." Stinson rolled his eyes.

"And how is it that you know about this New World place?" Sophia peered up at Jimmy. He was dressed in a dark Armani suit and crisp white shirt open at the collar.

"I used to dabble in the day."

"Dabble?" Sophia started to laugh.

"Yeah, me and some friends used to play Dungeons and Dragons online in a gaming room on New World. Just innocent shit."

"What other secrets do you have you want to share? How the hell did you pass the background?" Stinson folded his paper and dumped it in the trash can.

"I should see if my log on's still good." Jimmy walked back to his cubicle and scooted up to his computer.

"I wouldn't do that that on a network computer."

Jimmy stopped typing. "You're probably right."

Sophia leaned back in her chair and stretched. "I feel really old. I pretty much stopped being hip at Nintendo 64."

Stinson snorted. "Hip isn't a word I'd toss around too freely."

"You probably shouldn't give me any shit, old man."

Sophia sat up, pushed aside the Halifax file and grabbed the in-custody alert packet on the edge of her desk along with a pile of court subpoenas and mail. Since the suspect was in jail, she had seventy-two hours to file charges or he'd go free. She scanned for the reporting officer's name. Reggie Townsend was the report's author. That was a good start. She and Reggie went to the academy together and he was as squared away as they came. At least she knew the investigation at the scene would be thorough. The report was pretty straight forward:

"On the above date and time, the suspect was observed by several witnesses on top of the victim on a city sidewalk. The victim was screaming and struggling against the suspect. Witness Jackson pulled the suspect off of the victim and noticed his penis was exposed and erect. The

victim's pants were around her ankles and her underwear was torn in two and laying next to the victim's back pack. Both parties were extremely intoxicated. Victim Tilden stated that she had met the suspect at the Exterminate Homelessness feeding shelter under the freeway the day before and they had started hanging out. She stated that suspect Green, Walter A (DOB 01/23/62) made her feel safe and offered to accompany her to the Jungle where she had been sleeping recently. Victim stated that she and Green (whom she referred to as "Bug") bought some beer from Pete's Grocery when it opened. Witness Jackson stated that she was walking southbound on 12th Ave South approximately two blocks behind the suspect and victim, when Jackson observed the suspect push the victim to the ground and get on top of her. When Jackson reached the suspect and victim, she could see the victim was struggling against the suspect and that the act did not appear to be consensual. Jackson stated the victim said, "He's trying to rape me."

The phone rang. It was an outside number and Sophia hesitated as she always did when the caller ID didn't look familiar.

"Sexual assault unit, Detective Benedetti speaking." There was a pause on the line.

"Benedetti, it's Reggie Townsend. Sorry, I lost your cell number."

Sophia laughed. "Reggie Townsend. Why so formal?"

"Well, you being a detective and all, I thought that's how I had to identify myself." His voice was still smooth and dramatically low, like an after hours DJ.

"Yeah, that's me all right. Little miss formal." Sophia looked over her shoulder at Tommy. He was deep in a conversation on his cell phone, his hand rubbing the back of his neck.

"How are you?"

"Good. You know, things were a little strained for a while but now they're cool."

Reggie had recently come out, much to the surprise of just about everyone who knew him, especially his wife of fifteen years. Sophia hadn't talked to him since the gossip had made the rounds.

"I'm glad to hear it. And Brenda? How's that going?"

"She's still pretty pissed." The sound of the patrol radio droned in the background. "I mean, I can't blame her. We're just trying to get through the financial stuff with the divorce lawyers. She's going to take me to the cleaners. I'm going to be working until I fuckin' fall over." He paused to acknowledge a radio request. "Thank god we didn't have any kids." Reggie exhaled. "Did you catch the rape from last night?"

"I did." Sophia flipped open a steno pad and grabbed a pen.

"Maybe it'll get a decent look. I just ran past the shelter and your victim is sitting outside with a couple of other ladies. Do you want me to contact her?"

"No, just stay near and if she tries to leave, hold her there. We're just a couple of blocks away." She gestured to Stinson and hung up. "Let's go. The vic on this rush file is down the street. I want to see if she'll talk."

"She won't." He straightened his tie and grabbed his jacket.

"You're probably right, but we have to take a stab at it." Sophia grabbed her gun from her desk drawer and slipped the holster on over the top of her dress pants, to the right of her badge.

In the car, Stinson was uncharacteristically quiet. His right hand rested lightly on the bottom of the steering wheel.

"What's up with you?" She glanced at him and then looked away.

"The wife's on my nerves. She thinks I'm having an affair."

"Well, you are," Sophia laughed.

Stinson's face flushed. "She can't prove a thing."

"That's not the point, asshole." Sophia looked out the window. "And if you're going to keep screwing what's-her-name, Ashly, or Tiffany or Brittney…"

"It's Bethany."

"Ok, Bethany. Whatever. Evelyn is going to take you to the cleaners in a divorce. And over what? Some twenty something skank who can put her ankles behind her ears? That's going to be worth it? Do you want to be one of those guys who flags at a construction site until he has a heart attack because he's paying off ex-wives? Like you're going to marry her, right?"

Stinson took a deep breath and gripped the wheel.

"I don't know." He busted a red light. "And she's not a skank."

"Right."

Traffic was light and dominated by Metro buses jockeying for access to the curb where they could release their rush of passengers. Tommy navigated around the block to approach the shelter from the west, heading up Marion. Mary's Place provided a safe space to more than a few rape and domestic violence victims. Homeless women were especially vulnerable to attack if they didn't bed down at a shelter for the night. Sophia had spent many an hour camping out by the front door, waiting for a victim to come out and talk to her or catch one trying to avoid her. And because mental illness, alcohol and drug abuse were rampant for so many who lived on the streets, her efforts often led to dead ends.

"There's Reggie's car. And one of those two must be the victim." The two women sitting on a low concrete wall adjacent to the shelter, started to fidget. Sophia opened the door and jumped out of the passenger seat before the car had stopped.

"Jesus Benedetti, no wonder you've broken your leg twice." Stinson slammed the car into park.

Sophia walked over to Reggie's patrol car. He was tapping something into his MDC, a mobile computer allowing officers to communicate, run names and vehicle plates, and retrieve calls directly from dispatch.

Reggie nodded in the direction of the two women. "She's the one on the left. They started to walk off but I told them they had to wait for you."

Reggie stepped out of the cruiser. Sophia gave him a quick

hug. "You look handsome as ever."

"Girl, stop it."

He leaned closer to Sophia, "Just so you know, she's on to other things. Acted like she didn't even know what I was talking about." He looked over at Stinson, who remained by the driver's door. "Still like working with him?"

"He's fine. Just kind of making a mess of his personal life at the moment but other than that, he's a good guy. And a good cop."

Sophia motioned to Stinson. "Let's go get this over with."

"I'm going to take off unless you need me here," Reggie said.

"No, we're good. Thanks again, Reg. I owe you one."

Reggie smiled and folded himself into the car. Between the mobile digital computer, the radio, lights and camera, his huge frame barely fit. A kit bag sat on the passenger seat, exposing a jumble of papers, a dented metal ticket book cover and a myriad of gear stuffed in every pocket of the bag.

"See you around, Beni." He didn't acknowledge Stinson.

"What's the deal between you two?" Sophia asked as she and Stinson walked toward the shelter.

"It's his problem, not mine." He lit a cigarette and stood back to let Sophia take the lead. Stinson's interview technique tended toward the unsympathetic until he was convinced the subject wasn't a criminal or a con.

The women sat quietly, eyes downcast. Victoria Tilden, the one identified by Reggie as the victim, wore a heavy, soiled coat. The hem of her pants hung on the ground covering her shoes, making her look as though she had no feet. Her hair was full of mats. As Sophia and Stinson got closer, the odor of unwashed bodies hit them.

"Ms. Tilden, I'm Detective Benedetti. This is my partner Detective Stinson. We're here to talk to you about what happened yesterday. Can we speak to you for a moment?" Sophia held out her hand.

Victoria kept her eyes on the sidewalk. Sophia struggled to maintain her close proximity as the stench began to linger in the space between her and the two women.

"Your friend can stay here if that would make you more comfortable." Sophia put her hand down and stepped back. The woman sitting next to Victoria stood up.

"I got nothing to say to no cops, V. See you later."

"I've got nothing to say either." Victoria Tilden pronounced 'either' as if she'd just come from tea with the Queen.

Sophia looked over at Stinson.

"Where are you from, Victoria? You have an English accent."

"So do you, Detective."

Stinson chuckled and pulled out another cigarette.

Victoria looked up for the first time. "May I have one of those?"

"Jesus," Stinson muttered as he tapped the top of the pack and pulled out a smoke. Victoria took the cigarette and gracefully let it dangle from her lips, waiting for Stinson to retrieve his lighter. She cupped her hands around his as he lit the cigarette.

"We need to ask you some questions about what happened yesterday." Sophia sat down next to Victoria, careful to avoid the greasy stain left behind by another occupant.

"I don't know what you are talking about. I was having a grand time with a gentleman friend until some idiot interrupted us and now I fear I will not get a second date."

"So you had a 'date' on the sidewalk in the middle of the day with some piece of shit you met in the Jungle?" Stinson took a long draw on his smoke and shook his head.

Sophia looked at Stinson. She'd been down this road before with homeless women and every encounter ended the same way. This wouldn't even qualify as a domestic violence incident since the two had just met. At least then, she could have held Victoria's feet to the fire. And any woman who stepped foot into the Jungle, a stretch along I-5 with undergrowth so thick, a small village could camp out, was going to be victimized one way or another.

"Look, I know you don't want to cooperate with us. I understand but—"

"You understand nothing, my dear." Victoria stood, took a deep pull from her cigarette and flicked it at Stinson's feet. "I have nothing more to discuss."

Sophia pulled out two business cards, handing one to Victoria and stuffing the second one into the pocket of the woman's wool coat.

"Call me if you change your mind." She motioned to Stinson. "He doesn't have to be around for the conversation if you'd rather…"

"Oh, I quite like scoundrels like him." She smiled at Stinson and turned to walk away. Halfway down the block, she reached into her pocket and threw Sophia's card into the street.

"Should write her a fucking littering ticket," Stinson said, getting behind the wheel. "Ungrateful bitch."

"Jesus, Stinson. She's a crazy, homeless woman who's probably going to get raped a half a dozen times in her life. Give her a break."

"I'm done giving people breaks." He pulled into traffic, cutting off a Metro bus and bike messenger. Both the driver and the biker answered with a one-fingered salute.

As they drove past Victoria Tilden, the woman gave Sophia and Tommy her best royal wave with an extended middle finger.

Eldon Loveschild finished off the last bits of a week-old Mexican casserole and leaned over, placing the plate in front of his mangy cat.

"Who needs a dishwasher, right Pyewacket? Finish it."

Pyewacket started at the edge and worked his way to the center of the plate.

Eldon picked up the plate and nudged the cat away with his foot. He finished the last of the can of Olde English and cheerfully snapped open another. His landlady, Shirley, was restless tonight. The sound of her shuffling slippers, followed by the drone of the wheels of her oxygen tank taunted him from upstairs. Seventy-six years old and dying from an advanced case of emphysema, she was a nuisance. With no family and very few friends, she'd taken him in like a son, renting him a daylight apartment in the basement of her home for five hundred bucks a month, including utilities. He had access to her car and her banking records, having hacked into her checking account and helping himself to amounts of money small enough to go unnoticed.

Shirley's home sat at the back of a small cul-de-sac in north Seattle. Flanked by a rare in-city creek and greenbelt, it was a little too dark for Eldon's taste, but it afforded him privacy. His living quarters consisted of a small sitting room and windowless bedroom. Most of his apartment was jammed with spare computer parts, old Linux manuals, and an assortment of old school porn. His couch was bordered by a wood and glass coffee table that stood on wrought iron legs welded to look like entwined tree trunks. On top of the table sat his desktop, two monitors and a hard wired back-up large enough to support a small city. Dust, cat hair and cigarette ashes littered every uncovered inch of the table's surface, rendering it no longer translucent.

A bathroom, barely large enough for the shower and toilet, bumped up against the laundry room. Technically, it was *in* the laundry room, separated only by a Shoji screen. This particular setup provided Eldon with endless hours of amusement. Whenever Shirley came downstairs to do her laundry, he'd manage to magically appear from his shower, his flab extending over his semi-flaccid cock.

"Eldon, be more careful!" Poor Shirley, oxygen tank on one side and dirty clothes basket on the other would rattle up the stairs, slamming the basement door behind her.

I should just crimp that fucking tank tube and drop her in the creek.

By ten o'clock, the shuffling from upstairs had ceased. Cracking open his laptop, he double clicked on an encrypted folder and entered his password. The screen filled with light, and the image of a woman clad only in a black cape and leather leggings, breathlessly spoke.

"Welcome back, Gregor."

Eldon pressed a hot key and navigated through the gates of New World. He maneuvered through several screens, a safeguard he'd installed to make it harder for 'civilians' to stumble upon the more 'progressive' areas of New World, a virtual society predicated upon a crassly libertarian view of a truly free and limitless existence. It was a very exclusive club populated mostly by Internet outliers interested in socializing with those who believed, as they did, that free persons needed no rules.

He suspected Gwendolyn Majestic and her real life husband El Ray, were the admins for the night. That meant he had to tread carefully. New World was under scrutiny by the FBI. Worlders chatted nervously in the forums about the high likelihood that Feds were posing as pedos trying to ferret out the weak and lazy. It wouldn't be hard for Eldon to spot a cop.

They logged in with brand new accounts and photoshopped avatars. They struck up conversations in chat rooms that set off alarms even for newbies, who quickly scrambled off the site and scrubbed their browser histories.

And it helped that he worked for the City, often servicing computers at the police department. He had unfettered access to share drives and the network. He knew cops; how they strutted around, treating the civilian employees like servants.

Sometimes the undercovers lurked, careful to stay away from contact with other Worlders. Eldon could see everyone who logged on. If they didn't make any attempt to contact players or admins, or if they hung back and jumped from room to room without interacting with others, he'd call them out. Then it was easy to pull their ISP's off the site and use his contacts with service providers to trace them back to cold computers purchased in government bundles. It was so easy, sometimes it wasn't even worth the effort.

This was who he was and he was uninterested in changing anything about his life. He didn't care about a single solitary soul. He didn't want help. If he could stay out of jail, he'd take every ounce of scorn he'd get if the rest of world knew his secret. If he could get away with murder, if it wasn't so messy and time consuming, he'd choose that path. He was a psychopath in love with his pathology.

Eldon hesitated before entering the encrypted playground, changing his avatar from Gregor, a swarthy, thin man with the devil's goatee and horns, to a pale, blond eight-year old boy named Justin. His heart raced as he manipulated the keyboard and guided his playmate through the gate.

He felt it in his bones. His fingers trembled and his eyes widened.

He was going to get another chance to see the new little girl, the real life angel contained in a fully rendered interactive character.

CHAPTER THREE

The red message light on Sophia's desk phone blinked slowly. She punched in her password. The voice on the other end was professional and detached. It was Grace's father, Stewart Halifax, saying that he and his wife would be available later in the day to discuss the situation with his daughter. He paused awkwardly on the word 'situation' as though he was trying to find another descriptor. Sophia decided not to return his call, knowing people often excused their way out of hard conversations. She'd cold call them, show up at their house unannounced.

"I'm going to run by the victim's home and see if mom or dad will talk to me." Sophia was doing her best to not let Tommy get to her.

Stinson sighed. "I'm not in the best of moods. Can you do it alone or take Jess or Paulson?" He was packing up his desk, ready to call it a day before noon.

"That's why I used the pronoun 'I'."

"Jesus, Soph."

"I think I can handle it without you." Sophia brushed past Tommy before he could stand up. She grabbed the unit car keys and headed out to the parking deck.

* * *

Within a few minutes, Sophia was a stone's throw from Volunteer Park, land purchased by the city in 1876 for a cemetery and officially commissioned a park in 1901. It was a beautiful piece of land in the middle of the city.

But at night, the park and its dark corners became a notorious cruising spot.When Sophia had worked nights on third watch as a new officer in the East precinct, she often found herself driving through the park long after it had closed, painting the stands of Douglas Firs with her spotlight, looking for men crouching in the shadows or darting away.

She'd developed a bit of a reputation on the watch for sweeping the park after closing, leading some to accuse her of being obsessed with that peculiar set of humans who sought out anonymous sexual encounters. It had also garnered her more than a few complaints of harassment from members of the gay community.

"Why do you give a shit, Benedetti? They want to kill themselves, let 'em." It was not an uncommon refrain from her co-workers who had become resigned to looking the other way. They were 'damned if they did, and damned if they didn't' when it came to enforcing laws against lewd conduct in the park.

But for Sophia, it was personal.

Three years earlier, her oldest brother Matthew had been murdered in Buena Vista park in San Francisco. Although the crime remained unsolved, police believed he was one of several men targeted by a serial killer as they cruised for sex. Matty had kept his life separate from her and her other two brothers, Anthony and Michael. Her parents had no clue that their first born was living a life of duplicity, dating women until midnight and then cruising the park after hours.

Her last conversation with Matty was the night before he was killed. He'd called to say he had met someone special and was going to come up to Seattle for a quick visit in a month or two. He sounded happier than she'd remembered in years.

For Sophia, driving through the park shining her light on anything that moved wasn't harassment. She couldn't protect Matty. Maybe she could save someone else's brother.

Sophia drove slowly north down Federal Ave on what a Seattle Times reporter once called 'one of Seattle's most stylish streets.' Framed with Dutch and New England Colonials, English Tudors and Norman French manors, it was old money mixed with a side of diversity.

Sophia spotted the Halifax house on the corner of the intersection. It was a brick Georgian colonial, set back high on the property. Impeccably groomed shrubbery ringed the front yard, sitting atop a boulder barrier to the street. She imagined the house decorated during the holidays with tasteful lights and handmade ornaments, a Noble fir laden with Christmas decorations in the living room window.

Sophia pressed the doorbell and from inside came the opening bars to 'What a Friend We Have in Jesus.'

Sophia stepped back as the door opened and a small boy appeared on the threshold.

"Hi." The child revealed several missing teeth.

"I'm Detective Benedetti. Is your mom or dad home?"

"My mom is. My dad's not here." The boy looked over his shoulder and then back at Sophia. "You're here about my sister?"

"I'm here to talk to your parents. Can you let your mom know I'm here, please?" The child was probably eight years old, but even after two years of working child abuse cases, Sophia still was a bad judge of age when it came to kids.

"George, who is it?" The sharp sound of heels clicked against a hardwood floor.

"Yes, may I help you?" The woman pulled the door open and lightly pushed George behind her. She wore a light blue cashmere sweater and black pants. A petite strand of pearls hung around her neck.

"I'm Sophia Benedetti, the detective on your daughter's case. Your husband left a message on my phone this morning." She glanced behind the woman at George, who leaned against the wall in the hallway.

"That's strange. My husband didn't say anything to me before he left for work. That's par for the course, but still…" The woman looked at her watch. "Why don't you come in and I'll see if I can reach him. Perhaps he was planning on coming back to the house to meet you."

She held open the door and put out her hand. "I'm Ginny Halifax, Grace's mother." Sophia shook the woman's hand. It was soft and buttery.

George extended his hand to Sophia's holster, touching the top of her Glock. "That's a gun."

Ginny slapped his arm.

"Ouch," George cried.

Ginny glanced sheepishly at Sophia. "He's a curious kid. It'll get him in trouble one day, I swear."

Sophia squatted until she was eye to eye with George. "It's never a good idea to grab a police officer's weapon. Maybe someday you'll get to hold a gun but you're a little young now."

"Don't tell his father that," Ginny said. "If he had his way, Georgie would be packing a revolver to t-ball practice." She grabbed a cell phone from a table on the hallway. "Do you mind waiting here for a moment?"

George followed his mother, both disappearing around a corner before Sophia could respond.

Sophia stood in the entry way. It was formal but homey, decorated with handwoven baskets, a low bookcase full of children's books and a few framed photos of old Seattle. It led straight ahead to a long hallway that appeared to branch in two directions at the end. A tall and narrow window at the end of the hall opened to a view of the backyard. Sophia guessed the kitchen was to the right of the window. To her left was the living room, filled with white leather furniture and an ultra modern glass coffee table. The room was sparsely furnished and looked as though it belonged in a New York loft, not a Northwest home. *Nobody lives in that room. Why would you ever have white furniture with kids?*

Sophia glanced down the hallway and then quickly stepped into the living room. It felt as though her presence might cast a black mark on the pristine whiteness of it all. It reminded her of a hospital clinic. This was all for show.

"Ms. Benedetti?"

Sophia stepped back into the hallway. "It's Detective Benedetti, ma'am. Nice living room."

"We rarely use it. My husband insisted on having a formal living room for entertaining, which we never do." Ginny leaned over and picked up a pine needle that Sophia had tracked into the house. "Detective. Yes, I'm sorry."

"Where is your husband, Mrs. Halifax?"

"He's tied up at work. He's a doctor. It's not uncommon for him to not make it to appointments. We'll have to reschedule, I guess." Ginny walked toward the door. Sophia didn't move.

"Mrs. Halifax, this is not some student-parent meeting. Those pictures of your daughter…" Sophia hated having these conversations with parents. It was only slightly less painful than making middle of the night death notifications when she was in patrol. She looked over Ginny's shoulder and caught sight of George.

Ginny stiffened. "We need to reschedule, Detective. Besides, George is home sick today. I don't want to have this conversation in front of him." She walked to the front door and reached for the handle.

"We need to do this as soon as possible, Mrs. Halifax. And we have to get Grace in for a forensic interview at the prosecutor's office and she needs to be evaluated by a doctor, preferably a specialist. Is there a reason you and your husband didn't take her in right away?"

"We wanted to wait for a specific specialist — a friend of

the family — and he wasn't available. We have an appointment next week."

"What day?"

"I'd have to look at my calendar. I don't know off the top of my head."

"Do you know the name of the doctor?" Sophia pulled out a small notebook and pen.

"I don't." Ginny ran her hand though her hair, pinning back her long bangs. Her eyes darted between Sophia and the door.

"Mrs. Halifax, you just told me the doctor was a friend of the family, now you don't recall his name?"

"Frankly, I'm trying to wrap my head around this whole thing. I'm relying on Stewart to take the lead on this. I'm not good with this kind of…" Her voice trailed off and she stared at the floor.

"No one expects you to be good at this." Sophia pulled a business card from her pocket.

"Call me as soon as you hear from your husband. I need to interview the two of you and your son, Barrett. If he's not comfortable talking to a woman, he can talk to my partner Detective Tom Stinson."

"Barrett's very upset about this whole thing. He's not able to concentrate in school and he really can't afford to drop any grades. He barely eked his way into Stanford. Stewart would be devastated if they pushed him out at this late date."

"Of course he's upset, Mrs. Halifax, but we really need to talk to him."

"Oh, my husband talked to him at length. And of course that very nice police officer who came to the house and took a report. He talked to Barrett, too. I don't know that he can add anything more." Ginny opened the front door. "He's such a sensitive young man. I hope this experience doesn't change him. Thankfully, we have such a strong faith."

"Children are very resilient. You'd be surprised what they can overcome." Sophia stopped and turned back to face Ginny.

"I can expect to hear from you or your husband by the end of the day?"

"One of us will call you. I promise."

Back in the car, Sophia stared at the Halifax home. There was nothing but perfection about the place. A horseshoe of rhododendrons huddled near the driveway, poised to outshine the rest of the garden with their bombastic flowers. To the south, a line of cedars marked the end of the finely manicured lawn. It looked like a castle from a fairy tale. Something unsettling had just transpired between her and Ginny Halifax. Sophia couldn't put her finger on it but it was there – something malignant and ugly.

Sophia came around the corner of the cubicle she shared with Stinson, fully expecting, and secretly hoping his chair would be empty. He was studiously typing at his computer. He nodded his head silently in her direction but didn't take his eyes of the monitor screen.

"I thought you were taking off." Sophia dropped her bag and wiggled the computer mouse.

"I changed my mind." Stinson was still in a mood.

"Well, you didn't miss anything. The girl's parents basically blew me off."

He glanced over his shoulder. "How's that?"

"The wife was there. Her husband was 'too busy' to come and talk to me." She bent over her fingers in an air quote. "I have a really bad feeling about this whole thing. About this family, actually."

Sophia leaned back in her chair. "I'll bet you a paycheck they try and bug out. I think they're far more concerned about their reputation and their son, Barrett."

"Really? More than the five year-old?" Stinson returned to his computer.

"What are you working on?"

"I thought I'd wrap up a few loose ends on some old files."

Sophia had acquired a bad habit of half listening to her partner. She glanced at her computer and saw a phone message sitting in her inbox. It was from Victoria Tilden.

"Looks like that victim from yesterday called. Victoria Tilden. Your new girlfriend."

"Well, I didn't see that coming. She sure didn't seem to give a shit when we left." Stinson grabbed his gun from his top drawer, holstered it, and locked his computer screen. "I gotta do some PB. I'll be back in a bit."

"What kind of PB?" Sophia was used to getting ditched by Stinson so he could conduct personal business on-duty and she had long suspected it involved meeting his girlfriend on the side.

"The none-of-your-business kind of PB."

As he rounded the corner, she heard him say, "Looking good, Julie," to the admin specialist.

"Frickin' shameless," Sophia thought. She glanced at her watch. It was already two pm. He wasn't coming back.

She didn't recognize the number Victoria left. It didn't belong to the women's shelter. Voicemail picked up after one ring. It was a male voice that sounded drunk. Sophia feared it was the voice of Victoria's rapist. Hanging up, she walked out to Julie.

"Did you take that message from Victoria Tilden?"

"The British chick? She wasn't very pleasant."

"Is this the number?" She showed Julie the scrap of paper with the number scribbled on it.

"If that's a '7', then yes. There was a lot of noise in the background. I had to ask her to repeat herself four times. If I didn't know better, it sounded like she was calling from the jail. You know, it was all echoey, like she was in a tin can."

Sophia walked back to her desk. Was it possible Victoria was calling from the suspect's phone? Wouldn't have been the first time, but she knew Bug was still in custody. Sophia had one more day to file the case or cut him loose. It was too late to go across the street and try to talk to him at the jail, and she wouldn't go by herself, anyway. Despite the fact that he was probably an old drunk with one foot in the grave, it never paid to interview a suspect alone at the jail. Even the most feeble dirt bag could turn ugly and physical if provoked. Some guys looked forward to a fight, even in the jail, where the consequences for an inmate was always guaranteed to be brutal. Her one and only fight with an inmate provided her with a deep cut to her hand and a long internal investigation by the Office of Professional Accountability.

Sophia grabbed her bag and pushed her chair under her desk. Stinson's cubicle was freakishly clean. She pawed through a couple of files on his desk, self-conscious and slightly guilty over her curiosity at his sudden interest in giving a shit about his case backlog. Something in his scribbled handwriting caught her eye — it was the number to human resources, a note about retirement and a reminder to set a date for early next year.

"The bastard's really going to cut the cord."

CHAPTER FOUR

Sophia pulled into her garage, careful to leave plenty of distance between the Jeep and her Moto Guzzi that was tucked into the corner and protected by a heavy duty cover. It'd been months since she'd ridden, and the old itch was starting to beg for a scratch. She peaked under the cover and ran her hand under the bike's engine. It was dry and free from oil. Her last repair must have taken care of the leak. Carefully tucking the cover back around the cowling, she shut the garage door and locked it.

Between the muffled barks and the chaotic tap dance of her nails on the hardwood floor, Bodhi's favorite person in the world was home. Sophia bent down and let the dog wash her with wet kisses from her chin to her hairline.

"Okay, okay. Even I'm getting a little disgusted, girl." Sophia stood up and wiped her face with the back of her sleeve.

She dropped her bag in the hallway, placed her gun and holster on top of the only antique she owned — a beautiful oak bookcase — and peered into the living room.

"Well, I see you made yourself at home." She scratched the top of Bodhi's head.

Pillows lay in a haphazard half-circle in front of the couch. A pile of books leaned precariously next to her reading chair.

It was her last big group purchase of hardbacks before swearing off bookstores for a while. Bodhi had left a blonde trail of hair across the expanse of the couch after carefully pulling off the old blanket meant to protect the fabric.

"Jesus, Bodhi." Sophia threw the blanket back on the couch and tossed the pillows behind it.

After a quick change into tights, a Nike tee shirt with matching hoodie, and a pair of Adidas Supernovas, she leashed up Bodhi and headed out the door.

It wasn't quite summer yet, and the early evening, once the sun was low in the sky, could cut a brisk spell, especially near the Puget Sound. Sophia found her rhythm quickly, heading west on Admiral Way toward the beach. It was downhill for fifteen minutes, flat for twenty and then hellishly steep back to the house. The metronomic slap, slap, slap of her footsteps on the pavement reminded her more than once that she'd forgotten her iPod. Nothing silenced the rough edges of her breath.

Bodhi ran with her nose in the air, her nostrils practically vibrating with every stride. Rotting seaweed and algae bloom, pungent and on display with the low tide, braced against the breeze coming off the Sound. There was a storm surging in from the southwest, the smell of rain now mixing with dead shellfish. She'd memorized the word that named the smell; petrichor, the scent of rain on dry earth.

The day drew out behind her, her mind fixed on the strain in her knees and hips. Every year, it took longer for her muscles to warm and stretch. Where once she could bound up from the floor in a single unencumbered motion, she now labored to do it in two. Whether it was the wear and tear of the job or the stress of the last few years, she was not the pain-free athlete of ten years ago.

Robin picked up after two rings.

"You up for a quick couple of martinis? My treat, as previously promised."

"I just canceled a blind date. He sounded like my dad on the phone. So, yes. I'm in."

"Meet me in an hour. I have to take a shower."

"Please do. See you there."

The two women had met working opposite sides of a rape case, Robin representing the suspect and Sophia investigating the crime. They shared a love of good wine, bad men and Clint Eastwood movies. Despite their differences on the subject of criminals, they had become fast friends.

Sophia found a parking spot a half a block away. She spotted Robin, her head in her phone, walking on the opposite side of the street. She ran up behind her and slapped her on the ass.

"Dammit, Sophia. You scared the shit out of me." Robin fumbled with her phone.

"You should be scared. Just because it's Seattle doesn't mean it's safe. Remember what I always tell you? Head on a swivel."

Robin hugged Sophia, burying her face in her friend's neck. Robin's curly hair engulfed Sophia's face.

"How the hell are you?"

Sophia stepped back, holding Robin's hands in front of her. "You look fucking gorgeous."

"Oh please." Robin dipped her chin and sized up Sophia.

"You look skinny and pale. Are you eating or just chasing bad guys all day long?"

"Most of my calories these days seem to come out of a wine bottle. But hey, on that note, let's drink."

The two women found a small table near the back of the bar. They each ordered vodka martinis.

"Tell me about this guy you ditched for me tonight."

"One of the guys at work set us up - Jeff. You remember him, right?"

Sophia had met Jeff at trial, when he tried to flirt with her in the courthouse elevator.

"Yes I remember him."

"I got cold feet yesterday."

"You googled him, didn't you?"

"Maybe just a little."

"Robin." Sophia shook her head.

"I know, I know but I just had a feeling about him and I didn't want to ask Jeff. He was so excited about the two of us hitting it off."

"So he could get all of the sordid details from his friend if you two hooked up."

"That's disgusting." Robin ordered them both a second drink.

"And?"

"Cats. His social media profiles were filled with cats. If I wanted to date a lesbian, I'd just do it."

Sophia laughed. "So what's new with you, anyway?"

"I had a client bite me today." Robin held out her hand and tipped it up to the light.

"Jesus Christ. Did you go to a doctor?"

Robin ran her finger along the small red indentation on the top of her hand. "No. It was really more of a nibble anyway."

Sophia finished her first drink and pushed it to the edge of the table.

"I think Tommy's going to retire."

"Really? I just assumed he was going to go out with his boots on."

"The poor bastard is really looking tired. I'm worried about him."

"Guys like that live forever. He's lucky his wife hasn't shot him after all the bullshit he's put her through."

"I suppose." Sophia took a sip of her second drink. "I'm still going to miss him."

Robin's phone vibrated.

"Sorry, I have to take this. Give me a minute." She stood up and walked toward the restrooms. Sophia admired her friend.

She had a classic New York look to her - long, dark curly hair, flawless skin and a knack for fashion that made Sophia envious. She glanced back at Sophia and gave her a wink.

"I hate to do this to you, but you know that new city council guy, Shane Zimmerman? He just got picked up on a DUI. He's asking for me personally."

"So you're going to meet him at the precinct with a martini on your breath?"

"I'm fine. I only got through one." She pushed her drink over to Sophia. "You finish this one. You've got a get out of jail card anyway if you get busted on the way home." Robin leaned over and kissed Sophia on the cheek.

"Now, I'm the shitty friend. I promise I'll make it up to you. And next time, I want you to show up on that motorcycle of yours and give me a ride." She winked and blew another kiss.

"Drive carefully."

Robin ran out the door and across the street, several eyes in the bar following her every move.

By the time Sophia got home, it was nearly eleven thirty. She snuggled up to Bodhi on the couch and grabbed Patricia Cornwall's The Body Farm from the top of the pile.

A loud buzzing sound startled them both and Bodhi bounded to her feet, cocking her head toward Sophia's cell phone rattling on the dining room table. Sophia glanced at her watch. Her friends knew better than to call this late.

The caller ID showed a 425 area code. It wasn't from a city number and she didn't recognize it as belonging to one of the guys in the squad. She hesitated. The only reason to pick up was the time of night. Bad news always seemed to come in the dark.

"Hello?"

There was mostly static on the other end, but she could make out the sound of music in the background. It sounded as though someone had accidentally butt dialed her.

"Hello." She said it a little louder and looked at the number again.

"Sophia?" A man's voice barely cut through the noise.

"Who is this?"

"It's…" Another rush of static filled the speaker.

"I can't hear you. Who is this?"

"David."

Sophia's stomach jumped. She hadn't heard from her ex-husband in over two years.

"I can't hear you. Where are you?"

"I'm at Vito's. Sorry about the noise. It's mostly my shitty phone." He was drunk.

"What's up?" She tried to sound nonchalant.

"I have to talk to you."

"You do know there's still a protection order in place, right?" She closed her eyes and steadied herself against the table, a sudden vodka rush spinning the room.

"I know, I know." He paused. "But you've got to let me see you. I have something…

"Are you drunk?" She glanced out the front window. "Do you *want* to go back to jail?"

"Sophia, you've got to hear me out. It's got to do with that case." David lowered his voice as the noise in the background subsided.

"What case?"

"You have to trust me."

"Well that's pretty fucking priceless, David. And no, I don't have to talk to you, or trust you, for that matter. And if anyone on the department is talking to you about any case I'm working…" She stopped. "You don't have a clearance. You're not a cop anymore, David." Sophia shouted now, competing with the noise on the other end of the line. "And what case are you talking about?"

"That Halifax girl."

Sophia drew a short breath. Bodhi scratched at the back door, pushing it open enough to slide out.

"What Halifax girl? What are you talking about?"

"Stewart Halifax's daughter."

Sophia walked to the front door and checked the lock. "How do you know Stewart Halifax?"

"I can't have this conversation over the phone. I have to talk to you in person."

"Not going to happen, David. Tell me what you know now or I'm hanging up."

The connection started to cut out. "I can't Sophia. I just can't."

"Then I'm done." Sophia turned off the phone. "Goddamnit."

Leaving the back door ajar for Bodhi, she grabbed a half-full bottle of Merlot from the kitchen counter and emptied it into a tumbler. She sat on the couch and took a long sip.

"Piece of shit!" She threw the phone across the room and into the base of a brass floor lamp. By the time she finished the wine, she only vaguely recalled the conversation with David. A good red made everything better.

CHAPTER FIVE

Bodhi's rapid barking from the kitchen startled Sophia and she sat up. The room spun.

There was a steady, cool breeze coming from an open door. A gust burst through, slamming the back door against the wall. A strand of hair fluttered against Sophia's forehead.

Bodhi's barking was suddenly short and hoarse. Someone was tightening the collar against her throat.

Grabbing her gun from the bookcase, Sophia slid along the hallway wall toward the kitchen. She steadied her breath, slowed her heart rate. The house was dark. That gave her a tactical advantage but she'd have to make the corner without a flashlight. Bodhi's nails scratched and slid against the linoleum floor.

Deep breath. Finger off the trigger. Get a sight picture.

His back was to her as he struggled to hold the dog. A hunched stranger in a black coat and black jeans.

Aiming her Glock in the middle of his back, she yelled, "Let go of my dog you fucking asshole or I'll blow your head off."

"She doesn't recognize me anymore," the man said still holding Bodhi's collar.

"Release my dog, goddammit. Now."

When he let go of Bodhi's collar, the dog lunged against his lower legs, pushing him against the fridge, sending magnets and photos flying.

Sophia switched on the light. "Jesus Christ, David."

"Bodhi, come here." The lab bared her teeth and growled at David. She walked over and sat panting against Sophia's right leg.

"Good girl, Bodhi." Sophia reached over with her left hand and stroked the dog's head. Her right hand still held the Glock level with David's chest.

"I'm sorry. I'm sorry, Soph." David's hands stretched out in front of him, palms to Sophia. "Can you not point that at me?" He looked like the homeless men who lined up outside the St. Martin de Porres shelter on Alaskan Way every night with two days' worth of beard and hair that looked as though it hadn't been washed in at least a month.

"What the hell, David?"

David pulled out a kitchen chair and straddled it like a cowboy, with the back to her. He looked so different from the last time she saw him. Pathetic. Forgettable. Sick.

She lowered the weapon.

"You look like shit," Sophia said.

"I haven't looked in a mirror in a while, but I'm sure you're right." He shifted his weight and looked at the floor. "I didn't want to come over but you wouldn't meet me when I called you. When I drove by the house, I saw the open door and figured you were home. I forgot about Bodhi." He smiled at the dog. "Pretty good guard dog, you have there."

"If she was a good guard dog, she would have ripped your throat out."

"Oh, she tried but I don't think she really has the killer instinct. I think I broke my thumb holding her collar. She got a good twist on me." He held up his thumb to the kitchen light. It was cartoonishly swollen.

"I wish I could say I'm sorry." Sophia leaned against the doorjamb. "I almost shot you. God that would have pissed me off." She slid the Glock into the front waistband of her pants.

"Look, I have to show you something, but I need you to meet me tomorrow at that coffee shop on lower Queen Anne."

"Just tell me what it is, David. I don't have time for this. You're already in violation of a court order. What difference does it make?"

"I don't want to pull it up on your computer." He rubbed his hands together as if to warm them.

"Pull what up?"

"It's a website. That kid, Halifax's kid, she's on it."

"Grace?"

"Don't know her name."

"So how do you know it's his kid?"

"I just do."

Sophia moved closer to David. She rested her hand on the butt of her gun.

"How do you know Stewart Halifax?"

"I don't know him. I know who he is and I know who he knows." His hands shook. "I have something you need."

He looked at her for the second time. His eyes were soulless, black pools.

"David, you're not the one with the gun right now." His face sagged with fatigue. She was struck by how much gray had grown at his temples and crept down into his beard.

"Look, I'm going to leave before you call your buddies in to arrest me. I'm sorry I did this. It's just really important, Sophia. I wouldn't have taken this chance. I'm not stupid. I know what I've done here." His eyes filled with tears.

"If I was going to call the police, I would have." Sophia rubbed her forehead.She made a promise to herself at that moment that she would never touch red wine again. "You know I'm going to be just as much in violation of the no-contact order as you now if I meet you."

David stood up and gently pushed the chair away.

"This better be good."

"I promise you." He pulled open the kitchen door and looked back at Sophia.

He slipped onto the back porch, pulling the door closed behind him. Sophia flipped the lock. Pulling back the blind, she watched David jog into the alley and into the dark.

Sophia double-checked the locks on all of the doors and windows. Against the window panes, the soft tapping of rain reminded her that summer was still a month away. Bodhi followed at her heels, nearly tripping her.

Lying on top of her comforter still fully clothed, Sophia closed her eyes and tried to remember the David Montero she'd met almost nine years ago in the academy. He was different from the other guys in her class – college educated with no prior law enforcement or military experience. Quiet and disarmingly charming, with a dark complexion that made him popular with the other female recruits. She'd been drawn to him immediately, not because she found him attractive but because he made her feel comfortable.

But there was a darkness to David that Sophia noticed early in their friendship. He shifted quickly from sullen to elated but she dismissed it as stress from the rigors of the academy. Besides, he managed his mood well through training and graduated top of the class. And the day after they were sworn in, he and Sophia moved in together. She was sure he'd change, once he was able to relax into life with her.

It was not something she did normally – make a rash decision to commit to someone she really didn't know. She and David had kept their affair under wraps through the academy, although many of their classmates suspected. Sophia wouldn't know until much later what her decision would eventually cost her.

Bodhi stirred at the end of the bed, flipping over on her back and sticking her legs into the air. Sophia sat up and removed the dog's collar, the leather warm and supple. Bodhi snored though it.

It was almost three AM. The only light in the room was from the alarm clock, and it teased Sophia with the certainty of a five am wake-up. If she could just salvage two hours of sleep, she'd be able to stumble through the day.

She awoke to the soft light of the alarm blinking off and on. Reaching across to the nightstand, she faltered and failed to hit the snooze button before the ear splitting buzz began in concert with the flashing light.

Bodhi jumped to attention. Unaccustomed to the alarm, she let out something between a howl and a bark.

"It's OK, girl." Sophia reached out and stroked the dog's muzzle. She looked at the skylight above her bed. Raindrops beaded, then ran quickly down the glass, repeating a metronomic patter against the stifling silence of the morning.

Rolling out of bed, she pulled back the curtain and looked out to the street. It was part of her morning ritual, checking the kingdom for any signs of the enemy. She toyed with the idea of calling in sick.

"I know, I know. This isn't allowed. That's our agreement, isn't it girl?" Sophia scratched Bodhi behind her ears. "Let's go eat."

The kitchen light was still on and the chair David had commandeered a few hours ago sat in the middle of the room. Clumps of grass caked with dirt lay on the floor beneath the kitchen table. Leaning down to clean up the dirt, she steadied herself with one arm on the table, a heavy steel replica of a 50's dinette. Bodhi nudged Sophia's rear end with her cold nose. Sophia reflexively bucked, her head bumping into the table's trim.

"Goddamn it, Bodhi!" Sophia furiously rubbed the back of her head and looked up, fully expecting to see blood on the underside of the table.

That's when she saw it.

At first she thought it was an old piece of gum or a blob of plumber's putty haphazardly placed against the slide release. But as she moved closer and squinted into the dark corner of the table's underside, she saw the clear outline of a severed human thumb.

Sophia lurched back, propelling herself across the kitchen floor. She struggled to her feet, rising quickly as Bodhi reared back like a cartoon character on the linoleum.

CHAPTER SIX

The pounding on the door startled Sophia and as she headed to the living room to grab her cell phone, she glanced at the time again. She wasn't expecting company. Rounding the corner, she saw Tommy's hands cupped around his eyes, his face pressed up against the window trying to see into the front hall.

"You're never going to believe what I found under my table."

"Dust?"

Stinson was dressed in sweats. A pricey running jacket hung open over a gray Nike t-shirt.

"I take it you forgot that we were going for a run this morning?"

"Shit. Yes, I totally forgot." Sophia grabbed Stinson's arm and led him to the kitchen. "You've got to see this."

"Did you sleep in those clothes? And by the way, you look like hell." Stinson stopped Sophia and turned her to him. "Are you OK?"

Sophia pulled him into the kitchen. "I'm fine. I hit my head on the kitchen table."

"What the hell were you doing?" Stinson had stopped in the doorway and pushed Sophia's hand down. "Are you drunk?"

"No." She pointed at the table. "I had a couple glasses of wine last night. That's all."

"I'm looking at the table, Benedetti."

"It's under there."

"What's under there?"

"A thumb."

"A thumb?"

"Yes."

"Sounds reasonable." Stinson knelt on the floor, his knees cracking sharply and contorted himself so he could see under the table.

"I can't see a fucking thing under here. Get me a flashlight."

"I didn't have any problem seeing it, you moron. It's right there." Sophia fished in a kitchen drawer. She handed him a small tactical light.

Stinson turned off the light and pulled at something under the table. He swung around and sat on his haunches, a smile spreading across his face. "It's a thumb drive." He pulled on the severed end and revealed a small usb stick. "Oh, this is going to provide the squad with hours of hilarity."

Sophia grabbed the drive from him and rolled it over in her hand. "David must have put it there."

"David? What the fuck was he doing here?"

"He stopped by last night." Sophia pulled the end off of the drive to expose the male end of the plug.

"Since when does he stop by?" He stood up and arched his back. "I thought you had a restraining order."

The thumb drive looked like a severed and slightly decomposed thumb. Something right up David's alley.

She set it down on the table. "I need some coffee."

"I have a better idea. Since you clearly aren't going to accompany me on a lovely jog around the lake where I can check out the ladies without appearing to be a serial killer, why don't you take a shower and we'll grab some grub at Glo's." Stinson leaned over and scratched Bodhi's chest. "I'll feed the hound."

"I'm not sure I can eat," Sophia said.

"And I'm sure I can. Go clean yourself up." Tommy grabbed the bag of dog food off the sink and poured it into Bodhi's dish.

Sophia smiled at the sight of Bodhi inhaling her kibble.

"I won't be long." Passing a framed photo of the old Georgetown precinct that hung in the hallway, Sophia caught her reflection in the glass. She stopped to fix her hair and laughed. She and Tommy were now officially on the most informal of terms. She looked like warmed over death.

Sophia stepped out of the shower, wiped the steam from the mirror and wrapped her hair with the towel. She ran her fingers down the tattoo sleeve on her left arm. Jason had finished the last piece two months ago. She'd given him a black and white photo of a marshy field, smothered in fog. From the field, a murder of crows flew up from her elbow to the top of her shoulder. It was exquisitely beautiful in its texture and nuance. And yet, she'd shared with no one the fact that she'd spent well over a thousand dollars to ink her skin. She'd started the process over two years ago, savoring the secret that she shared only with the tattoo artist.

Her hands reached her shoulder and brushed the scar on her neck. It had faded but was still visible, especially when she got hot. It stood slightly raised, teasingly adjacent to her carotid artery, a reminder of how close she came to dying the day David decided to kill himself.

It was almost two years ago and against her best instincts, when Sophia had accepted an invitation to meet up with her academy mates at the pub where they'd spent many a Friday after a week of classes. She'd hoped David wouldn't be interested and she could go alone, but he'd enthusiastically encouraged her to RSVP and told her to include him in the count.

The first one to call her was Darryl Parker.

"Uh, do you think it's a good idea to have David come to this thing? I mean, isn't he going to be a little uncomfortable and all?" Daryl was not known for his tact but he had a fondness for Sophia, and like all of her classmates, he wasn't happy that David was coming. Despite graduating at the top of the class, David had crashed and burned during the final field training phase and was summarily terminated. It was a rookie's worst nightmare, enduring months of grueling training at the academy only to wash out once on the street. His field training officer noted several instances of hesitation when dealing with suspects, so much so, that he'd been pulled out of rotation for remedial training. In the Academy, he was smooth and decisive - on the streets, he froze under pressure. It was a deal breaker for the department and he was fired. Suddenly, he wasn't part of the blue clan.

"He wants to be there with me. He's fine. He's moved on. And he said he wants to see all of you again." She didn't really believe a word coming out of her mouth.

The dinner had been fun and Sophia had been surprised at how comfortable and calm David was listening to the stories of pranks and spectacular failures shared by the survivors. The laughter was good for him, she thought. It'd been awhile since she'd laughed so hard, and he seemed to be enjoying himself.

She hadn't noticed how much David had to drink, and she was only slightly conscious of her own level of intoxication. He was the designated driver, and she deserved to let loose with old friends.

On the way home, the silence was toxic.

"Did you have fun? You looked like you were enjoying yourself." Sophia turned to face him.

"I'm so much better than all of them." He shook his head.

"Including me?"

"Yeah, including you."

"Fuck you, David. I knew it was a mistake to have you come."

Sophia looked through the windshield at the traffic ahead and then at the speedometer. It read 65.

"Slow down. The speed limit's 55. That's all you need is a DUI." I-5 was busy despite the late hour. David darted in and out of lanes, barely missing cars.

"I graduated at the top of the class, don't you remember? I scored number one at EVOC" He swerved around a container truck.

"David, slow down!"

She expected something more grandiose, more elegant and less homicidal of him. He stomped on the accelerator as if he had mistaken it for the brake. The car lurched forward, narrowly missing an SUV as David yanked the steering wheel sharply to the left and toward the center median.

"No, fuck you Sophia."

The car veered violently toward the jersey barrier and went airborne. She remembered enough to testify in the civil case but little else. She had no recollection of the piece of windshield that separated her shoulder and sliced her neck.

Despite David's best efforts, they both had survived, and it was David who filed for divorce, not wanting to be the one who was left in the marriage. She accepted service graciously and returned the favor by cooperating fully with the prosecutor's office when David pled out to vehicular assault with time served.

Sophia let the steam obscure her reflection in the mirror until she was once again a shadow.

Stinson yelled from the hallway."Are you going to be done soon? Like this year, maybe? I've run out of ways to entertain Bodhi."

"Just trying to figure out what to wear."

"It's not like it's a special occasion, you know. Just throw something on. Nothing too splashy, though. I don't want you to look better than me."

Sophia chuckled despite a pounding headache. Throwing back some aspirin, she noticed the vial was almost empty. She'd gone through the Costco sized bottle in a little over a month.

She pulled on some black slacks, a white long sleeved shirt that was thick enough to hide her ink, and slipped on a lightweight lavender sweater. A quick blotting of makeup completed her prep. She grabbed her holster and slid it over her belt. On her left side, she affixed her handcuff and magazine holder. She snapped her detective badge on her belt.

Stinson sat at the kitchen table, flipping the thumb drive like a poker chip. Bodhi lay under the table on top of Stinson's running shoes.

"So, what was he doing here, anyway?"

"Just so you know, I haven't seen him in at least two years. Swear on my life, Tommy. But he scared the shit out of me last night." Sophia bent down to scratch Bodhi.

"Well, did he call you first? Or did he just show up?"

"He called earlier. He sounded drunk and begged me to meet him. I told him to fuck off, basically."

"Basically."

"Yes." Sophia opened the fridge and poured herself a glass of milk. "Want some?"

"Jesus, I'd rather kiss Bodhi on the mouth."

She drank half the glass and licked the edge to keep a drop from running down the side. "I told him I wasn't going to meet him. And then I proceeded to drink too much wine."

"That happening a lot, lately?" Stinson looked at her and stopped flipping the drive. He was sober twenty years.

"Only when I have to deal with assholes." She emptied the glass and placed it in the dishwasher. "Perhaps I should have a glass now."

Stinson glanced out the window. "Like I said…" He slid his hand over Bodhi's ears and stepped out of the back door. "Let's get going." He dropped the thumb drive into his pocket and jogged down the stairs to his car.

CHAPTER SEVEN

The neon sign at Glo's flickered into the restaurant. Tommy and Sophia sat at a table against the wall and ordered their usual - Eggs Benedict for Tommy and homemade corned beef hash for Sophia. She'd bested the nausea on the way to breakfast. The small room was empty except for an older women sitting alone and fully immersed in a book. The place was a mainstay of Capitol Hill, nestled on the western slope on E. Olive Way. Tommy had eaten there almost every day when he worked patrol in the East precinct.

"I thought you weren't hungry?"

"You thought wrong." Sophia cupped her hands around the heavy mug of coffee and looked out the window.

"There's the bitchy gal I've come to love." Stinson said, digging into his food as the plate hit the table.

"Hey, I'm sorry about the scene in the kitchen and…" She trailed off, not ready to concede. That wall was still firmly in place.

Stinson didn't look up. "I'm really not happy that you let that shit-bird into your house."

"He let himself in."

"Through an unlocked door." Stinson finally looked at her. There was a softness to his eyes but a gravitas to his tone.

"You know better, Beni."

"Yes, Dad.."

"This isn't a fuckin' joke, Sophia."

She leaned back in her chair and frowned. Stinson never used her first name like that.

"Look, I know you can take care of yourself and all that…" Stinson looked up from his plate. "But that guy is, I don't know, he's just - he's just bad news."

"I appreciate your concern, Tommy. I really do." She took a sip of coffee, weighing her next few words.

"I'm not sure what's going on. He looked terrible." Sophia said.

"Don't really care what he looked like." Stinson glanced at his watch.

"But he was really freaked out about something, and he didn't want to tell me. He wanted to show me something, something about the Halifax case."

"Halifax?" For the first time in months, Tommy seemed concerned about something other than his personal life.

"Yeah, he said he had information on the case. Maybe that's what's on the thumb drive."

"Well, let's just set aside the fact that he knows something about a case you're working on. That's fucked up enough." Stinson slammed down his fork on the plate. "You need to be more careful, OK? That means at home and at work. And lay off the wine. Seriously." Stinson nodded at the waitress and tapped his coffee cup. "I'm done with the lecture." He scooped up the last of his eggs. "And I'd give the drive to the forensics guys. Let them look at it on a cold machine."

The waitress filled up his cup. She smiled at Sophia. "More for you, detective?"

"I'm good, thanks," Sophia said.

The waitress brushed Sophia's shoulder with her hip on her way to the kitchen.

"I bet you are," she smiled.

Stinson slumped back against his chair. "Jesus. I'm the one with the ego that needs stroking, not you. We need to stop coming here for breakfast."

"Relax. She may just be immune to your charm." Sophia finished her glass of water and tucked her napkin under her plate.

"Hey, let's go to the high school and talk to Grace's brother, Barrett. It may be our only chance. I got the feeling from the mom she didn't want the kid interviewed."

"So remind me again what this case is about?"

Sophia pulled the case file out of her bag and flipped back a couple of sheets. "Says here he found the images of his sister while on his father's computer."

"He doesn't have his own? What kid nowadays doesn't have his own computer? I'm still paying off a loan to Best Buy for the PC's and Mac's and whatever else I bought for my boys, and I still haven't seen a dime from those two knuckleheads." Stinson finished his coffee. "So they were actually on the father's hard drive? Or was he surfing porn on a website and happened to be on his old man's computer?"

"Sounds like he accessed the website from dad's computer. We'll ask him. That'd be a whole other ball of crap if they were on the hard drive." Sophia tucked the manila file back into the bag and drank the rest of her coffee.

Stinson looked out the window. A young man walked slowly by cars parked on East Olive.

Sophia followed Stinson's gaze to the street.

"I spy with my little eye." Tommy craned his head toward the figure. "Troy Watkins prowling cars. God, I can't believe he's still alive. He was a hardcore tweaker when I worked the streets ten fuckin' years ago. Jesus, that guy's made of kryptonite."

Troy's filthy clothes hung from his body. Scabs covered his face from years of picking at imaginary bugs, a common side affect of meth. A large, green backpack was slung low against his boney ass. His eyes darted between the cars and the street, keeping a watchful eye for an east precinct cruiser. Suddenly he stopped, apparently mesmerized by something on the front seat of a Honda Accord. He bent closer to the passenger window while reaching into his front pocket.

"Here we go." Stinson stood up, slid his chair back and walked to the door.

Stinson didn't wait for Sophia, reaching Troy just as the young man tapped the passenger window with a spark plug sending the tempered glass onto the front seat and sidewalk.

"Goddamnit, Watkins. You piece of shit." Stinson grabbed the skeleton in street rags. Troy swung around and managed to squirm from Stinson's grip. He squared up on Tommy, then suddenly dropped his fists.

"Stinson!"

"What the fuck, Watkins?" Tommy shoved Troy back against the car.

"Hey man, this window was already broken." Troy shifted his weight and scrunched up his shoulders.

"Listen dumb shit, I saw you break it."

Troy looked at the sidewalk and fished his hands deep into his pockets.

"Hands out of the pockets," Sophia said.

A few people paused but didn't stop to intervene. With their messenger bags slung over their shoulders and their white ear buds implanted in their ears, they were on a mission. Perhaps it was the broken glass next to the car, a sight common in the early morning on Capitol Hill, or they just recognized Troy from his years in the neighborhood.

Sophia pulled her badge off her belt and waved it to a couple of hipsters who were beginning to get that look on their faces that meant they were going to intervene. Being in a plainclothes division had its perks but the downside was that citizens didn't recognize you as the police and neither did three quarters of the patrol guys.

"Hey Stinson, you know me. I'm sick. Cut me a break, man."

"You busted the fuckin' window, Troy. You know how much it costs to replace that thing?"

A young couple stood several feet away. Out of the corner of her eye Sophia saw one them fingering a set of car keys.

"Excuse me. Can we get to our car?" The female tapped Sophia on the back. Her deep purple hair was offset by almost translucent skin.

"Hey, you're going to cut him on that glass." Her male counterpart, wearing the obligatory black skinny jeans and Comet Tavern t-shirt, stepped forward and reached for Stinson's arm.

"Sir, you need to step back, now." Sophia pushed his hand down.

"Well, you don't really have to be so rough with him," the man said. "He clearly has a drug problem.You people are always up here harassing people like him. You should be ashamed."

Stinson squinted in the direction of the couple. "Tell that to the owner of this car. I'm sure they'll appreciate the busted window that he's never going to pay for."

"It's just a window. It can be fixed."

Stinson shot a look at Sophia.

She pulled out her cell phone and called the back line to radio. "Hey Donna, it's Sophia. Can you send me a car to Glo's? Stinson found himself a car prowler."

"We don't want to press charges"

Sophia turned. The couple stood at the car, peering inside.

"This is your car?"

"Yes. And we don't want this guy arrested." The male said as he pulled off his Herschel tote and threw it into the backseat.

"Hey Donna let me call you back." Sophia hung up and looked at Stinson. His mouth was tight.

"That's not your call, buddy."

"I'm not your buddy. I pay your salary."

Sophia put her hand on Stinson's arm.

"See, Stinson. No harm, no foul, right?" Troy straightened up and hoisted his backpack. "They don't wanna do nothing about it."

"You're not going anywhere until I say you are." Stinson pushed Troy back against the car.

"We got a history, Stinson. I threw you some good stuff back in the day." Troy chewed on his thumbnail.

"Let's get a car here and at least run him for warrants." The dance was about to start. Delicate and unpredictable, it was always Sophia's job to run interference and keep them both from another internal investigations beef. But Stinson was nearing the end of a very long rope. The less contact he had with an unappreciative public, the better.

"I'm not putting him in a patrol car. He shit himself." Stinson said.

"Jesus Christ." Sophia looked at the couple. They both put their hands to their mouths.

Stinson pulled Troy away from the car and shoved him toward the couple. "He's your problem then. You don't care, I don't care." Tommy pointed at the restaurant. "I'm going back in to have another cup of coffee."

Troy scurried down the sidewalk, pulling up his pants and yanking on his backpack straps. He looked back twice before jaywalking across Olive Way and disappearing into a side street.

Sophia leaned over, and made eye contact with the female, who sat gingerly in the front seat, fragments of broken glass clinging to the headrest. "You're sure about this?"

The car sped away before she could answer.

Back in the restaurant, Sophia sat down and took a sip of lukewarm coffee.

"What was that all about?"

Tommy squinted out the window and shrugged.

"I'm out of fucks."

"Clearly."

The bags under Tommy's eyes were fuller than usual. He looked exhausted. An hour ago, he was giving her a pep talk in her kitchen and practically begging her to run with him.

"Are you OK?"

"Let's go." Tommy stood up and threw down a five for a tip.

Sophia finished her coffee and grabbed her bag, quickstepping to keep up with Tommy as he headed to the car.

Tommy pulled into traffic and got onto I-5 north. He turned on the radio. The Eagles 'Hotel California' hummed softly from the speakers.

"Did you notice how that waitress looked at you?"

"No. I guess I wasn't paying attention."

"She was totally checking you out."

"Stop it, Tommy."

"Maybe you should consider batting for the other team since you're striking out with mine."

"I'm just fine on the bench right now."

"Just sayin'."

"Keep it to yourself."

"You do know that Vance is gay, right?"

"What?" Sophia turned and looked at Tommy.

"No, she's not."

"Yep. Certified."

"How would you know?"

"Let's say I have friends in all places." He winked at Sophia. "I don't have a problem with it. Do you?"

"Of course not. I just didn't get the…"

"Maybe you don't have as finely tuned gaydar as me."

Sophia laughed. Her own ingrained homophobia had tricked her before. Jess did not fit a stereotype. She was tall and lean with shoulder length blonde hair. She dressed out of the high end of Nordstrom's and wore a diamond encrusted Tag Heuer watch and a simple white gold band on her ring finger. For the first month she worked in the squad, Sophia assumed she was married.

"Well, good for her." She reached for her work bag. "And there's nothing wrong with my gaydar."

Sophia pulled out her file and double checked an address. She confirmed that Grace Halifax's brother, Barrett Halifax, attended Lakeside, a private school in north Seattle.

"Don't you think you should have changed into a suit, Tommy?" Sexual assault detectives were expected to wear suits and ties, unlike other plainclothes units, where almost anything was acceptable.

Stinson ignored her question and swerved around a Ford Escort straddling two lanes on I-5, driven by an old man.

"I just don't get people like those two outside of Glos, I really don't. I mean, I'm all about compassion, but do they have any idea that they've prolonged that kid's pathetic descent? At least if he'd gone to jail, he would have gotten three hots and a cot. He's just gonna head around the block and bust another poor schmuck's window." Stinson turned on the air conditioning.

Sophia nodded but her mind was a million miles away.

David's visit had rattled her. She swore that had she passed him on the street she'd never have given him a second look. His reappearance unsettled her carefully crafted life without personal chaos.

Stinson took the North 145th street exit and headed west. The school was just off the freeway, tucked inside a modest neighborhood and shrouded in tall evergreens.

"I don't think I've been here before." Sophia glanced around the campus at the Colonial red brick buildings with their crisp white trimmed windows. "Very nice."

"My close, personal friend, Bill Gates is an alumni."

"Really? I didn't know he was he was a friend." Sophia smiled as Stinson rolled the car to a stop in a faculty parking spot. He looked over at the gaggle of students milling around a black BMW 325i.

"Bet that's your boy. Rich kid with a Beemer." He nodded in the direction of a blond kid leaning against the driver's door. The window was down and Skrillex blasted from the stereo. Barrett Halifax wore dark blue pants, the crease settling perfectly atop his Nike Lebrons. His white polo shirt was partially tucked into his pants. Several teenaged boys stood in front of him laughing and fidgeting despite the impressive size of their backpacks.

"Ten bucks says as soon as we move in, the rest of those mutts are going to bounce," Stinson said.

Sophia opened the door and stepped out of the car. Teenagers were not her forte and she firmly believed that they sensed her unease, like Bodhi sensed fear. The group looked over and Barrett reached in to turn down the stereo. Two boys nodded at him and ambled off.

"We're looking for Barrett Halifax."

Barrett looked at Stinson and then back at Sophia. "That's me."

"I'm Detective Benedetti. This is my partner Detective

Stinson. We'd like to talk to you for a minute."

"I've got class in a few. Can you come back later?" He shifted from side to side, fumbling with his car keys.

Stinson leaned in to talk to him. "Your class can wait. We cleared it with the principal."

"Shouldn't my dad be here or something?"

"You're not a suspect, Barrett. Just a witness." Sophia touched his arm. "Let's go sit in our car so we can talk privately."

He pulled away from her.

"Relax, Chief. We're not hooking you up, just having a friendly chat," Stinson said.

Barrett walked ahead of them, pausing to press the lock button on his key fob.

Stinson opened the door to the backseat. "Why don't you slide in there."

Barrett glanced toward the school and then bent over and plopped into the backseat of the car, his legs bumping up against the driver's seat.

Sophia got into the passenger seat and shifted forward, tilting her head so she could see him. "We just wanted to go over a few things, and then we'll have you come in for a formal statement. I figured you'd be a little more comfortable not talking about all of this in front of your parents."

"I'm not crazy about talking to anyone about it." Barrett clenched his hands, then rubbed them on his pant legs.

"You hot? I can roll down the windows if you want." Stinson put the keys in the ignition and cranked up the air conditioner.

"Yeah, thanks."

"So, why don't you tell us how you came to find the pictures" Sophia pulled a legal pad out of her bag.

"Some guys at my school told me about this website. It's this site for LARPs. They thought it was totally lame and messed up..."

"LARPs? What the hell is that?" Stinson turned around.

"Live action role playing. You know, the losers that dress up as superheroes and go out and film themselves doing stupid shit. We thought one of our classmates was into that, and I was curious. They're the same guys that are into RPG's." He paused. "Role playing games."

"Well, was he? I mean, it's not illegal." Sophia looked at Barrett.

"It's just generally for dorks, that's all. I couldn't really tell. He's a weird dude. Very much into geek speak and goth shit. He's a loner. We all figure he'll go all Columbine one of these days."

"Does the loser have a name?"

"Jared Poppins." Barrett looked at Stinson. "Yeah, like the movie."

"Well, that explains his attitude problem." Stinson shifted in his seat. "So how does this fit with the pictures of your sister?" Stinson looked at Barrett in the rear view mirror.

"There was this thing on the sidebar." Barrett looked out the window.

"And..." Sophia glanced up from her notes.

"And it had this really hot chick who looked my age in this picture and I clicked on it."

"Like any red blooded American guy would do." Stinson said as he followed a young, attractive woman walking across the parking lot.

"It went to this webpage that had these weird content warnings. I didn't really think much about it."

"Who would?"

"I know, right?" Barrett said. "Anyway, I clicked through it and all these images came up. Mostly run of the mill pussy shots."

Sophia rolled her eyes and kept on writing.

"And I thought, well this is boring and so I kept clicking through the site. And then I saw it."

"Saw what?" Sophia seemed to snap him out of his pornographic trance.

"Sorry, I..."

"Keep going." Sophia poked Stinson on the arm with her pen. He was far too engrossed in the stray co-ed running late for class.

"I saw the link for New World."

"Oh, for chrissakes. What the hell is that now?" Stinson turned around again.

"New World. It's like Second Life..." He glanced at Stinson and Sophia. "...a virtual world where you create an avatar and live your fantasy." He ran his hands through his hair and put his head against the backseat head rest. "I guess that's what you do. I don't really know anyone who's into it. It's kind of for people who don't have much of a real life, I guess."

"You sure guess a lot," Stinson looked over at Sophia.

"I'm telling you what I know." Barrett crossed his arms and looked down.

Sophia tapped her pen on the pad. "Then what happened?"

"I just started clicking around and I found this area on the site called the Playground and I went in there."

"And...?"

"And there were all these avatars that looked like kids, and they were just kind of hanging around this place that looked like a water slide or some amusement park kind of thing. I don't know what it was, exactly. And then a chat window popped up and some guy asked me if I was there to play."

"Did this guy have a name?"

"I don't remember. I got really creeped out. He asked me if I was a cop."

"And what did you tell him?"

"I didn't answer at first. I just waited. And then he asked again and I said no. Then he sent me a jpeg."

"A jay pig? What's a jay pig? And what the hell is an avatar? I'm sorry, but Jesus Christ." Stinson stepped out of the car and took off his jacket.

”A jpeg. J-P-E-G. It's a digital image. A picture. And an avatar is kinda like a digital representation of what you want to look like on the Internet.”

"And what was the picture of?"

"Of a girl, like someone, my age. She looked kinda virtual, not real. And I thought, OK this is a little weird but whatever..."

Sophia shifted her weight. Her back was still stiff from her last run and her hamstrings were tight.

“He started asking me if I wanted a playmate and I thought he was, you know, talking about a chick my age or something, and I said I was just looking around. Then he sent me his email address and told me to write him if I came back. He said he was sort of an unofficial greeter at the playground and would be happy to introduce me to others."

"And that was it?" Sophia’s pen paused over the paper.

“That time, yeah."

"And the next time? When was that?"

"A couple of days later. I went to school the next day and told a couple of the guys and they thought it was cool that I got in and they wanted to check it out so we logged in on one of the guy's netbooks. That same guy was in there and one of my friends started goofing on him. I think he got spooked. And then another friend typed in my email address as a joke…”

"Did he write to you?" Stinson asked.

"Yeah, like that night. I tried to Google his address to see if could find him. You know, to see if he was really who he said he was. But it just came back to New World. I figured maybe he was an admin or something."

"Do you remember the email address?"

"It's on my Dad's computer. The one the cops took. It was something like'playing with fire at yahoo dot com.' There could have been a number in there."

Barrett stretched out his right leg. "How much longer do I have to sit back here?"

Stinson looked over at Sophia. "Why were you on your dad's computer? Don't you have your own?"

"Yeah, I have my own, but I dropped it in the pool last week."

"Of course you did."

"We need you to get to the part where you saw your sister." Sophia turned up the fan.

"A couple days later, he sent me another email."

"What was in the first email, the one he sent you the first night?"

"He just asked me why I gave him my email address, if I thought he was a loser. That's what my friend Josh had written in the chat room. I wrote him back and told him that my friend wrote the stuff about being a loser. I figured that was going to be the end of it. Then he wrote me again and invited me to what he called a 'members only' thing at the playground. He said if I was into pretty girls, I'd like it. He gave me a temporary password and username to get in. He said he was cool with people goofing on him."

"We're going to need that username and password. Do you still have them?" She looked back at him. He didn't want to talk about his sister. She couldn't blame him. She hadn't really liked the kid. She thought he was a privileged asshole who got busted looking at porn that turned out to feature his little sister. But now he was starting to seem more sympathetic.

"I know this is hard, Barrett. We're almost done."

"I don't think so. It was just a bunch of letters and numbers. Nothing I would have remembered anyway."

Barrett looked up at Stinson. "I didn't think any of it was illegal. So he sent me the link and that night I went in and kind of walked around..."

Stinson piped in. "Walked around where?"

"Not really 'walk' around. Like, my avatar walked around in

the playground. In New World."

Stinson closed his eyes and sighed.

"Go on..." Sophia said. Barrett might as well have been speaking Chinese.

"So I went in and there were like all of these rooms. No one really talked to me except this one guy."

"The email guy?"

"Not the email guy. At least I don't think it was the same guy. His avatar looked like a surfer dude. He asked me if I was a cop, too."

"That should have been a clue," Stinson murmured.

"I guess I'm sort of stupid when it comes to some things."

"Go on Barrett. You're doing a great job." Sophia flipped over another page and scribbled the words "we need him to get to the point" and showed it to Tommy.

"He said the area we were in was kind of like a video game and that you could win stuff if you figured out what door went where and that kind of stuff and I thought that was cool."

"So you thought you'd crack a code to some pussy, basically." Stinson leaned over the seat.

"Yeah, I guess." Perspiration beaded up along Barrett's hairline and ran down the side of his face.

"So I followed this guy into this one room, and it had all these doors, and he said 'Hey, figure it out.' I'm kind of a gamer so it didn't take me long to get through a few levels and I think he was surprised. And I get to this one room and the door opens and there's like this kid, this little girl on a swing and she looks like Grace." Barrett looked out to the parking lot.

"Keep going. We're almost done."

"The girl, Gracie, she talked to me. And I started to freak out 'cause she looked so much like my sister, and I thought I was being punked or something. She told me to click on this flower that was near the swing set, and I did, and that's when the pictures popped up on the screen."

“What sort of pictures?” Sophia stopped writing.

"They just started filling the screen, like they wouldn't stop, and I was panicking. They were horrible. They were of my sister. She was naked." Barrett started to shake.

“The guy, he sent me a chat that said, ‘You like? There’s more’ and I wrote back that he was a fucking pervert and I said the girl was my sister and then the screen went black. Like he was controlling the computer. And then it just fucking shut off.”

"I'm going to be sick. I have to go." He pushed open the back door and jumped from the car, sprinting for the front stairs of the school.

"That went well," Stinson said. "Let's get out of here before the principal calls his dad."

Some days Sophia really hated her job.

CHAPTER EIGHT

North Seattle faded behind them as Stinson headed south on the freeway. There were seven messages on Sophia's phone. It had been vibrating endlessly while she interviewed Barrett. She was certain that there was a family emergency or something had happened to Bodhi. But none of the numbers were familiar. The first voicemail was from radio. The dispatcher was asking if they wanted to clear the call from earlier. Three other voicemails were unintelligible, the audio cutting in and out so frequently, she couldn't make out enough to piece together the message. The fifth message was Victoria Tilden calling to say she now wished to "lodge a complaint against the rapscallion who'd attempted to spoil my good character."

"Your girlfriend Victoria wants to cooperate."

"Jesus. Let me guess. She's suddenly a victim."

"Behave. I kind of liked the old girl."

Tommy chuckled.

Sophia saved the message from Victoria and played the next one.

"Soph, it's David. I need to talk to you again. It's urgent. Please call me."

Two minutes later there was another message from David.

"You need to call me." The rest of the message cut off

before he could finish. She checked the number against the first three calls and it was the same.

"More calls from crazy town?"

"No." She didn't want to tell him but if she didn't, he'd know anyway. "A bunch of calls from David. Five, to be exact."

"What the hell does he want? Is he drinking again?"

"He wants to talk to me about this case."

Stinson tapped the brakes so he could look at Sophia without rear-ending the car ahead of him. "Again, I gotta ask, cause clearly you aren't. How could he know anything about this case?"

"I have no idea, Tommy. It's really not even a case for our unit. We should hand it off to the ICAC guys."

"Well, there's a big problem here if your ex-husband is involved in some way. Or someone on the department is talking to him."

"I don't know that he's involved. He just claims to know something about Stewart Halifax. And trust me, I don't think David has any friends left on this department. He didn't have many to begin with."

"It hasn't made the papers yet. Don't you think it's a little odd that he not only knows about the case but he knew you were the case detective?"

"Why are you jumping all up in my shit, Tommy? He called me. I didn't call him."

"Because I think you're acting like a helpless little girl, like you just don't know what to do. I'll tell you what to do. Tell him to fuck off."

"I don't need you to give me advice on how to handle David. I need you to get your own head out of your ass and help me work this case."

"Save your breath. I was doing this shit when you were getting your first training bra." Stinson pulled into the parking garage.

"That's helpful. Jesus, Tommy."

Stinson slammed the door and headed across the lot to the seventh floor building entrance.

"Asshole."

The she-beast screensaver spread out across the computer monitor, half seductress, half demon. The computer hard drive swirled to life as it had been programmed to do every morning. Jared Poppins peered out from under the covers into his darkened room, not needing to look at the alarm clock. He knew he was late for school by over an hour.

The light from the computer monitor bathed the room in a fluorescent flush, his favorite color. It was really no color at all, and that was just right. His sheets smelled like sweat and teenage boy, unwashed in over a month. The room was his own brand of organized chaos. Programming books, game consoles, black jeans and empty Cafe Vita coffee cups littered it. The curtains had long been closed, so natural light never penetrated. Only the glow from four computer screens atop a desk, a dresser and two TV trays pilfered from the family room, made anything visible.

Jared climbed out of bed. His feet landed on the cover of Resident Evil 4. Kicking it away, he listened for sounds of life from the rest of the house. His stepfather Ed was probably gone. His mother was, for sure. She was worthless as mother, but second to none as a defense attorney. His real dad used to say that the city set their clocks to the sound of Jared's mother opening the door to her office. Sherry Poppins may have taken a ton of shit for her name, but she was ruthless in the courtroom and at the negotiating table, never failing her clients and garnering respect within the bar association. Her only transgression - and it was a biggie - was screwing Ed Sanderson, a three time convicted felon, two weeks before his trial for embezzling a half a million dollars from a local children's charity. Recusing herself from the case set it back two months but gave her time to throw out Jared's father and rearrange the house to accommodate Ed's humongous garden gnome collection. They arrived by the truck load, ceramic miniature animals and Disney replicas, that Ed promptly organized into custom made glass and wood collector's boxes. More than once, Jared had imagined taking a baseball bat to the entire lot.

It was the worst time of Jared's life, exacerbated by an outbreak of acne and a growth spurt that left him looking like Gandalf . His father, Theodore had moved out of the city to Federal Way, into an apartment complex populated mostly by Somali and Eritrean refugees. Jared saw his father only sporadically after Ed convinced Sherry that Jared needed a stable influence like himself, and that Theodore Poppins was an unmotivated loser who'd only managed to stake a claim in a failed landscaping business. Jared's sister Angie was a freshman at Western Washington University and lived with her boyfriend off campus in Bellingham. She'd never gotten along with their mother, so she was ecstatic when she was accepted to WWU. When she first moved out, Angie emailed Jared frequently and then started Skyping him on the weekends. Soon a series of boyfriends took all of her time, and the calls to Jared dwindled until they came only on special occasions. His only ally soon ceased to be a part of his life.

After Ed was acquitted, he moved into the house and tried to engage Jared by buying him a new X Box and taking him to Game Stop for one hundred dollar spending sprees. Jared ate it up, taking advantage of Ed's generosity with Sherry's hard earned paycheck. After all, she would have never have spent that kind of money on Jared but when Ed did it, he was being a good stepfather.

But it was always clear to Jared, Ed was never interested in the boy's heart. Securing Jared's loyalty would go a long way to securing access to Sherry's bank accounts. Jared may not have been motivated at school but he wasn't stupid, and he had Ed's number within hours of meeting him.

"Jared, you have to give Ed a chance, for heaven's sake," his mother would say on her way out the door, coffee cup in one hand and discovery binders in the other. "He really wants to be a part of your life."

"He can suck my dick."

"Please, Jared. Enough with the language." And then the door would close and his day would rewind just like the one before.

He got out of bed, slipped on some jeans and shuffled to the kitchen. It smelled like coffee and Cheerios. Jared pulled the box of cereal down from the fridge and ate it dry. He'd grab an espresso on his way to school, knowing that no matter what the principal said about his tardiness, his mother would dismiss it as just another example of the failure of public transportation.

He jumped the express bus and arrived at school just as a large gray sedan sped out of the parking lot. Jared ran up behind Barrett Halifax, who walked slowly toward a set of double doors. Barrett ran his hands over his hair as though he was petting a dog, tucking the sides behind his ears.

Jared stepped in front of Barrett and held the door for him.

"How's your sister doin'?"

"Fuck you, Poppins. You fuckin' fag."

Jared laughed and loped down to his class, leaving Barrett alone in the hallway.

CHAPTER NINE

By the time lunch period arrived, Barrett had recovered his swagger. He shoved his backpack into his locker and slammed the door. Deke Jenkins stood behind him waiting patiently to head to the cafeteria.

"So what was up with that chick and the old man this morning?" he asked.

Barrett scanned the hallway for Poppins or one of his crew of goth nerds. He looked at Deke and shrugged. "No big deal."

"She was pretty hot. Was that her dad or something?" Deke walked alongside Barrett, his massive girth creating a wide berth in the sea of students. He was a scholarship student, meaning no money but lots of talent on the football field. At six three and two hundred and five pounds, his black skin and bulk made him stand out at a school of mostly white kids.

"I don't think female cops work with their dads, Deke." Barrett smiled but his stomach was still in knots from the conversation with the detectives. "But yeah, she was pretty hot. I'd hit that."

He slapped Deke on the arm and smiled. It was going to take a lot of will power for him not to hunt down and beat the shit out of Jared Poppins today.

The lunchroom smelled like tomato soup and Axe body spray. Students sat at tables, lunch trays or bags scattered on top. Laughter and fevered conversations bounced off of the hard walls

Barrett scanned the cafeteria. The goths and nerds generally sat apart from the rest of the school. Pimply and greasy, they huddled together like ferrets. They were worthless oxygen thieves, taking up space at his prestigious school. He was tired of the diversity speeches and anti-bullying rallies. These idiots were his energy drink, his drug of choice. He had convinced himself that Jared was involved somehow with the pictures of his sister. Those detectives had caught him off guard, but he was ready to engage in a little troll smack down.

"Hey Deke, let's go look for some retards to play with."

Deke laughed and headed up to the lunch line. "I gotta eat, little man. That shit takes a lot out of me." His hands engulfed the lunch tray as he pushed it along the metal tray rail.

The smell of food caused Barrett's stomach to lurch. He'd grab something after school before heading to soccer practice.

"I need to hunt me some gothtard. Especially that faggot, Mary Poppins." He glanced to the back of the room. A small group, clad mostly in black, sat huddled together at one end of a long table.

"That fucker actually had the balls to ask me about Gracie this morning. I should have pounded his shitty ass right then." Barrett walked alongside as Deke took one of everything from the cafeteria workers.

Deke paid for his food and shuffled to a nearby table. Barrett sat so he could keep an eye on Jared and company.

"'Sup?" Chad Weaver and Mason Tolsen dropped into the plastic chairs next to Barrett and Deke. Their lunch trays were piled with food.

"Where the fuck were you this morning?" Chad checked out four girls at the table next to him.

"I had an appointment." He glanced at Deke, who was too

busy shoving forkfuls of food into his mouth to notice his white lie.

Mason followed Chad's eyes to the girls. "Shit, that Mallory Turner has got a bangin' body. Damn."

"Yep, that is some fine ass right there."

"Look at those fucktards," Barrett said nodding in the direction of Jared's table. "That Poppins fag can't even dress himself. Look at that shit he has on."

Jared wore a variation of the same thing every day - black jeans, black t-shirt adorned with some anime character and laced, steel-toed boots. Despite the warmth of the lunch room, Jared wore a flannel shirt.

The other kids at the table, Darren Johns, Perry Finnagen and Petra Slovof were also draped in black. Their thin frames were accented against almost translucent skin.

"Hey Jared, your boyfriend Barrett is eye fucking you." Petra scratched at the scabs on the inside of her arms.

"Whatever." Jared looked in Barrett's direction and gave him a large and very uncharacteristic smile.

"Jesus, you're gonna get us all killed if you keep that shit up." Perry picked at the last of the food on his plate, avoiding eye contact with the jock table. Chipped, black fingernail polish covered the ends of his long fingers. "It's not like they need any more reasons to fuck with us."

"Grow some balls, Perry."

"I don't care one way or the other. I just don't want to take another beating. I'm done with it." Perry glanced over at Petra. "And you should be, too. I just want to graduate and get the fuck out of this place."

"He's still looking at us. He's gonna come over here with his bottom feeder friends. Fuck it, I'm outta here."

She pushed out her chair, the legs scraping along the linoleum with a loud screech that settled the room.

Petra froze. "Shit."

Barrett and Deke were on them so fast, Petra didn't even

have time to steady herself before Deke's hand pressed against her breasts and shoved her into the wall.

Perry's lunch tray flew skyward. His food splattered across two tables. Barrett grabbed him by the back of his head and slammed him to the floor. He scrambled under the table and ran toward the exit. Deke grabbed the back of Jared's coat, twirling him around until he launched him into a jumble of chairs. Barrett leaned over and grabbed Jared by the collar, close enough for only the two of them to hear.

"Listen you little shit bag. If you ever mention my sister's name again, I will fuck you and then I'll have my friend Deke fuck you. And after that, we'll fuck all of your little retard, faggot friends."

"Aren't you tough when you're with your fuckin' mutants," Jared spit.

Activity in the lunch room had come to a standstill. Vice-principal Truscott quickly walked across the room just as Barrett aimed his fist at Jared's face.

"That's enough." Truscott was a big man with a tiny voice. He grabbed the back of Deke and Barrett's jackets with his giant rubbery hands and pulled them together with a hard thud. "You two are done here." Both boys shook off Truscott's grip and stepped back.

"He assaulted me, Mr. Truscott," Jared said. "I want to file charges. I know my rights." Jared had practiced a series of phrases his mother had taught him should he be stopped by the police.

Truscott placed his hands on his hips and surveyed the mess. His eyes darted between the two groups.

"Jared, you can take it up with the principal. We're not calling the police and no one is pressing charges." Truscott grimaced and rubbed the back of his neck. "Show's over everyone." He turned to the three boys and waved his hand. "Let's go."

The room erupted in conversation. There was still ten

minutes left of the lunch period.

From the car, Sophia watched Tommy walk across the parking garage to the building entrance. He was moving slower these days, limping slightly. She was watching his last days as a cop.

She grabbed her file and stepped out onto the concrete deck. Tommy wasn't going to let her dodge the subject of David. But he needed to let her handle the problem - not jump in and fix it for her. And knowing Tommy, he was one bad day away from 'accidentally' putting a round into David's skull.

Tommy and Jess were alone in the squad room. Twenty-eight, tall and slender, with a boyish figure that confused her male co-workers and produced nothing but envy in Sophia, Jess was listening to Tommy when Sophia walked in.

"So, Tommy was just saying that you guys talked to the kid brother. How'd that go?" Jess tucked her hair behind her ear and wedged a pen on top.

"Ask him." She pulled her chair up to her desk and shook her computer mouse to rouse her desktop.

"Jesus, Soph. Don't take it out on Jess. She didn't piss in your cornflakes, I did."

Sophia typed her password in on the keyboard. "Hey, I'm sorry. It's just that captain asshat there can't seem to keep his mouth shut when he gets a chance."

"Oh, not Tommy. He's always got something interesting to say." Jess walked over to Sophia and leaned over. "Remember, he's a guy. He can't help himself."

Sophia chuckled despite her deepening bad mood.

Stinson swung his chair around and picked up the newspaper. "Oh, I see how it's gonna be."

The main line rang and Jess picked up the phone. She looked at her watch and covered the receiver with her palm, snapping her fingers to get Sophia's attention.

"Hey Benedetti, it's for you. I think he said he name was Halifax. Sounds like an angry man." She only mouthed the last two words.

"Put him on hold, will you?"

"Hold on for one minute, Doctor."

Sophia glanced over at Tommy, who had suddenly become engrossed in his email inbox. She picked up.

Sickly sweet hold music droned on the line. "I don't think so," Sophia said to herself and hung up.

"Did I drop the call?" Jess peered over Sophia's cubicle.

"He put me on hold. That's not going to cut it for me today. Asshole can call me back." She looked up at Jess and smiled. Jess was the only person who wasn't getting on her last nerve.

The phone rang again and Sophia quickly picked up the line.

The man's voice was hurried and distracted."This is Dr. Stewart Halifax. I got disconnected. I'm calling for Detective Benedetti."

"Speaking. What can I do for you."

"Look, I'm a busy man, Detective so I'll make this quick. Don't speak to any of my children without clearing it through me or my wife. Barrett is extremely upset. He called my wife practically hysterical and told her that you and your partner yanked him out of class and put him in the back of a patrol car."

"We thought it would be more comfortable to let him sit down in an unmarked car while we talked to him. And we figured he didn't want to do it in full view of his classmates. And frankly, sir, he's not a suspect. He's a witness, and he's old enough to talk to us without parental permission."

"I don't care what your policies are Sophia, I don't want you talking to him again without me in the room."

"How about you and your wife meet with me and my partner later tonight so we can get a few things ironed out?"

"Tonight won't work. Call my wife and have her call my office. I have a patient waiting for me. Please don't talk to my children again, Detective or I'll call Marcus Burton myself." The line went dead.

"Well, that was productive." Sophia turned in her chair.

Jess walked around the corner and leaned up against the cubicle wall. "Did he hang up on you?"

"Yep." Sophia leaned back in her chair. "God I hate men like that."

"Now, as much as you hate me right now, I'd never do that to you." Stinson had an impish grin on his face.

"As much as an asshole as you can be Stinson, I'll give you that one." Sophia stood up and rubbed her lower back. "That guy sounds like a real peach. No wonder his wife acted like such a broken bird. But hey, here's the best part." She tapped her pen on the cubicle wall. "He told me that if I talked to his kids again, he's going to call Marcus Burton.'

"As in Assistant Chief Marcus Burton?" Stinson's eyes widened.

"Isn't that a fun fact?"

Jess grabbed a chair and scooted it over to Tommy and Sophia's cubicle space. "This case just became a royal pain in the ass for you two. I'm surprised he hasn't been down here sniffing around."

"Now that's the kind of guy I like to fuck with," Stinson said.

"Who, Burton or the nice doctor?" Jess smiled and clasped her hands behind her neck and leaned back in the chair.

Stinson stroked his chin. "Now that you mention it, both."

Sophia liked the sound of the challenge. "He's a condescending prick."

But something about Stewart Halifax rubbed her the wrong way. It wasn't just his arrogance. He was a controlling bastard who was going to try and direct her investigation and she was going to have none of it.

Tommy spent the rest of the day quietly typing at his desk. He left for an hour and then returned, smelling like cigarette smoke and french fries.

"Where did you disappear to, partner?"

"I ran down to Burger King and then ate in the car and smoked. I felt like flaunting all of the rules today. Even left a french fry under the seat." He smiled and leaned back in this chair.

"You're really turning into a rebel at the end of your career."

Stinson grunted. "I've got a doctor's appointment later, so I'm going to take the last two off."

"I'm going to type up my notes on our interview with Barrett. You were so busy lecturing me on the way back, I didn't get a chance to ask you what you thought of the kid," Sophia asked.

"He's an equal mixture of good kid and turd. I just don't know which one we're dealing with yet. Seemed to me he was being straight with us. I'm still trying to wrap my brain around all that digital avatar shit."

"Then we're on the same page."

"For now." Stinson locked his computer, grabbed his bag and headed out. "See you in the morning."

The rest of the squad filtered out as the day drew to a close. As she finished up the last of her supplemental of Barrett's interview, Sophia remembered the thumb drive in her pocket. Stinson had turned it over to her after they left her house.

She slid the nail end of the drive back until the connector was exposed and plugged it into the USB port on her computer. Double clicking on the computer icon, she looked for the device and found something named 'hitchhiker' come up on the E: drive. She paused, realizing that she was about to embark on a fishing expedition that might or might not have something to do with her case. This really called for someone far more versed in computer forensics. Since she was certain David had left it behind, for all she knew, it contained personal information about her or about their marriage. That was something she didn't want floating around the department.

Her mouse hovered over the device drive. She right clicked and pressed 'open.'

The only item on the drive was a single Word document which she opened. It read: *If you've found this, I'm dead. David.*

She grabbed her phone and dialed David's number. The phone rang once and went to voicemail.

"David, it's Sophia. I found the thumb drive under my table and I read the message. Meet me at the Uptown on Queen Anne in the morning at ten. Don't call me. Just be there." She paused. "This better be good, David. By the way, if you don't show up, I will send patrol to your place and have them hook you up. I'm serious."

Grabbing her bag and gun, she headed to her car.

CHAPTER TEN

The following morning, Sophia dropped Bodhi off with her neighbor Candy, who spent three days a week using the dog to try and meet eligible men in the Junction. It worked perfectly for both women - Bodhi got some badly needed attention, and if she was lucky, so did Candy. Her home sat across from the park at the end of the street. It always smelled of garlic and tomato sauce, a poignant reminder of Sophia's own mother's kitchen.

"I should be home at the end of shift unless something comes up. I'll call you."

"I'm home all day. We'll hang out. Have a good one." Candy held Bodhi by the collar and stood on the porch, as the dog wagged her tail furiously.

The West Seattle bridge was a mess of red brake lights, as far as she could see. Blue and red emergency lights flashed a half-mile east. There was only one way off the bridge now and everyone was attempting to get on Highway 99 northbound.

Sophia dialed the main office line but it went to voicemail. She tried Sgt. Pierson's cell. He answered after three rings.

"Hey sarge. There's an accident on the bridge. I'm going to

be late." It was a formality that she followed from patrol. Pierson didn't care one way or another. He was three years from retirement, and all he wanted was to be left alone.

"Your partner called and left a message at four AM saying he wasn't coming in, so you're on your own today. You can take Vance with you if you have to go out."

"Sure. I'll get there as soon as I can."

Sophia looked for any missed calls from Tommy. Her screen was clear. She called Robin.

"Calling to schedule a date for general debauchery?"

"No. That'll have to wait. I'm up to my ass in alligators at the moment."

"Sounds like fun. More work for me, then?"

"I need tell you something…" Sophia hesitated.

"What?"

"David showed up a couple of nights ago."

There was silence except for the sound of typing on a keyboard.

"Wait, what did you say?" The typing stopped. "David Montero?"

"He called me, and after I hung up on him, he showed up at the house. Scared the shit out of me. I almost shot him."

"Well, that wouldn't have necessarily been a bad thing."

"Funny."

"What did he want?"

"I'm not sure, exactly. He wants to talk to me about a case I'm working."

"Ok, that's pretty weird. I don't like the sound of that at all." Robin had resumed typing.

"What are you working on that's more important than giving me your undivided attention?"

"I'm just reading some email. I'm backlogged from that stupid conference they sent me to last week."

"How was that boondoggle in Las Vegas anyway? Get smarter?"

"Whoa."

"What?" Sophia tapped the brakes to get the jerk behind her to back off.

"I've got an email from David."

"Seriously?"

"Where are you right now?" Robin asked Sophia.

"I'm driving. What's the matter?"

"Call me when you get to work," Robin said and hung up.

Sophia hit re-dial but her calls went directly to Robin's voicemail.

She tossed her phone onto the passenger seat and started straight ahead. It was going to be at least an hour until she made it to the office.

By the time she got into the squad room, she was anxious and pissed. Pissed at Robin for hanging up on her and then not picking up her phone, and at Stinson for not answering his. She dialed Robin again so she could scold her.

"Are you at work yet?"

"What the hell, Robin? Why didn't you answer your phone?"

"I didn't want you to be driving when I read you the email."

Sophia's stomach dropped.

"It says, 'Please ensure that Sophia gets the copy of my will.'" Robin paused. "And then it says, 'If you are reading this,

I'm dead.'"

Sophia walked out into the hall. Scuff marks marred the off-white walls from years of officers bumping their leather gear into them.

"Are you there, Soph?"

"Yes."

"Well?"

"I can't really talk to you about this. I think it's about this case I'm working."

"Ok, well I may be just a dumb defense lawyer but it seems to me that David's about to end up, well…"

"Dead."

"Yep."

"I'm going to have to call you back. I'm supposed to meet him today. He's just probably being a drama queen."

"Maybe so. And Soph?"

"Yes"

"Please be careful."

Jess, Jimmy Paulson and Anthony Grover were already in. It was nice to hear the sound of other voices, the tapping of computer keyboards and the shuffling of pages. It'd been too quiet in the office yesterday.

"Hey, nice of you to show up to work." Jimmy Paulson leaned back in his chair and took a break from his keyboard.

Ignoring Jimmy, Sophia headed to her desk.

"Someone's in a good mood." Jimmy looked around his cubicle wall as though he was afraid Sophia was going to punch him.

"Shut up, Paulson. You're way too perky for this early in the day." Sophia dropped her bag and looked at her phone. The message light was illuminated. Maybe Stinson had left a message for her.

Paulson continued. "I met my future wife last night," he said. "I think I finally know what love is."

Anthony snorted.

"That line is just as bad coming out of your mouth as it was coming over the radio," Jess said.

"Getting a happy ending at a skanky rub joint does not constitute love, Jimmy." Sophia stood and peered over her cubicle at the young detective. He was impeccably dressed as always, a pressed shirt tightly woven to his impressive upper body.

"Oh snap, Beni," Jimmy laughed. "You kiss your mama with that mouth?"

"I do. And my dog." She paused. "On the lips." Sophia called her voicemail. There was a message from Stinson and the sounds of a party in the background.

"Hey Beni, it's Tommy. I'm taking tomorrow off. See you Friday. Bye."

Tommy had called Sophia's desk phone because he knew no one would answer. If he'd called her cell phone, he would have felt compelled to explain. He was probably with the girlfriend; the twenty something legal assistant he'd met during a deposition last July. Tommy was a notorious philanderer but he generally kept his affairs on the down low, not forcing Sophia into lying for him to his wife Evelyn. His children were grown, married and on their own. Evelyn had a good job – she was a comptroller for a large telecommunications company, and certainly didn't keep Tommy around for his money. Their relationship made no sense to Sophia. It seemed as though Tommy was cutting off his nose to spite his face. But she wasn't naïve enough to think that there weren't issues in that marriage that she wasn't privy to, or that Evelyn had always been a saint. The fact of the matter was that Tommy and Evelyn seemed to genuinely love each other. They just couldn't love each other exclusively.

Sophia looked at her watch.

"Hey, I've got to go meet up with a witness. Who's coming with me? Stinson's poking the pooch today." Sophia waited for a response, hoping Jimmy would speak up. David wouldn't probably pull any of his usual crap knowing Jimmy was within earshot.

Jess piped up from around the corner. "I'll go. I need to get out of this cubicle farm for a while."

Sophia walked over to Jess' desk. "I need to go up to Queen Anne and meet this guy. The problem is, I don't think he's going to talk to me if you're there, so I need you to just hang back in the car. You OK with that?"

"Sure. Who are you meeting?" She threw on her jacket and pulled her gun from the top drawer of her desk.

"I'll tell you in the car."

"See you girls later," Jimmy cooed. "Hey Vance, sounds like Benedetti is making you her wingman today. Make sure you take notes."

"Whatever." Jess looked at Sophia and rolled her eyes.

Sophia checked out a car from motor pool, the only way detectives could get to interviews. Unmarked cars were shared by all of the detectives in Headquarters and were always in high demand. She snagged a three year-old Impala with lights in the grill and a police radio.

Sophia headed down James St. to 4th Avenue. "Ok, so here's the deal, and I'd appreciate it if you didn't talk to the guys about this."

"Okay." Jess glanced at Sophia as though she was going tell her something that would prove Jimmy right.

"I'm meeting up with my ex, David. You know the story, right?"

Jess nodded. "I've heard the department version."

"He's been calling me incessantly. Even showed up at my house the other night…"

"That's kinda creepy."

"And yes, there's a protection order in force so I'm not only in violation of policy but of the law by meeting him. You didn't hear that from me, though."

Jess looked out the window, and absentmindedly wiped a smudge off.

Sophia stopped for a light and surveyed the intersection. A bike messenger screamed through the red light. "Asshole."

"We can go get him," Jess said, smiling.

"We could, but the last time Tommy and I did that, we got a big, fat complaint out of IIS."

The light turned green and Sophia gunned it, hoping to catch up to the biker. She slowed the car down.

"Forget it. I don't give a shit if he gets flattened into mist." The biker was long gone, replaced by another two-wheeled menace, darting in and out of traffic.

"Anyway, he showed up at my house, scared the shit out of me and apparently left a thumb drive glued to the bottom of my kitchen table." Sophia was suddenly struck by the absurdity of the story she was telling.

Sophia shifted in her seat. Jess poked her in the arm.

"Hello? Where did you just go?"

"Sorry. I just sort of had a bit of a moment there…"

"Did you hear my question?"

"No, sorry."

"Did you look at the thumb drive?" Jess looked out at the road ahead of them.

"Yes." Sophia slid her hand down the steering wheel to the bottom and rested it there.

"And?"

Sophia pulled into a parking spot, two stores down from Uptown Espresso. She threw up an official police business placard in the window.

"I'll call you if I need you."

"What's this meeting about, Beni?"

"David says he has information on this case that Tommy and I are working.

Sophia stepped out of the car and leaned down. "I'll be quick."

Slamming the door before Jess could protest any more, Sophia scanned the street for David. The sidewalks were full of people on their way to work and moms pushing Bugaboo strollers.

The coffee shop smelled like warm chocolate and dark roasted beans. It was empty except for a couple near the back, studiously ignoring each other but practically making out with their smart phones. Sophia stood at the door to let her eyes adjust to the dim light. She glanced at her watch. It was ten on the dot.

He'd get fifteen minutes and then she'd leave. She dialed Jess and told her he wasn't there yet and to just sit tight. Ten minutes passed and she heard the barista pick up a call on the business phone.

"Is there a David Montero here?" the barista asked.

Sophia stood up. "I'm supposed to be meeting him here. Who's asking?" The barista looked at Sophia and shrugged.

"I don't know. Some woman. Do you want to talk to her?" The barista held out the receiver.

Sophia took the phone. She could make out the faint sound of a TV.

"Hello?" said a woman's voice.

"Who's this?" Sophia asked.

"I called for David. Who the hell are you?"

"I'm a detective with the Seattle Police Department. And you are?"

"I'm looking for David. Is he with you? He said he was meeting someone named Sophia at Uptown on Queen Anne. He didn't say he was meeting a detective. Are you the detective or Sophia?"

"Both."

"Oh."

There was silence at the other end.

"I'm sorry to be so rude. This is Melissa Walker. I'm David's landlady."

The barista pulled shots for a new customer. Between the espresso machine and the milk steamer, Sophia strained to hear.

"Why are you calling?"

"I'm pretty sure I heard him leave the house, like really early this morning. I heard the door slam. But I just tried to call him and I can hear his cell phone ringing in his room. He's not answering when I knock on his door."

"Are you sure he's not there?"

"Well, I don't go in his room when he's not home."

"Where are you calling from?" Sophia realized that she had no idea where David lived.

"I'm in the valley at 6710 Rainer Avenue South. Hang on and let me look and make sure he's not down there."

Sophia took a breath. She knew the area well from working patrol. It wasn't generally a good place for someone with mental health and substance abuse issues to hang his hat. Sophia could hear the woman calling David's name.

And then came the most blood curdling scream she'd ever heard in her life.

CHAPTER ELEVEN

David's room was in a daylight basement with two doors - one to the house and the other to the outside. Someone could have gotten to him without going through the house.

A patrol officer had let her past the crime scene tape when she identified herself as a detective, and David's ex-wife.

"Don't got too far in. It's a mess," he'd said.

"Oh, God." Jess stopped in the doorway.

The room was a chaotic jumble . Either David was a first class slob or someone had tossed it. A few laptops lay scattered across the floor. An unmade bed, the sheets crumpled into a ball against the wall, and a small desk, were the only pieces of furniture. The strong smell of sweet cologne lingered in the air. It wasn't a run-of-the-mill aftershave either. She'd never known David to use cologne - he had a sensitivity to perfumes and strong scents, that always made him congested.

David's body had come to rest against a wall, his head hanging on his chest.A gaping hole was left where the round had exited the back of his skull and passed through the plaster. A blood trail on the wall followed his head to the floor. He'd been standing against the wall, like a traitor facing execution.

Sophia hunched down to look at his face. He was barely

recognizable. Tiny white fibers clung to the entry wound in his forehead. His white tee shirt was soaked with blood that dripped down to his blue jeans. The pool of blood on the floor was strangely deformed as though it had fallen on something in a slightly rounded shape - something that wasn't there anymore. Both of David's arms were splayed open as if in one last effort of surrender.

A bloodstained pillow lay on the floor next to him, a smudge of blood surrounded a bullet hole. No wonder his landlady didn't hear anything. The killer had used the pillow as a silencer.

Sophia had been almost clinical in her attempts to guard her privacy and here she stood, a few feet away from her ex-husband's body, and she was about to become a witness in his homicide investigation. She was going to have to tell homicide detectives that she was waiting to meet him at the coffee shop. The past was once again going to consume her present.

Sophia felt as though she was intruding, as she always did at a crime scene, peering into the most private of places at the worst of times.

She'd hated him for so long it was difficult to feel anything. But she knew better than anyone, the emotions were there, waiting to come to the surface.

"Hey, you doing OK?" Jess touched Sophia on the arm. "You want to step out and wait for homicide?"

"I guess." She continued to survey the room, hoping for a clue, a dropped weapon, a shoe print.

Something. Anything.

"Let's go out and get some fresh air. They're going to want to talk to you, anyway."

Sophia took one last glance at David's body. "Sure."

Rain had started to fall in sheets. Sophia and Jess got into the car and turned on the engine to get the defroster going.

"This has to be related to my case." Sophia took a deep breath.

"So let me get this straight. He told you that he knew something about the Halifax case but he couldn't just tell you over the phone. Didn't he come to your house? Why didn't he just tell you then?"

Sophia pushed a wet tangle of hair back from her face. "He said he had to show me something. I got the impression it was something on a web site. He didn't want to use my computer. Honestly, I thought he was full of shit, that he was just using it as an excuse to see me. Before a few days ago, I'd had zero contact with him. I thought he was either dead or had moved back to California." The adrenaline was beginning to subside and a heavy fatigue was settling in.

"Oh, lucky you. Here comes Taylor from homicide. He's a real piece of work."

Drew Taylor was one of three homicide sergeants. He was famous for stonewalling on every case and brewing up a contemptible reputation as an asshole just for the sake of it. Sophia had run afoul of him when she was a new patrol officer, making the big mistake of telling a reporter that she was responding to a homicide just as she got out of her patrol car. Taylor hated the press so much that he took delight in holding back as much information as he could, even going so far as to give a fabricated cause of death to some rookie who promptly dropped the nugget on a local reporter. The station manager was furious when his 'exclusive' turned out to be as far from the actual facts as possible. It took the department's media unit months to mend the damage.

Sophia stepped out of the car.

"Detective Benedetti, what are you doing out here?" Taylor pulled up his hood and looked past Sophia at the front of the house. Rain ran down the front of his cap.

"It's a bit of a long story."

"Make it as long as you want. I'm on overtime now. You can talk to me all night."

"The victim is my ex-husband, was my ex…"

"Ok, must say I didn't see that coming."

"Nor did I."

"And…?"

"And he called me out of the blue a few days ago and told me he had some information for me on a case I was working…" Sophia looked at Jess.

Two homicide detectives came up the walkway. They were the on-call guys, not necessarily the ones who would investigate the case. Sophia knew them both. Terry Shriver was in his late forties and recently widowed. His partner, Rodney Stringer was pretty new to homicide.

"Sorry to interrupt. Have you been in there yet?" Shriver didn't acknowledge Jess or Sophia.

Taylor nodded in the direction of the house. "Just got here. Go ahead. I'll be there in a minute."

Rodney smiled at Sophia but kept walking.

Sgt. Taylor turned to Sophia. "Feel free to cut to the meat of this, Detective."

"I was supposed to meet him for coffee this morning over on Queen Anne."

"So you two were not on good terms?" Taylor smiled.

"No, we actually weren't on any terms. I hadn't heard from him in over two years." Blood began to course to Sophia's face. Taylor knew full well what had happened between her and David. Everyone on the department knew the story. It was department lore.

"Any idea who might have wanted him dead?" Taylor started walking to the house ahead of Sophia. She waved off Jess and pointed to the car.

"Well, if he had something that implicated a suspect in my case, then I guess that would be a start. But I don't even have a suspect yet. I've just started working it."

Sophia steadied herself down the stairs to the basement. Moments earlier, she'd been fine. Now she struggled to summon the will to remain detached.

"I hope this doesn't bother you to come back in here, detective." Taylor looked over at Sophia. "If it's too much for you, we can do this back at the office."

Sophia took another deep breath but kept her eyes off David. "I'm fine."

"You know, I've been through a few wives and a couple of them were raving bitches, I mean absolute cunts." He slid on a pair of latex gloves and leaned over David's body. "But I can't say that I'd ever want to see them like that. Poor bastard."

"Hey sarge. Look at this." Stringer waved Taylor over. Sophia followed.

Holding his flashlight to a bullet hole in a kitchen cabinet door, Stringer opened the door and ran his hand over the back.

"Bastard dug out the round."

"Make sure you take a hard look. Maybe it ricocheted somewhere." Taylor yelled over his shoulder. "Anyone find a casing yet?"

"Nope. But this place is a mess. It could be anywhere," Shriver said.

"Someone wanted to make sure they weren't identified." Taylor looked at Sophia and frowned.

Sophia suddenly wanted to leave, to stand out in the pouring rain with her face to the sky so she could cry without anyone knowing.

"Tell you what. Why don't you head back to your office and I'll have one of my guys call you for an interview." Taylor pulled out his cell phone.

"And don't worry detective, I don't really think you did this. But hey, we gotta do that old due diligence, don't we?"

Sophia and Jess barely spoke on the way back to headquarters.

She let Jess drive, fearing she was too distracted to make the short trip without running someone over. Her reaction to the surgical strike of David's homicide surprised and alarmed her. Maybe she wasn't cut out to work murder cases. She'd only responded to murders as a patrol officer. There was no crossover on the department. You worked the cases assigned to you based on the crime. If a homicide had a sexual assault component, homicide worked it. Sexual assault detectives only worked rapes and child abuse cases. She wouldn't be allowed to work a case in which the victim was known to her, but still - Taylor was one of the sergeants who had to approve her transfer. This could change his opinion about her readiness.

"That was awkward."

"Give yourself a break. Taylor's an asshole. You did fine."

"I don't think he likes women."

"He likes women but only the ones he thinks he can get into bed."

"I wasn't very strong out there." Sophia laid her head back against the head rest.

"You were a rock star."

Sophia laughed. "I'm not sure I'd go that far."

"Name one other officer on this department who's had to deal with something like."

Jess was right. Sophia wanted to find the bastard who killed David herself. There'd be nothing left of him when she was done.

It was a little past one o'clock when they arrived at the office. It was Friday, so the hallways were empty, most detectives having skipped out early to golf or hit the bars. The rain was going to make the bar a lot more likely destination. She was relieved she wouldn't have to answer a million questions.

As soon as she and Jess rounded the corner into the bullpen, they ran into Pierson.

"Walker from homicide was looking for you." Sgt. Pierson said."What do those guys want with you?"

"We sort of fell over a homicide, " Jess said.

"Who's dead?"

"My ex-husband."

Pierson looked at Sophia for a long time. He mouth twitched as though he was suppressing a smile. Then it went slack. Even he could see by the look on her face that Sophia wasn't joking.

"I'm sorry."

Sophia told him about David's visit to her house, the thumb drive and the crime scene.

"I see." Pierson leaned against the wall and buried his hands in his pockets. "How did he die?"

"One shot to the head."

Pierson grimaced. "Go talk to Walker and then take the rest of the day off."

Guys on the department said a lot of shitty things about Pierson, but he usually had the sense to realize when detectives had reached a breaking point.

Detective Avery Walker sat at his desk reading email.

"You were looking for me?"

He stood up and grabbed a legal pad. "Let's go some place more private."

"Here is fine. I've got nothing to hide nor do I think I'm going to be able to tell you much that's going to be helpful."

"Have a seat then." He pulled over another detective's chair.

The homicide unit was surprisingly open. Given the sensitive nature of the cases they investigated, it was a bone of contention with many of the detectives that they didn't have an enclosed and secure space to work their cases.

"So what's your relationship to this incident again?"

"The victim was my ex-husband."

"Right."

"But you knew that." Sophia crossed her arms and looked at

Walker.

"I got a very quick brief from one of the guys at the scene." He made a note on his pad.

Sophia made it easy for him. She knew the questions he had to ask and she gave him a running narrative. They were done in under an hour.

As she reached her desk, her cell phone rang. It was Tommy.

"What the hell happened, Soph?" His voice was hoarse.

"Where are you? I just had the most fucked up day and it would have been nice for you to have been there."

"I'll take that as a compliment, I guess."

"Don't."

"What happened to Montero?"

"I don't know. He was supposed to meet me. He didn't show."

"Aren't you leaving something out?"

"I'm really not in the mood."

"Ok, so he's dead. What does his death have to do with our case? My cell phone is blowing up with calls from guys on the department."

"Screw it. People can talk to me if they want to know what happened."

"For fuck's sake, I took a day off. I had some shit I needed to do. It's not personal. I can take time off without permission from you or anyone else. Jesus, I'm just trying to find out how you are. If you don't want to talk to me, that's fine."

"Maybe we can talk about it tomorrow." Sophia hung up the phone.

If it was related, David's death had changed the dynamic of her case. But knowing David, he could have been involved in a million other things that could have produced the same outcome. She'd long suspected that when they were still married he was not just programming software or re-building computers for his geeky buddies. He had lots of unexplained income that found its way into a bank account he didn't know she'd discovered by accident. They'd fought about money often. He was furious about how much she made, how she could supplement her income by working off-duty while he had to scrape by working under the table repairing computers for friends. He hated being the one with the shitty job. Despite his protestations to the contrary, he was still inextricably bound to his macho hispanic heritage. He was a failure. A failed cop and a failed breadwinner.

Sophia swung by Candy's house and picked up Bodhi. Her tail could barely keep up with her wiggling butt. The dog could get her to smile even in the worst of moments.

Sophia's cell phone was on vibrate but she still heard it buzzing on the counter in the kitchen. She glanced at the number. It was the Chief Dispatcher. The CD only ever called when something was a high priority or a sensitive incident.

Sophia picked up.

"Homicide's out on a reported kidnapping. Your name came up on the call. Does the name Grace Halifax ring a bell?" He clicked over to radio before Sophia could answer, updated a robbery call and got back on the line.

"She's victim in one of my cases." The sound of several other voices competed for the dispatcher's attention. "Who's reporting her missing?"

"The mother, I assume. The call is a cluster."

"This whole case is a cluster," Sophia murmured.

"Now a homicide sergeant is asking for you to call the office. Here's his cell."

Sophia scribbled the cell number on a post-it pad.

"Thanks."

She hung up, and pulled her jacket over her sweats. She didn't even want to know how bad she looked. *Thank God I work mostly with men. No one will even notice what I'm wearing.*

Bodhi nuzzled her leg as she dialed Stinson. She stroked the dog's neck.

"Ok, first off, I'm sorry for being a bitch earlier. Secondly, I need you to meet me at the Halifax house. Ginny Halifax is reporting that Grace has been kidnapped."

There was music in the background of Tommy's phone. "Not a great time, Soph."

"Stinson, I don't give a shit if you are about to stick it to Cindy Crawford. I need you to come in."

"Cindy Crawford is way too old."

"Stinson!"

"I'm having dinner with my daughter. Give me an hour. That's the best I can do."

"Tell Tina I'm sorry I busted up some father/daughter time."

"She's used to it. Drive carefully. Lot's of fruits and nuts on the road."

CHAPTER TWELVE

The Halifax house was overflowing with cops, some taking copious notes, others hanging out in front waiting for something to do. True kidnappings were extremely rare and when they involved a child, every cop in the city wanted to help.

Rumor had it that the FBI had been called in to consult but so far, the scene was mostly guys Sophia recognized from SPD.

Ginny Halifax sat on the couch in her pristine living room, surrounded by her white furniture. Her eyes settled on the group of detectives and patrol officers oblivious to the 'no shoe rule.' George sat next to his mother, hands folded in his lap. When he recognized Sophia, a slight smile lit his face but it was vanquished by a stern look from his mother.

Ginny stood up and lunged towards Sophia. "This is all your fault, you bitch. You went to Barrett's school and harassed him and now those sickening people, those… those creatures, took my Grace." Tears streamed down her taut face.

All eyes in the room fell on Sophia.

From behind Sophia came a familiar voice. It was Tommy.

"What people you are talking about, Mrs. Halifax? Where's your husband?"

"I haven't been able to reach him. I assume he's in surgery."

She settled back down on the couch. "And those people," she said, "are the animals that Barrett is exposed to at that school." She put her arm around George's shoulder and pulled him close.

Ginny Halifax was the kind of woman who hated other women. Sophia turned back to Tommy and let him take the lead. In other circumstances, she might have challenged Ginny.

"I think we need to talk to your husband, ma'm. You know, just to make sure there's no misunderstanding here. Maybe he's with your daughter." Tommy pulled out his phone. "What's his cell number?"

Ginny Halifax rattled off the number. One of the homicide guys moved over to her and squatted in front of George and let him hold his badge.

Tommy stepped into the foyer. Sophia followed, squeezing by three patrol officers. Tommy signaled for Sophia to come closer.

"I don't think she's been kidnapped. I think she's been taken somewhere by the family because they don't want her to talk to us. I'll bet you my left nut she's with the father. Or he knows where she is. And I think Barrett's in on it."

"I'll bet you your right nut, you're correct."

Tommy grimaced. "I don't want to be that right. I'll be out of nuts."

"This family is giving me all kinds of creeps." Sophia glanced into the living room. "I'm going to take a look around."

"Sure. I gotta make a phone call anyway." Tommy opened the front door and stepped out onto the porch.

Sophia walked into the kitchen where a lone officer stood by the back door. He was easily a foot taller than Sophia with sandy blond hair and deep brown eyes.

"Hey, it's Tim, right?"

The officer pointed at his name tag. "Tim Johannes. We met a few months ago at that rape on Broadway. That was a nasty one."

He lowered his voice. "Hey, so why are you guys out on this one? This isn't a sex case, right?"

"It started out that way. Photos of this little girl showed up on some child porn site."

"Isn't that an ICAC issue?"

"Funny you should mention that, but yes," Sophia said.

Sophia scanned the room. Her eyes came to rest on a picture of the family tucked into an alcove. She bent down and picked up the ornately framed photo. It was the first time she'd seen Grace, this tiny little girl who had suddenly become the center of attention of half of the department. The picture had been taken on a boat, maybe on Lake Chelan. Ginny Halifax stood on an ice chest behind her husband, her hands on his shoulders. George stood next to his mother, his right hand reaching up and clinging to her left hand. Barrett sat in front with his legs pulled to his chest. His smile was forced, not easy like his father's. Stewart held Grace with his arms extended, as though he was displaying her to the camera. She wore a tiny orange life vest over a blue, one-piece bathing suit covered in yellow seahorses. Blonde, curly hair partially covered her face. But her eyes were lifeless little pools of blue, sitting atop perfect cheek bones. It was a bizarre photo to display in a family area. Certainly they had something happier to frame.

Sophia slapped the officer on the shoulder. "Hey, I've got to find my partner. It was nice seeing you again."

"Maybe sometime we can chat when we're not at a crime scene." He sank his hands into his pockets and smiled.

"That'd be nice."

Stinson walked into the kitchen, sliding his phone into its holster. "Let's get out of here. Patrol can deal with this bullshit until the feds get here."

"Did you reach Stewart Halifax?"

"The phone forwarded to his office and according to the very helpful nurse, he was out of surgery two hours ago so either she's lying, or he's lying. I'm betting on both."

"Any doctor worth his salt, has a very devoted and loyal nurse."

"Probably banging' her, too. Shit, I would after meeting the wife."

Tommy and Sophia moved quickly down the hall and out the front door.

"Maybe we should mention to the homicide guys that we think this might be a little drama produced by Barrett or his father. This is going to hit the news any minute and it's going to be hard to walk it back if it's not a good kidnapping."

"Not our problem." He pulled her by the sleeve through the front door. "Leave your car parked around the corner and come with me. I grabbed a pool car. Let's go see if that that little shit bird Barrett's at school."

Tommy inched the Crown Vic around several patrol cars and headed north to the freeway. Sophia's phone rang within minutes of leaving the Halifax house. It was Shelly Torres, a reporter with a local alternative newspaper and a friend of Sophia's from college. Shelly was like a chihuahua with a rag when it came to certain stories. She liked to write about bad cops, the scandals in city government and get exclusives on active investigations. Sophia had lost track of the number of times she'd said 'No' to Shelly. But Shelly still asked because that was her job and it was the stuff that brought in the advertising dollars and occasionally, a Pulitzer.

"Hey, Shell. What's up?"

"Sophia, I heard about David. I'm sorry."

"Thanks but you know I can't talk about the investigation."

"I know. Is there anything you can tell me? Your media guys are being more tight lipped than usual, and you know I have a pretty good relationship with them."

"It's not my case. It's a homicide."

"Ok, fair enough but can you at least confirm that he left some sort of suicide note at your house?"

Sophia shut her eyes."How the hell did you hear that?"

Shelly laughed. "Well now, you know I can't tell you that."

"Off the record, and you're not hearing it from me," Sophia glanced over at Stinson, who was frowning at what he was about to hear, "He didn't leave a note at my house."

"That's not what I heard."

"Fucking leaks piss me off."

"It's the bedrock of my business." Shelly said.

"Your paper isn't exactly a friend to this department. You must have something pretty impressive on someone to get a nugget on a homicide."

"Just good sources. I'm not interested in blowing the investigation. Just want to confirm something."

"Well, you heard wrong. Look, when I can, I'll see what I can pass on. It's way too early right now to comment." Sophia waited for a question about Grace's disappearance.

"Ok, so on a personal note, how are you really doing?"

"I'm fine but busy. We'll talk in a couple of days, OK? I really have to go."

"Call me."

Sophia ended the call. "I don't want to hear it, Tommy."

"Actually, I thought you handled that pretty well."

"Well, slap me on the ass and call me shocked. Did I just get a compliment from Tommy Stinson?"

"Are you really OK, or was that just some bullshit you were dishing out to that reporter?"

"Honestly Tommy, I'm just numb. I hated David so much after the accident, and I'd been able to maintain that hatred for a long time, but when I saw him the other night looking so weak and shitty, all that anger just kind of subsided."

"You still loved him?"

"Oh god, no. It wasn't like that." She turned away from Tommy.

"I don't get it. I always figure that when shit heads die in some terrible way, it's just God doling out almighty justice. Maybe what you would call karma. I've never thought of it as a bad thing."

Stinson smiled and pulled into the school parking lot. It was empty except for a few cars parked along the fenceline.

"A Camry and an Accord. Those are teachers' cars. These kids drive high-end rides," Sophia said.

"Yep. Spoiled little bastards."

Sophia stepped out of the car. "Let's go and see if anyone here knows what's going on. Maybe he talked to someone before he left."

"Fat chance." Stinson got out, locked the car and lit up a smoke.

"Put that out. It makes you smell like a horn." Sophia whispered as they neared the front door of the school. Tommy flicked the end of the cigarette, carefully keeping the smoke intact for when they left.

"Jesus, you sound more and more like my wife."

Sophia tried the door but it was locked. The halls were vacant except for a janitor's bucket in the hallway along with a large plastic garbage can. She banged on the door. An older black man peered out from a room and squinted toward Sophia and Tommy. Sophia held her badge up against the window.

"School's closed, officers." The janitor pushed the door open with one hand but blocked the entrance.

"We need to come in and take a look around for a missing kid." Sophia pushed past the man. Tommy followed, slamming the door behind him.

"You're just the kind of citizen we love to talk to." Tommy put his hand on the man's shoulder. The man straightened his back and tucked his shirt farther into his pants.

"Hey brother, any teachers still here that we might talk to?"

"Not really. There's a couple of teacher's aids still in the gym playing basketball. I could take you there."

"Sounds like a plan, my man." Stinson and Sophia followed the janitor down the hall.

The hallways smelled of cheap perfume and gym clothes that hadn't been washed in months. High school had been a pretty good time for Sophia. She'd been a band geek who hung with the popular girls. She did well scholastically which also put her in a unique camp, but she didn't flaunt it. Her parents saw great things for her like law or med school and she often thought she'd let them down becoming a cop. At least she'd finished college and gotten her degree in English from San Fransisco State before moving from San Fransisco to Seattle and applying to the department on a dare. She'd worked for loss prevention at Nordstrom's between semesters and she was so adept at spotting bad guys her boss had encouraged her to ditch college and become a cop. Once she graduated, she applied to several departments on the west coast before settling on Seattle. It was just far enough away from family to afford her a sense of independence.

Two young men dressed in cut-off sweat pants and soaking wet t-shirts glided around the basketball court. They were jawing at one another, insults flying but mixed with laughter. The younger of the two was black and wore a blue and gold Notre Dame shirt that clung to his toned chest. The second man was white with a stubble of beard. They stopped when they saw the two detectives enter the gym. Fighting Irish spoke first.

"Hey Roger, what's up? You know the school's closed right?"

"Yep, but these are cops," the janitor said. He turned to Sophia and Tommy. "I didn't get your names."

"Detective Benedetti. And this is Detective Stinson."

Sophia addressed the younger man. "And you are?"

"Kenton Charles. I'm a teacher here. Folks call me Ken."

"I'm Chuck Ferrel, also a teacher." He started to extend his hand and then pulled it back and wiped it on his shirt.

"I'm going to go back and finish cleaning up. You can find your way out?" Roger walked backwards as though he was afraid to turn his back on the group.

"We're good. Thanks, Roger." Sophia said.

"So we just want to ask a few questions about Barrett Halifax." Stinson looked over at Sophia. "We really need to talk to him about his sister. She's come up missing."

"Grace?" Chuck looked at Kenton.

"Is that a surprise?" Stinson pulled out his note pad.

"Well, uh…" Kenton looked at Chuck again.

"Well, uh what?"

"Barrett had his sister with him today. I saw him walk her out to his car." Kenton lifted his shirt and wiped sweat from his face.

"What time was that?" Sophia glanced at Tommy.

"Probably around five or five fifteen. It was long past the end of school. And it was an early day. Chuck and I came back to the school to hoop. I think Roger was the only other person here."

"Where was he when you saw him with Grace?"

"Out behind the school," Chuck said. "It looked to me like he'd been inside and was taking her out to his car. I didn't think much about it. Barrett's a pretty squared away kid, for the most part. He's very protective of his sister."

"As long as he stays away from the goth squad. Those guys don't mix." Kenton laughed but stopped when he saw the look on Stinson's face.

"Ok, gentlemen. I hate to break up your game, but you're going to have to come downtown with us. The homicide detectives are going to want to get statements from you." Stinson picked up the basketball and lobbed it through the hoop. He looked at Sophia and winked.

"Lucky shot," she said and turned her attention back to Ken and Chuck.

"Did something happen to Barrett and Grace?" Ken asked.

"Well, based on what you two have just told us, they're both just fine."

Sophia pulled out her cell phone and hung back in the gym. The two men grabbed their bags and followed Stinson.

She called Barrett. He answered right away.

"What's going on, Barrett?"

"What do you mean?"

"Don't play me. You know what I'm talking about." Sophia's voice was suddenly hoarse.

"I wanted to give Grace a break from my mom."

"So you took her without letting your mother know Grace was with you? You didn't think your mother would be worried sick?"

"My mother wasn't worried. It's all an act."

"Where are you?"

"I took her to the park. She's on the swings. She's safe."

"You need to take her home now."

Sophia hung up, then dialed Andrew MacGrory, the homicide captain, as she slowly walked out of the gym.

"Captain, just wanted to let you know Stinson and I located a couple of witnesses who put the girl with her brother earlier today." She took a deep breath. "And I just talked to the kid brother. The girl's with him. She's fine."

The silence on the other end was excruciating.

"So you two took it upon yourselves to initiate an investigation on a matter outside of your unit?"

"Sir, this case started with us."

"This is being investigated as a kidnapping. It's not your call to make, detective."

"I have a relationship with the brother."

"What the hell is going on, detective?"

"I wish I knew. Barrett Halifax took his sister to the park

without telling his mother. It was all a misunderstanding."

She should have waited until she got the teachers to headquarters and then dropped the information on one of the homicide guys. This wasn't going well.

"Are you at least bringing these witnesses down so one of my guys can talk to them?"

"On our way."

"And don't call me directly again. You shouldn't be jumping your chain."

Stinson stood outside the car smoking.

"What took you so long? These two apparently have something better to do than go talk to the cops."

She motioned him away from the car.

"I talked to Barrett."

"And?"

"He has Grace. He took her to, in his words, give Grace a break from their mother."

"I hope you told that little fucker that I'm going to kick his ass."

"Something's wrong here, Tommy." Sophia moved upwind from Stinson's cigarette. "You saw Ginny Halifax. She seemed legitimately upset. But Barrett made it sound like it was all an act. I'm missing something."

"You're making it too complicated. Let's get these mutts down to HQ. This family is just your run-of-the-mill messed up, that's all."

Sophia stopped Tommy. "I also called MacGrory."

"Jesus. Why the hell did you do that?"

"My ass is already sore. I don't need to hear it from you."

"It went that well."

"He's pissed. "

"Fuck him."

"Easy for you to say. My name's all over this now. Hopefully dropping these guys off will make up for it." She walked over and got into the car which smelled like the inside of a gym bag.

"That and solving the big mysterious kidnapping." Tommy climbed into the car, gunned the engine and drove out of the parking lot.

Stinson and Sophia escorted the two men to the seventh floor of headquarters and put them in an interview room. Sophia walked across the hall into the homicide bullpen and let the administrative assistant know there were two witnesses waiting to talk to a detective. The admins curt answer told Sophia everything she needed to know - detectives were expecting the men and weren't happy.

She took the stairs down to the sixth floor and found Stinson at his desk. It was well past seven o'clock and Sophia suddenly remembered she'd left Bodhi home alone. She called Candy and begged her to run by the house and feed and water her fur kid.

"That poor dog, having you for a mother." Stinson propped his feet up on his desk.

"I agree. But I'm too damn selfish to let her go to a better home." She swore she loved that dog more than any human.

Sophia looked over at Stinson. "New shoes?"

"Not really. I've had them for a while."

"What happened to your favorite ones?"

Stinson blinked. "I still got 'em." He took his feet off his desk. "Why are you so interested in my shoes all of a sudden?"

"No reason. I've just never seen you in anything but those stupid wingtips."

Sophia's cell rang.

"It's Tim Johannes. Patrol guy. Talked to you in the kitchen a few hours ago."

"Hey Tim. What's up?" Sophia hoped he wasn't moving in for a date this soon.

"I've got a license plate for you if you're interested. The father came home shortly after you left and I grabbed the tag as I was leaving."

"Was he alone?"

"Yeah. And seemed pretty cool for someone with a missing kid. I'd be losing my shit if that was my little girl."

Sophia decided to let the homicide guys break the news to the troops that Grace was never missing.

"What's the plate?"

He gave her the plate and the hit came back within seconds to a black BMW 325i registered to Stewart Halifax. That was the car they saw Barrett get out of the day they talked to him at the school.

"Thanks, Tim. I owe you one."

"So maybe I stand a chance for a cup?"

"Seems like I'll be buying."

"Works for me. Talk to you soon, detective."

Sophia hung up.

"Who was that?" Tommy said. "And what are you buying?"

"A patrol guy I chatted with at the house. Said Stewart came home acting like it was no big deal that his daughter was missing. And he drove up in a black Beemer."

"The same one as the kid was driving the other day?"

"Sounds like it."

"Daddy probably lets the kid drive his car to school so he makes the right impression."

"And Stewart doesn't have a care in the world because he knows Grace is with Barrett."

"You think Barrett and his dad are in cahoots? Fucking with Ginny for some reason?"

"I don't know."

"If you want my opinion, I think Stewart Halifax's stink is all over this case."

Stinson stood up and grabbed his bag."I think I've done enough damage for tonight. This one's in homicide's court." Stinson turned off his desk light. "Remind me to do an overtime slip on this one. I'm not doing this shit for free."

Sophia ignored Stinson and looked through the returns on

vehicles registered to Stewart Halifax. He had two cars currently registered to him, one black BMW and a white Lexus.

"Lexus must be Ginny's." Sophia said to an empty room.

Stinson was right about one thing, she wasn't doing any of this for free.

CHAPTER THIRTEEN

Jared cut through the school parking lot and jumped on the bus just before the doors slammed shut. He maneuvered to the back where he had more latitude to choose his seat. The odor of alcohol and cigarette smoke hung in the air, and as soon as he sat, he spotted the culprit - an old man hunched over and passed out near the back exit.

Jared hadn't taken out his earbuds since leaving last period. As the bus rolled over the Aurora bridge, he pressed the volume button up on his iPhone and let Rozz Williams and Christian Death moan at him from the grave.

He was supposed to meet his mother at her office but he'd texted her earlier and told her he was going over to a friend's house to play video games. She'd be working late and he'd be left alone at home to deal with Ed, and that meant listening to that insipid idiot drone on about football or baseball. Jared couldn't remember a time when he hated Ed more. He thought it would be hard to beat the first few months after his mom married Ed, but the bastard had managed to outdo himself by trying to pry into Jared's personal life like some kind of social worker cop. Ed was never going to be his father, no matter how hard he tried.

It was close to four-thirty when Jared jumped off the bus at

Third and Pine across the street from McDonald's. It was a notorious intersection, known for its gang banging and dope slinging. Drive-by shootings had slowed down and moved to south-end neighborhoods, but it was still a good bet to score some rock or a bag of low grade pot.

Jared scanned the block for a familiar face, a knowing glance or a chin-up acknowledgment that a transaction was possible. A boy no older than he walked by and brushed his backpack. Jared grabbed his straps and pulled them tighter, running his hand along the back to make sure the zipper was up. He turned and followed the kid north along Third Avenue, and then turned west on Pine Street. Jared knew not to get too close in case he'd misread the cues. A skinny white boy like him would get jumped in a flash, and explaining a beat-down in that part of town to his mother would be a hard one.

He followed the kid into an alley that smelled like a urinal. Buildings on either side blocked out most of the sun, their fire escapes casting eerie shadows into the puddles below. The kid ducked behind a dumpster. Jared paused and looked around for bike cops, then stepped over against the wall furthest away from the boy. The kid pulled out a small baggie from his pocket and shook it. Jared couldn't see whether it was crack or pills and he wanted neither. He shook his head.

"Weed."

The boy sneered and waved the bag again.

"Not interested." Jared grabbed his shoulder straps and jogged south, dodging a puddle of urine. As he neared the sidewalk, he picked up the pace. The sound of footsteps accelerated behind him. Jared took the corner hard and flattened himself up against the side of a building.

Jared waited, his breath ragged and halting.

Suddenly it was quiet. No running boy emerged. Jared held his breath.

"Yo, bitch." The boy stepped around the corner and lifted his shirt to reveal a pistol in his waistband.

Jared stumbled back, catching himself on a railing that surrounded a sunken stairwell.

"You buying or not?" The boy moved closer to Jared.

"No, dude. I'm looking for weed."

The boy lowered his shirt and clucked. "I ain't your dude, bitch." He stared at Jared as though he was collecting his thoughts.

Jared turned and ran, sure a bullet was about to rip into his back.

The lobby of the apartment building was lit up like Christmas. Two old men sat on a couch, their bodies canted awkwardly, as though they were leaning in to hear one another. Jared wasn't even sure they were breathing. He slid past the empty front desk and made his way to the elevators. He could have walked up the five flights of stairs to Adrian's apartment, but he was so out of breath from running he thought he was going to throw up.

The door to the apartment was cracked and a thin stream of smoke snaked out into the hallway. Jared lightly pushed the door open and stuck in his head. The light from the TV illuminated two men in the room. Jared recognized Adrian. His stomach sank when he saw Eldon.

"Hey," he said softly.

"Hey kid, how'd you get in here?" Adrian sat on a red vinyl couch, a beer and a bong between his long legs. He barely looked up, concentrating on the video game on the TV monitor. His thumbs deftly moved around the game controller in his hands.

The apartment had one chair, a couch and a coffee table held together by duct tape. The only light came from the sixty inch flat screen that sat atop wooden produce crates. The dark brown carpet was barely visible under strewn clothing and pizza boxes.

Adrian laughed. "Get that look off your face. The maid took the day off, man." He shifted over on the couch.

"You know Eldon, right?" Adrian waved toward the fat little man sitting in an overstuffed armchair. It was hard to tell where the man ended and the chair started, his body was wedged into it so tightly.

"Of course he knows me, dipshit. I'm his youth minister." Eldon nodded in the Jared's direction but didn't look up from the game blasting away on the flat screen.

Eldon Loveschild was the youth minister at the Church of Venus Mountain, a hipster house of worship where Jared'smom and his stepfather attended services. It was full of clueless sheep who hung on every word sputtered by the Reverend Damien Copeland, a skinny, jeans-wearing asshole who filled his sermons with the Bible, bloodshed and bullshit.

Eldon gave Jared the creeps. He was overly familiar with the teenagers and way too interested in the youngest members of the congregation. The only saving grace of hooking up with Eldon was meeting Adrian, a low level drug dealer who appreciated Jared's gaming abilities and often supplied him with free weed.

Jared sat down next to Adrian and grabbed a game controller.

Eldon leaned back, took a long pull off a joint and offered it to Adrian.

"Take your backpack off and make yourself comfortable. And grab a beer if you want." Adrian took the joint from Eldon.

"He's a kid," Eldon hissed.

"I'm good. I'm just here to kill some stuff."

"Good boy."

"So how's your old man?" Eldon said. "Haven't seen him at church lately."

"My old man doesn't go to that church. He goes to a real

one."

Eldon chuckled and then his face went slack. "I'm talking about Ed."

"Whatever. He's not my father. He's just some guy who screws my mother."

"Whoa, there, kid. Let's keep it civilized around here," Adrian laughed. "Seriously, go get a beer and chill."

"Mind your manners, Jared." Eldon shot him a look.

Jared ignored him and concentrated on the game, executing a headshot from a hundred yards out.

"Nice shot, dude," Adrian said, taking a long toke on his joint before handing it off to Eldon.

Jared and Eldon had each other in a pretty little vise. Eldon didn't want to be outed as a pot smoking youth minister, and Jared had no interest in his after school antics getting reported to his mother. But there was something about Eldon - a layer of smarmy topped with a good dose of criminal. And he long suspected that whatever it was, his stepfather Ed was at the edges of some shady shit that involved Eldon Loveschild.

Adrian and Eldon were so consumed by their new video venture, they didn't even notice when Jared left the apartment. Back at home, he lit up a joint in the backyard before going into the house. His mother was still not home, and through the kitchen window he saw Ed toss his dinner plate into the sink. By the time he finished smoking, Jared felt sufficiently baked to deal with his stepfather.

"Where the fuck have you been?" Ed pulled a beer out of the fridge, slammed the door and twisted off the top. He flipped the cap across the room and into the sink.

"I had a school thing." Jared brushed past him.

Ed caught him by the sleeve. "Hold up. Why you leaving so

fast?"

"Homework." Jared pulled away.

"Listen, you pot smoking little freak." Ed grabbed Jared again. "Don't think you can pull one over…"

"Get the fuck off me."

Ed stepped back then took a swing. It landed on the left side of Jared's jaw, throwing him against the sink. Jared swung hard but missed, twirling forward. He fell to the kitchen floor, blood from his mouth dropping onto the light gray linoleum.

"Your daddy never taught you to fight, did he?" Ed laughed and stood with his hands on his hips.

Jared assessed his options. He could make another pass at Ed but his jaw was throbbing and the pot had taken the fight out of him. He stood up and looked around the kitchen. Grabbing his backpack, he threw open the kitchen door and stumbled out into the backyard.

"Come back here, you little faggot." Jared ran around the side of the house, across the front lawn and into the street. He kept running until he got to the bus stop on 35th NE and threw up in the corner of the bus shelter. He could hang out until his mother got home and then confront Ed with her support or he could call her, tell her what happened and wait for her at the bus stop.

She picked up on the second ring. "Hey, J. What's going on?" She knew why he was calling.

That bastard already called her.

"Hey mom. Just wanted to tell you that I'm going to stay at Petra's tonight. Her cat's real sick and she's not taking it too well. That ok with you?" His mother trusted Petra's mom and rarely challenged him when he spent time with Petra's family.

His mother didn't answer right away. He was right. She knew.

"Sure, honey. Anything wrong?"

"Nope. I just need to get going, ok? My bus is here."

"All right. Did you get a change of clothes? You don't want

to wear the same thing two days in a row, do you?"

"Do you really think anyone at the school gives a shit what I wear?" Jared hung up.

Jared was pretty sure Petra's mother would narc him out if he actually spent the night with her. She wasn't as strict as some of the moms, but Jared didn't think she liked him much. And besides, she would notice the split lip and start asking questions.

He got on the number seventy-two bus and slumped into a seat. The inside of his lip was still bleeding, the taste in his mouth reminded him of when he used to lick the monkey bars as a little kid. He spat into his hand and wiped the blood on his pant leg. His fingers tingled and his heart pounded. This was how his panic attacks always started. It had been a few years since his last one, and he thought he'd outgrown them. Laying his head back against the plastic frame of the seat, he closed his eyes and took a deep breath. He focused on the sway of the bus. His heart slowed and the tingling stopped.

He texted Adrian.

"Got in shit @ home. Can I chill at ur plc?" Jared held his phone loosely and closed his eyes again. Adrian was usually too baked to find his phone, much less answer a text in a timely manner.

The phone vibrated.

"Im not there. Use key dont touch stuff."

Awesome, Jared thought. He'd have the place to himself. That took care of everything. He could smoke some weed, play on his computer and come up with a plan for Ed.

The walk from the bus stop to Adrian's apartment was far worse at night, when the street dealers and homeless settled in. Jared was fresh meat for predators. He was young and skinny and still didn't shave. He had no sense for assessing threats. His mother the true believer, raised him to believe that every bad guy was misunderstood and set up by the cops. Everyone was innocent until proven guilty, even when they were cocking their fist back and about to knock you out. He found it best to keep his head down, avoid eye contact and walk as though he had a mission.

At night it was also a lot harder to get by the front desk at Adrian's apartment building. There was usually a clerk or concierge stationed in the lobby to discourage the homeless from sneaking in and setting up camp in vacant units. Invariably, someone would overdose or start a fire and then the police or the fire department would crawl all over the place, asking questions that led to fines the building owner wanted to avoid.

Jared didn't recognize the woman at the front desk. She looked like she belonged in a strip club. Intricate tattoos sleeved her arms. Her black tank top hugged obscenely large breasts.

"May I help you?" The clerk was as bored as Jared was nervous. She barely looked up from her book.

"No, I'm just heading home."

"Sure you are." She gave him a quick look and went back to reading.

Jared picked up his pace to the elevator.

The only light in the apartment came from the TV. Jared threw his backpack on the couch and turned on a table light.

Jared peered into the fridge, knowing the potential for anything edible was minimal. He grabbed the second to last beer and cracked it open.

Checking his phone, Jared noticed a missed call from home. It could be from his mom or from Ed, but either way, he decided not to return it. If it had been important, his mom would have left a message. He texted Petra to let her know he was staying with a friend downtown and asked her not to say anything if his mom called.

Jared fired up his laptop and spent the next few minutes

trying to remember Adrian's wireless router password. It didn't take long; the idiot had used his own name. Navigating to the Start button on his laptop, he logged into the remote desktop connection and typed in "Poppins." Up came the desktop of his mom's computer at home. It was the only computer in the house, and he knew Ed spent hours on it buying useless shit on Ebay. He jumped on the browser and pulled down the history tab.

Jared ran the curser down the list of websites Ed had visited in the last few weeks. Mostly, it was what he expected –junk sites, sports betting portals and an occasional porn site. He flicked through the porn sites, not seeing anything he hadn't already investigated himself. He closed the browser history window and went to the bookmarks bar. It was short – neither Ed nor his mother seemed to have interest in visiting any sites more than a few times. But then he saw it. It was a bookmark for New World. Jared never used his mother's computer, so he was certain he hadn't saved it, and he was even more certain his mother wouldn't even know how to get to the site much less have any interest in delving into a virtual world.

But Ed did.

Jared opened the bookmark. Of course, Ed the idiot had asked the login page to save his user name and password.

He clicked himself in through the portal. Jared knew where to go and he made his way through the various rooms until he hit the lobby.

Suddenly, the screen lit up with chat requests. Colored bubbles bleeped and competed for monitor space.

"Hey bud, 'bout time you logged in. What's up? LOL"

"Hey sexy. Cum see me. Brandi"

"BL Conqueror, see me in a private room. Need to talk now."

Jared navigated deftly through the digital noise. These people didn't have a clue that he wasn't Ed. This was going to be fun.

He moved into a private room.

"Are you safe?"

"Yes. Alone."

"Good. I've been off the grid for a few days. May have a problem with a project. May have been compromised. Will need to stay out of playpen for a while."

"What's your issue?"

"Police."

"OK." Jared's heart started to race. What the fuck was Ed into?

"What do you want me to do?" Jared typed.

"Sit tight. Don't troll for BL's on the playground."

The only thing Jared could think that BL meant was 'barely legal,' but he was afraid to tip his hand.

"K."

"And btw, may hv to figure out what 2 do with the old lady ;) on my ass and getting nosey."

"K."

"UR man of few words 2nite."

Jared paused. This guy was going to figure out that he wasn't talking to Ed if he made a misstep.

"Busy day. Ballbuster just got home. Hv to go now." Jared held his breath. The screen stayed still and silent. Jared jumped when the sounds of voices erupted in the hallway.

"Kbye."

The chat room was empty.

He popped back to the lobby and navigated to Ed's favorite locations. Each portal was secured behind a door. Some were password protected, others opened when the avatar stopped in front. Jared didn't care about the free doors – he was curious about the protected domains.That's where Ed was vulnerable.

He moved to the door labeled 'playhouse' and tried it. A warning popped up about age appropriate content and then a prompt appeared for a password. Jared tried Ed's full name. It didn't work. He tried to think what a rookie would use as a password, aside from birth dates and social security numbers, but the program would have a lockout feature after a limited number of tries. That would put Ed on alert. As it was, the next time Ed logged in, he was probably going to see the account activity.

He typed in 'barelylegal.'

The door swung open and a computer synthesized child's voice said, "Welcome. We're glad you're here."

It was a virtual playground filled with dozens of very real looking children. They laughed and skipped rope or played hopscotch. The grass was a deep green, oak trees with huge canopies swayed overhead. The sound of children playing came from the computer speakers.

Jared felt something in his stomach tumble. Why would they need a content warning for a playground?

Jared used the mouse to move around the playground. As he passed them, the children smiled and waved. In the distance, was a swing set. A lone child swung slowly. It was only when he got closer, that he saw her. She was sitting on a swing, legs covered in white leotards that led down to black patent leather shoes. Her dress was pink and rested just above her knees. Blond curly hair fell around her face. She looked at Jared and smiled.

"Hi there, Conqueror. It's me, Grace."

CHAPTER FOURTEEN

Eldon was surprised to see Shirley's lights still on. She was an early to bed, early to rise kind of woman. On the weekends, she'd rummage around upstairs, her oxygen tank clanking into the furniture and overturning tables. It frequently woke him up an hour or two after he'd passed out from half a case of beer the night before. But he couldn't beat the deal he got living in her basement, and the free food and money more than outweighed the noise she made or the nagging when rent was due. And for five hundred bucks a month, he could put up with anything. She rarely came down into his den, and he was reasonably sure that even if she did, she wouldn't have the vaguest idea of what he was doing.

He dropped his coat on the floor. The room was illuminated by the light from his monitors. They were carefully lined up and daisy chained together. The servers hummed gently, their fans coming on and off to cool the hard drives. It was a lot of work to run his enterprise but it was helped enormously by the wi-fi Eldon paid for with Shirley's money. The old bitch still watched TV using rabbit ears. Oh, the world she was missing.

He grabbed a beer and twisted off the top.The door opened at the top of the stairs.

"Eldon, are you up?"

Fuck. Go away.

"Eldon?"

He walked over and looked up the stairs. Shirley stood backlit by the kitchen light. Her thin nightgown was sheer enough for Eldon to make out her spindly frame. He looked away, embarrassed by the sight of the nearly naked old woman.

"What do you want?"

"I need some help with my oxygen tank. It's not working. I can't sleep."

"I'm busy. Can't it wait until the morning?"

"No. I can't sleep."

"So take some cough medicine or whiskey. I'm not coming up there."

"Damnit, Eldon, I'll call the fire department again, and they'll come and then start asking questions like last time."

Eldon set down his beer. All he needed was a bunch of firemen snooping through the house, asking questions and staring at his belly spilling over his pants like he was a heart attack waiting to happen. He hated those fuckers almost as much as the cops.

The last time she called 911, he had to talk his way out of letting them into the basement so they could check the breaker box. He'd be screwed if they saw his server setup and the pirated cable and electricity.

"Give me a minute. I have to take a leak."

"Hurry up."

As he stood at the toilet, he caught a glimpse of his ruddy and pockmarked face. His thinning hair stuck to his scalp from a mixture of sweat and hair gel. He wasn't a handsome man, but he never thought he'd live his life alone, forever trapped beneath the floor of a dying old woman.

Shirley sat at her kitchen table, legs spread open with her nightgown tucked between them. She was sucking air, her boney chest heaving with every breath. Her thin fingers struggled with the tubing coming out of the top of the green tank.

"It's not coming out strong enough." Dirty fingernails clawed at the tank valve.

Eldon opened her fridge peered in and grabbed a Miller Light Tallboy.

"That's my beer. Keep your goddamned hands off of it."

"Really? You want me to help you and you're bitching about me drinking this piss water?"

"You can't talk to me like that, you little queer."

Eldon swung around in one fluid motion. He'd never moved so elegantly. The bottle landed just below her right temple. He was startled by the sound it made against her skull. He expected the bottle to break but it remained intact, scraping off the thin skin of Shirley's forehead. The contact sent her flying from the kitchen chair. Her nasal cannula ripped from her nose and snapped back against the green tank, which fell to the floor with a huge clang.

He stood for a minute over her body, surveying the nightgown wadded up above her waist. The almost imperceptible hiss of the oxygen tank and the low murmur of the television in the front room were soothing. A sliver of hair and skin clung to the bottom of the beer bottle. He wiped it off on his jeans and tipped back the bottle, taking a swig as he squinted through the amber glass into the dim kitchen light.

The office was a den of clicking keyboards, detectives chatting on the phone, and good natured ribbing. Sophia was relieved to find her unit back to full strength. The cases continued to pour in, and Pierson had no compunction about piling up the work on the desks of the detectives who were there, not the ones who were on vacation or in training. Sophia hadn't even cracked open the latest. And then there were the three messages on her phone from Victoria Tilden. She'd been so obsessed about the Halifax case, she hadn't returned a single phone call.

Stinson wasn't at his desk. He was the only one not there.

"Where's your boy?" Jimmy asked.

"I'm not in charge of him today."

Jimmy's tie was loose, his top button undone.

"What's with the casual look?"

"I've been here since five am. Totally forgot I have court today. A little last minute catch up. 'Sides, I fuckin' hate ties. Hate 'em." He looked over at Tommy's desk. "Seriously, where's the old man?"

"Seriously, I don't know." It wasn't like Tommy to be late. He left early on occasion, but she could set her clock by his punctuality in the morning. His desk was uncharacteristically clean. She walked over, looked around and flipped open a file lying on his desk. Inside were papers from the city on his benefit and retirement package.

"Can I help you with something?" Tommy said.

Sophia jumped. "Looking for a ransom note or something. You're late."

"Did you find what you were looking for?" Tommy threw his bag on the floor and pulled out his chair.

"Are you thinking about retiring? Why didn't you tell me?"

"The operative word is 'thinking,' that's all. Calm down."

"I hate it when you tell me to calm down."

"Did you hear from homicide last night?"

"No, did you?" The answer had better be 'No' or she was going to be really pissed. She hated it when Tommy got the follow-up calls and she didn't because she was 'the girl.'

"Nope." Tommy picked up his phone. "I'm going to call Ken Thomas."

Thomas was the old timer in homicide. Sophia was lucky if she got a grunt out of him when they passed in the hallway. A hundred pounds overweight, he moved like a caboose, as though he was at the end of a long, heavy load. He was a brilliant detective, scoring confession after confession. Ken was an intimidating guy. His girth alone was impressive.

"Hey, Ken, it's Stinson." Tommy licked his thumb, leaned over and rubbed a smudge off of the toe of his shoe. "Yeah, yeah. Back at you, asshole." Stinson smiled at Sophia. "So, what's the deal on the kid? We left the office at about eight last night. Neither one of us heard from you guys."

Sophia wanted to be on that call, wanted to hear the news, one way or another.

"Really?"

"What?" Sophia whispered.

Stinson nodded. "No kidding. So, did you hook the kid?" Another long pause. "You're shitting me."

Pierson appeared at Sophia and Tommy's cubicles. "Come see me when he's done."

Not unlike grade school, a collective 'ooh' went up in the office.

On top of whatever Tommy was hearing from Thomas, the two of them were probably about to get an ass chewing for yesterday.

Tommy hung up. "You are not going to fucking believe this."

"Make it quick. Pierson just called us into his office."

"Well, I think I know what's coming." Stinson stood up. "Don't you have to use the restroom before we get our administrative enema?"

"Sure." She nodded to Tommy and they walked toward the door. She looked into Pierson's office. "Be there in a second, Sarge."

The two headed down the hallway toward the restrooms. Tommy looked behind him and then grabbed Sophia and pulled her into an empty interview room. He shut the door.

"So check this out." He lowered his voice. "Barrett showed up at the house last night with his sister and all hell broke loose. The Captain got into a big smack down with the dad, accused the mom and dad of knowing the whole time where the girl was, and then the dad got on the phone and guess who shows up?"

"Who?"

"Marcus fuckin' Burton."

Sophia felt the bottom drop out of her case. "You're kidding…"

"Nope. That asshole showed up and shut down the investigation – the whole thing. Sent everyone packing. I'm telling you, Soph, something is seriously fucked up with this case. I felt it from the start."

"You remember Halifax telling us to play nice or he'd call his friend Marcus?"

"Well, fuck him. I got nothin' to lose at this point. I'm going after that Halifax jerk-off, I think he's involved. And I'm starting to think Burton is, too."

"Let's not get ahead of ourselves. Well, at least not until we hear what Pierson's got to say."

"Oh, I can tell you right now what he's gonna say. He's gonna say we're off the case, that he's inactivating it."

Sophia hadn't entertained that thought. Sometimes she wanted to slap herself for being so gullible and naïve when it came to department politics. That's why, despite his womanizing and hot temper, she loved working with Tommy. He knew the players. He always called it, every single time. He'd been around thirty years and had seen it all. He knew who the workers were, who was trustworthy and who was a climber. He never backed down from a fight – which wasn't always a good thing – but she knew he always had her back.

"I can't believe I'm saying this, Soph but you need to call that friend of yours, that reporter. You need to put a bug in her ass. This is bullshit."

Sophia and Tommy walked back into the office.

"Ready for us, sarg?"

Pierson didn't look up from his computer. "Is Stinson with you?"

"Right here, boss."

Pierson was at this desk. Behind him was a wardrobe, a printer and a bookcase. Family photos dotted the shelves. Sophia took a seat at a table that sat adjacent to the desk so they were facing him. Tommy leaned on the door jamb.

"Close the door, Stinson and have a seat."

Pierson pushed back his chair and crossed his legs. "So, I take it you both know that that child was found unharmed, right?"

"Yeah, she was with that turd of a brother the whole time. And probably with the permission of her equally shitty parents."

"Anyway," Pierson turned his attention to Sophia, "the bottom line here is that this case is going to be inactivated."

"No shit," Stinson said.

"Stinson, you have no idea where this is coming from."

"Oh, I know exactly where this is coming from."

Pierson uncrossed his legs and leaned forward, glaring at Stinson. "It's an order, Stinson. You still remember how that works, right?"

"No problem, sir," Sophia said. "We're officially off the case. I don't need to hear anymore." She stood and motioned for Stinson to move.

As Sophia and Tommy left his office, Pierson pressed on. "I don't want to have this conversation again. Am I clear?"

"Let's go get some coffee." Sophia grabbed the Tilden case file, her jacket and her bag. "I need to call this victim."

"I need to punch someone in the face." Stinson pulled on his jacket and followed his partner out the door.

CHAPTER FIFTEEN

Sophia and Tommy walked across the street and grabbed a cup of coffee at the Starbucks in the Columbia Center. They took an escalator to the second level of the atrium and found a table in a corner.

"Can you believe this bullshit?" Stinson took a gulp of coffee and grimaced. "Shit, this is hot."

"Ok, don't go having a damn heart attack about this." Sophia looked over her shoulder at the escalator. "Maybe it's just as well we're out."

Stinson winced again from the hot coffee. "What is wrong with you? Don't you think David's death is connected to this?"

"I don't know. But I think we can stay on top of this through other channels. I need to find out who's the lead on his homicide, and I need to do that by avoiding that ass-hat Taylor. That guy totally creeps me out. He treated me like a suspect at the scene."

"Well, with David being an ex and all…" Stinson smiled.

"Whatever." She took a sip of coffee. "Taylor is still an idiot."

"I was serious about you calling that reporter." Stinson leaned back and smoothed down his tie. "I think she needs to look into Marcus Burton's connection with this case."

"Well, your personal beef with Burton doesn't make you the most credible source." Sophia watched a woman balancing several cups of coffee on a brief case as she navigated the escalator. "I can call Shelly, but I want to settle some things first."

"Like what?"

"Like I need to work this rape case first and give myself a break from the Halifax family. I haven't even given the thumb drive to the homicide guys yet."

"Yeah you might want to get on that if you don't want to fall back into the suspect box again." Stinson said.

"Funny."

"Seriously, you need to get that thing to them."

"There was nothing on it except for that one file."

"That you know of."

She stood up and pushed back her chair. "God, I hate it when you're right."

Sophia logged the thumb drive into evidence, did a quick supplemental to her follow-up report and sent an email to the homicide admin asking for a call from the case detective so she could explain their new piece of evidence. She should have stopped by in person, but all of the detectives were on a call-out. Besides, the further away she stayed from homicide, the easier it would be to avoid the temptation to snoop for the file on David's death. It was going to be nearly impossible to find someone to talk to her about the investigation, but a detective would have to talk to her at some point, because David was in contact with her the day before his murder. She was still a cop, and if nothing else, a good witness.

Sophia's desk was covered with case files, stacked without any thought to organization.

Her message light was bright red. Victoria Tilden had now left four messages. Sophia expected to get an earful.

The call back number rang to the women's shelter. An

employee put her on hold.

"Detective Benedetti, thank you so much for taking my call," Victoria said.

A woman screamed in the background about 'touching her stuff.'

"I'm so sorry, Victoria. I've been taken up with a few things over the last several days."

"Yes, dear, I heard. That child and that man dying."

There'd been a virtual blackout in the media on Grace's disappearance, and the coverage on David's death had peaked during an otherwise busy news day.

"So, I understand you'd like to meet with me again and talk about what happened a few weeks ago. Can you come to my office?" Sophia didn't want to talk to Victoria at the shelter with its parade of crazy and curious.

"Actually dear, I think it would be a good idea for you and that handsome partner of yours to meet me under the freeway, over by the feeding place. Do you know where I'm talking about?"

"Just north of James?"

"Yes. I can be there in say, half an hour."

"Sure, but can I ask why you want to meet us there? It's pouring outside."

"I just must show you something, dear. I just must." Victoria hung up.

Sophia stood. "Victoria wants to meet us across the street near the feeding tent."

"Have a nice meeting. I'm not going out in that." The rain was coming down in sheets.

"Come on, Tommy. She's a little crazy. I'd like to have some company."

"You really want me to go out there in this seven hundred dollar suit?"

"My curiosity is piqued. What could she possibly want to show us?"

"Oh for chissakes, Soph." He opened his locker and pulled out a rain coat. "I hope you know you'll owe me big time for this. And I'm going to drive over there."

He grabbed a set of keys off of Jimmy's desk. "And yeah, you heard me right. I'm going to drive across the goddamned street."

Victoria was twenty minutes late.

"I fucking knew this would happen." Stinson gripped the steering wheel.

"It's not like we have anything better to do."

"I have plenty of better things to do than wait on some nut job."

Victims and witnesses like Victoria often lived in an alternate time zone. The rain was still coming down, but it was dry underneath the freeway. The parking lot was confined to carpoolers during the day. At night, it became a makeshift homeless camp. Mostly covered by I 5, it spanned an entire city block.

"You know it's only a matter of time before we on-view some car prowl, don't you?" Stinson sat with his head back and his eyes closed.

"Yeah, you look like you're really keeping an eye on crime here." Her shirt sleeve had crept up her arm, exposing part of her tattoo.

"I don't know why you think we don't all know your left arm is covered in ink."

"It's personal. I don't share it with anyone."

"Well, at least not now, since no one's seeing you naked. But I'm assuming you're not counting on that for the rest of your life."

"Leave it alone, Tommy."

"Just trying to be helpful, Beni." He depressed the button on the seat to move it back and stretched out his legs. "I'm going to keep checking for cracks in my eyelids. At my age, it could happen any day and then you're screwed."

In the corner of the parking lot, a figure disappeared between two cars.

"I think that's her. What is she doing?" Sophia got out and walked closer, then turned and got back into the car.

"She's peeing between those two cars."

"Of course she is." Stinson turned off the car and got out.

Victoria stood up, adjusted her clothing and walked over to Sophia and Tommy.

"Detectives, so nice to see you." She extended her hand.

"Hey there, Victoria." Stinson put both hands in his pockets. "I'm coming down with a cold. Wouldn't want to give it to you."

Sophia said a quick prayer. *Please don't expect me to shake your hand.*

Victoria turned to Sophia.

"So, I'd like to tell you a story, if I could." Victoria began walking north through the parking lot.

"Whoa, Victoria where are you going?" Sophia went after her.

"Up here detective, where the men come." Victoria moved in the direction of an area near the freeway entrance that had been fenced off to keep people from clamoring up the concrete supports to set up camp. A small hole had been cut near the bottom of the fence. It wasn't visible from the street and it wasn't likely that department of transportation people checked the area very often, since it was populated heavily by homeless 'urban campers' who didn't welcome the presence of noisy city workers. Sophia waved Stinson over. Victoria slipped through the gap in the fence and stood on the other side like a triumphant explorer.

"What are we looking at?" Sophia peered up into the space between the bottom of the freeway and the support. An abandoned sleeping bag lay partially shredded in the corner.

Stinson pulled out a small flashlight and shone it up into the cavity. The light caught something glinting.

"That is where they come at night."

Stinson looked at her, inadvertently shining the flashlight in her face. "Ok, when you say this is where they come at night, are you speaking literally or figuratively?"

Sophia shook her head.

Victoria threw back her head and laughed. "Oh, you are such a rogue, detective." She slapped him on the arm. "Figuratively, of course. I'm not the tramp you think I am."

"Victoria, we really have no idea what you are talking about." Sophia began to shiver in the wet and cold.

"At night, I've seen them. These pathetic little men climb up there and stay for only a moment. They usually have one of those things." She put her finger to her head as though she was trying to solve a difficult problem. "One of those computers. They're portable."

"You mean a laptop?" Stinson said.

"Yes, a laptop. They carry a laptop up there and then come back down and get into their cars and drive away."

"Well, what do you think they are doing up there?" Sophia asked while Tommy climbed up the steep concrete incline in his new Bruno Magli's.

"I have no idea, dear. But I saw that man up here last week."

"Who?"

"That man who died." Victoria cocked her head and looked at Stinson.

"The man who died in Rainer Valley?" Sophia asked.

"Yes, dear. I didn't know he was once a police officer."

"Where did you see his photo, Victoria?"

"In the paper or on the news. Frankly, I don't recall."

Stinson climbed to the top of the concrete embankment and sat on his haunches. Snapping on a pair of latex gloves, he reached up into the area where the base of the freeway met the concrete wall and pulled out a small box.

"I've got something." He turned and displayed the box.

"Bring it down." Sophia pulled out her notepad. "When did you see the man, the man who died?"

"Well, there are a lot of them who come here. Let me think…" Victoria looked out at the northbound on-ramp. "I believe it was a week ago. Yes, that's right. He came here with a woman, but she stayed in the car. He didn't actually go up there," she said pointing under the freeway. "He stood near the street, down there." Victoria pointed to Sixth Avenue.

"Can you describe the car?"

"It was white. Sort of large and probably American. A sedan, not one of those giant gas eating things."

"And the woman?" Stinson had climbed down and stood next to Sophia. In his hand was a small steel box, the lid opened.

Victoria glanced into the box. "She was caucasian, probably in her 40's, with a little fat around the middle. I only know that because at one point she stepped out of the car when she saw me. I was only passing through to my sleeping spot. She gave me a stern look. Which, I might add, I did not appreciate at all."

"What did the man do?"

"Sweetie, I was busy. I didn't pay that close attention. I was looking for a place to sleep." Victoria hiked up her skirt. "But I believe he was taking pictures of something. Or someone."

Sophia pulled out her phone and called Jess.

"Do you remember seeing any cars at the homicide scene?"

"Why are you calling on the homicide, Beni?" Jess lowered her voice.

"I'm not working it. Tommy and I are out on another case and I just thought of something and wanted to run it by you. Might be helpful, who knows?"

"So do you remember any car?"

"I only remember an old light colored Chevy Caprice parked right out in front. You know the kind. Big, old boat. It's kind of a popular car in that neighborhood so I really didn't think much about it."

"No word to anyone about this, ok?"

"Ok, but the chief was crawling around here after you left. Spent a half an hour in Pierson's office, and now Pierson looks even more pathetic than usual. I don't know what's going on, but people are in a serious mood around here."

"Thanks for the heads up."

Sophia hung up. Tommy had opened the box and pulled out a thumb drive.

"My, that's a strange thing to attract such odd group of men to this god forsaken place." Victoria had sidled up alongside Tommy.

"Yeah, it is." He looked at Sophia and then, realizing Victoria was practically in his lap, he stepped aside.

"I want to take a look."

"You think we need a search warrant?"

"For what? It's not evidence of anything, as far as I know. It's out in a public place and no one's claiming ownership, right? I don't see why we can't plug it in and take a look." He walked over to the car, grabbed an evidence envelope from the trunk and dumped in the thumb drive.

"Victoria, these men you see coming out here. Is that all they do, just climb up there and go to this box?"

"With those computer things, yes."

"And would you recognize any of these men if you saw a picture?"

"Well, I recognized that one poor fellow, didn't I? And I also recall seeing that policeman."

Tommy looked at Sophia.

"What policeman?" He closed the lid on the box and placed it on the hood of the car.

"He's one of those types that talks on TV a lot. And I've seen him with your Chief of Police when they appear at events for the homeless. But mostly, I've seen him on the news, talking about murders and such. I do find the shelters are very good about keeping us all abreast of the news." Victoria picked up her bag of belongings. "Oh, and there were two others with him that night. I couldn't see the one person, but I recognized the man in the nice suit."

Stinson sighed. "Jesus Christ."

"No dear, that fellow with the same name as the actor who married dear Elizabeth Taylor." She paused and then smile. She clapped her hands together.

"Burton. Yes, his name is Burton."

CHAPTER SIXTEEN

Sophia and Tommy dropped Victoria off at the shelter with a promise to call her in the morning. She bummed a couple of cigarettes from Tommy and insisted he hold the shelter door open for her.

"I think we need to take this to ICAC. Didn't you go to the academy with George Anderson, the forensics guy down there?" Sophia said as they drove toward headquarters.

"Why not just plug it into one of ours?"

"Oh, hell no. I have no idea what's on this thing but I know enough that it needs to go into a cold machine. It could have a virus or a whole slew of stuff on it that we don't want to pass on to the city network. That'd get us both canned."

"Well, let's just head down there and see if he's in. Hopefully, he'll do us a favor."

"And while we're down there, I want to run by evidence and check out Halifax's laptop so we can take it to the guys on the Secret Service task force. I want them to do a forensic analysis on the hard drive."

"You got a warrant I don't know about, Beni?" Stinson pointed the car south onto I5 and then took the Airport Way South exit.

"It's definitely too late to ask for consent."

"We can talk a judge into a warrant. Don't worry about it." Stinson said.

Sophia held up the evidence bag with the thumb drive. "I guess we should see what's on this thing first. Halifax's computer isn't going to walk out of the evidence unit."

Detective George Anderson was probably just shy of fifty-five. He could have retired two years earlier but he loved his job and it only required him to sit in front of a computer all day long, which meant he wasn't likely to hurt himself and then have to go out on a disability retirement.

He was exactly where Sophia expected to find him, sequestered in a windowless room tucked in the corner of the Internet Crimes Against Children unit. He spent his days looking for some of the worst images imaginable. Although Sophia thought it would be awesome throwing pedophiles and child pornographers into jail, it meant having to look at those pictures and videos day after day. An old timer had told her once, "Once that crap gets in your head, it's there forever. There's no going back." It was hard enough to deal with sexual assault cases, but at least she didn't have to see it replayed on a computer monitor every day.

Anderson leaned back in his chair. He wore a black polo shirt with the initials 'ICAC' above the left breast pocket, and khaki BDU pants.

"Well, I'll be damned. What brings you two into my den of depravity?" George stood up and extended his hand to Tommy and then to Sophia.

"A favor." Tommy smiled.

"Of course. No one comes in here to just hang out." George laughed.

"I still don't know how you do this shit day in and day out.

I'd eat my fuckin' gun after I put one in the head of any one of these monsters you babysit."

"A strong faith helps." George smiled. "And you're not the first guy to threaten to eat his gun after spending time with me."

"Probably a couple of women, too." Stinson chuckled.

"Still the same old Tommy Stinson." George sat back down and tipped back in his chair.

"Hey George, remind me to buy you a beer someday so I can hear those stories." Sophia smiled and took a seat at an empty desk.

"He's a freakin' Mormon. Maybe you could buy him some fancy sparkling water or something." Tommy said.

"No worries, Detective Benedetti. And yes, I'd love to regale you with some Tommy Stinson lore."

"Ok, spare me the threats to expose my complicated past. We need a serious favor from you."

"Can you take a look at this?" Sophia handed the evidence envelope to George.

"You have a warrant, I assume?"

"Nope."

"A case number?"

"It's a little complicated," Sophia said.

"I'm generally not a fan of complicated but try me."

"This thumb drive was in a box under the freeway. As far as we know, it doesn't belong to anyone, so we figured we were good with looking at it without paper."

"Sounds like a dead drop." George opened the envelope and let the thumb drive drop on his desk. "How did you come to get this?"

"A dead what?" Tommy looked at Sophia and back to George.

"A dead drop. It's an anonymous peer-to-peer file sharing practice that takes place in public spaces. It's sort of a new take on an old espionage trick used during the Cold War mostly.

Now, it's popular with gamers and artists and…" George paused."Cretins who traffic in child pornography. They load their pictures on a thumb drive, another user comes by, uploads what's on the drive and then leaves their own stash for the next guy." George put on a pair of oversized glasses and picked up the drive. "Although they tend to be a whole lot more discreet. Must be a newbie. No one with an ounce of brains would leave a drop somewhere the cops would find it."

"We didn't find it. A rape victim took us to it."

"So we should be good without a warrant, right?" Tommy said.

"Is this connected to the rape?"

Sophia spoke up. "Oh, no. Not at all."

"Are you expecting to go forward with a case on this? Is this going to be evidence?" He knew how hard defense lawyers fought child porn cases, and mishandling of evidence was often the focus of many a suppression motion.

"We don't know. It may be nothing, completely unrelated." Sophia didn't look at Tommy.

"Look, I didn't just fall off the turnip truck, guys. You wouldn't be bringing this to me if you didn't think it was going to lead you to someone or something. I can take a look. But if there's anything bad on here, we'll have to stop and get a warrant."

"It's a deal, George."

George looked at Sophia.

"I can live with that," she said.

George got up and walked over to a stand-alone tower while donning a pair of latex gloves. He slid down a cover, inserted the drive and clicked it open on the desktop.

"There's just a readme.txt document on here. I'm guessing it's just instructions on using the drive." He opened the file.

"Nothing special on here. Pretty much what I expected."

"There's nothing on there? What's the point?"

"You might have grabbed the drive in between shares. The

last guy may have just taken something but not left anything." George closed the drive window.

"Well, that blows." Tommy put his hands in his pockets and slumped into a chair. "Not that I wanted to see a bunch of naked kids, but I was sort of hoping it was going to lead us to our guy."

"So you are working this as a case." George looked at Sophia.

"Not anymore. We got pulled off by Chief Burton."

"Burton?" George furrowed his eyebrows and frowned.

"Yeah, he pulled us off from SAU but not ICAC. This has always been a case better suited for you basement dwellers. What if we went forward with, say, a referral from SAU? What if you guys took a look?" Tommy said.

Sophia looked at George. He smiled slyly.

"I hate that guy, Burton. And he absolutely hates this unit. Won't approve any training or overtime. He's made some pretty serious enemies down here. Why does he care about this case anyway?"

"He's friends with the father of our victim, Stewart Halifax. And Halifax has been less than helpful from the beginning on this case."

"Is that the kid who went missing a couple of days ago?"

"Yep. And as soon as she showed up with her idiot brother, Burton shut down the case, pulled us off and put the fear of God into our sergeant."

"Aside from the fact that he's a pussy anyway," Tommy added.

"And how does this drive play into things?"

"Our witness puts Burton at the scene along with Halifax."

"Really? Of course there could be a number of reasonable explanations as to why he was there. That parking lot is across the street from headquarters." George pulled up the browser window and started typing in the address bar.

"There's too many coincidences right now. Too many fingers

in this pie for me to believe he doesn't know something." Tommy said.

George turned his chair towards Sophia and Tommy. "I have an idea but it's going to be a huge gamble."

"Can't get any worse, right?" Sophia said.

"We could load a software program on the thumb drive that would install secretly on the computer of the next person who tries to dump something on it. I can put a keyword logger on it and then I can access it remotely. We could probably pull an IP address off of it, get a warrant for the records and identify the user. It might take a while to pull it off. These guys are usually pretty sophisticated about these things. Smart guys will scan the device for malware before taking anything off of it. If that happens, we're screwed, and they'll probably ditch the drive."

"We could set up on it, watch it for a while to see who shows up. I'd love to catch one of these assholes in the act," Sophia said.

"The only problem will be the warrant." George flipped a ballpoint pen through his fingers like an experienced baton twirler. "That will be tricky."

"Could you guys open a case, maybe on the down low or at least until we have enough to go above Burton, and convince them we've got some legitimate bad guys? The chief of all police is not going to want to be caught up in a scandal that makes the department look like they're protecting a child raper." Tommy had started pacing.

"Well, I am acting sergeant this month and this has been brought to my attention by two well respected detectives on this department." George spun his chair and winked. "I'll assign it to myself. That way we can keep the other guys out of it until we know what we are dealing with."

"You're a genius, George. You are a fucking genius." Tommy slapped George on the back.

They were treading on thin ice. It this backfired, she and Stinson could be looking at some serious discipline, maybe even land on the prosecutor's Brady list, a distinction that could follow them both until the end of their careers.

George loaded the keyword logger on the device and set up a remote access point he could check once the software was downloaded on the unsuspecting computer. Sophia and Tommy headed back to the office with the dead drop ready for an unsuspecting mark.

Tommy pulled into the garage. It was the safest place for he and Sophia to talk. They were well out of earshot of anyone and any cop would have to pass them to get to their car, including a chief.

"We're gonna have to do the surveillance on our own dime, you know," Sophia said.

"I've stolen more time from this city than they've ever paid me for. I'll get over it. Besides, this is personal now."

"Tommy, that's not a good…"

"I know, I know. It's just that Burton has always bugged the shit out of me, and I don't trust that fucker. He's up to his ass in this. And so is Stewart Halifax. And who knows, maybe that little prep school prick Barrett is also involved. Maybe he made up all that stuff about what he saw to take the heat off of him or his old man."

Sophia nodded in the direction of the roof access from the garage elevators. "Speak of the devil."

Marcus Burton pulled out a cigarette as he walked to his black Toyota Highlander. He leaned against the car and looked up at the Municipal building parking garage.

"What's he looking at?"

Tommy craned his neck to look through Sophia's side window. "I don't see anything."

Sophia grabbed a pair of binoculars out of her go bag.

"See anything?"

"There's someone standing there but they're back from the edge. I can't get a good look."

Burton dropped the cigarette and ground it out with his foot. He nodded at the figure across the street and then got into his car. As he passed Tommy and Sophia, he looked straight ahead.

"Did you see that?" Tommy said.

"His brake lights lit up just after he passed us."

"He saw us. Just didn't want us to think he did."

Sophia took another look at the parking garage. "Not there anymore. Whoever it was, ditched the same time as Burton."

Tommy stepped out and walked over to the edge of the garage. Sophia followed and the two looked over so they could see the Cherry and 6th Street exits.

"I think there's an exit on Columbia, too."

"We can't cover everything."

Two white Prius' pulled out.

"Pretty sure those are city rides," Tommy said.

"Tommy. Look." Sophia pointed up 6th Ave. A black BMW sedan pulled slowly out of the garage, pausing for southbound traffic.

"Can you see the driver?"

"No. Fuck." Sophia ran along the garage wall to get a better angle but the car quickly sped south on 6th and out of her view.

"Get a plate?"

"No, goddamn it."

Back in the office, Sophia cradled her phone and leaned forward, both elbows on her desk.

"Hey, it's Detective Benedetti. Can you check on an item that was booked in under case number 13-555467? It should be a laptop."

The warehouser put her on hold and as she listened to some horrible, one-percent-for-art band, Jimmy and Jess walked past her hauling file boxes.

"Where's that stuff going?" Sophia asked.

"I'm finally getting rid of all that crap from the Franklin case. It's been piling up under my desk," Jess said. "Trying to start a trend in the office." She looked at Sophia's desk.

"Maybe it'll rub off."

"Fat chance," Tommy laughed.

"Detective? I'm a little confused," the warehouseman said.

"About what?"

"According to the paperwork I'm looking at, you released it to the owner yesterday."

"No, I didn't."

"Yes, you did. I have the slip right here.Your signature's on it."

"I never released anything yesterday. I was here all day."

"Don't know what to tell you. I've got the slip in front of me."

"Who released it from your shop?"

"Looks like the sergeant did it." There was a long pause. "That's kind of weird."

"What's weird? Who's the sergeant?"

"Sergeant Burton, ma'am."

Marcus Burton's ex-wife.

Sophia hung up.

"You are not going to fuckin' believe this."

Tommy nodded and laughed.

CHAPTER SEVENTEEN

That night under the freeway, Sophia and Tommy huddled in an unmarked car.

"What's that smell?" Tommy wrinkled his nose.

"I'd rather not think about it."

"It smells like ass in here. "

"Yes, it does and again, I'd rather not think about it. I'm sure some has been acquired in here."

Sophia looked into the backseat. "Hopefully back there."

"It's pretty quiet now. Put this back up there." Sophia handed him the box. "Fingers crossed, no one noticed it was missing."

Tommy took the box and jogged to the corner of the parking lot. He looked around quickly before scaling up the incline.

Tommy returned to the car, opened the door and grabbed his cigarettes from the center console. "I'm gonna have a smoke." He leaned against the front of the car and lit a smoke.

The image of David's body came back to Sophia in waves. Sometimes the images appeared like strobe lights, passing quickly in and out during a busy moment. Others arrived with a tsunami-like wall of emotion, blindsiding her with grief. He was not the love of her life, not even close. And things changed so fast, much of the time was a blur between the fighting and his drinking. Soon the make-up sex turned into long stretches of silence and passivity. He was never a mean drunk, but the rage that bubbled just beneath the surface was palpable most days. Sophia always suspected that one extra glass of whiskey would be just enough to tease out the violence, and she'd see him as he truly was. And that one day was almost her last.

"Whatcha thinking?" Tommy got back into the driver's seat.

"Nothing."

"Figured as much." Tommy rolled down the window. "Montero was a self-centered asshole. He tried to kill himself and take you with him. Don't forget that. He wasn't good for you. He should've never come back here."

Sophia smiled. "It's weird how you can hate someone and wish them dead but when it happens, it's so surreal. I never understood how people could say they didn't believe someone was dead even after they'd seen the body. How they'd talk about their husband or wife in the present tense, like they were going to walk in the door any minute. I used to think, you know, they're dead, right there, right there in front of you, and you're referring to them as though they're alive. But I get it now." Sophia looked away from Tommy.

"That's always a good clue to a perp's guilt," Tommy said. "When they refer to a missing loved one in the past tense. They know they're dead."

Sophia wasn't interested in talking anymore. She suddenly hoped someone would come up and try and jack them so she could have an excuse to hit something. Thank god Tommy was there.

"Hey, lookie there." Sophia grabbed the binoculars.

A car backed into a parking space across from the concrete ramp to the dead drop.

"Come on you little fucker, get out and haul your fat ass up there." Tommy also looked through a pair of binos.

"Gee don't we look unsuspicious," Sophia laughed.

"It's just us and the dopers and car prowlers. These guys aren't looking for cops."

"God, I'd love to beat the shit out of one them."

"Hang in there, terminator. You'll get your chance."

The figure in the car stayed behind the wheel.

"Can you see anything? I can't see shit." Sophia adjusted the lens on the binoculars.

"I can see part of the car. Fucker has his dome light turned off. It's too dark to see anything. If he gets out, I won't be able to tell from this angle."

"Wait. Someone's crawling up to the box."

The figure resembled a troll. Long hair protruded from underneath a large floppy hat and trailed down the back of a mid-length coat. He - and that was a guess - couldn't have been much taller than Sophia but he scrambled up the steep concrete ramp like a seasoned rock climber. A messenger bag was slung over his shoulder.

"Jesus, he looks like a fuckin' monkey. Obviously done this a time or two."

At the top of the ramp, the figure turned back in the direction of Sophia and Tommy's car.

Sophia slid down in her seat. Tommy leaned over toward the center console, too tall to slide anywhere. The beam of a flashlight struck their car and lingered over the front window.

"Do you think he made us?"

"He made something. Just stay down for now. I want him to plug that drive into his laptop, assuming he has one."

Sophia started developing a cramp in her leg. "I've got to move. I'm dying here."

She sat up slowly. The troll was gone. But the car was still parked in the stall.

Sophia looked out the passenger window.

"Jesus!" A man stood next to the door holding a flashlight directly in her face. She struggled to grab her gun and push the door open. The door knocked the flashlight out of the man's hand and he fell backward. Tommy jumped out and ran around, grabbing the man by the shoulders just as he rose and tried to run.

Sophia stepped out of the car. "Hey, where you going?" She took one arm and pulled it behind the man's back.

"You're hurting me!"

"Seattle Police, settle down." Tommy turned the man toward them.

He looked to be in his late twenties, a sparse beard covered his chin. His hair was stringy and flat.

"I'm not doing anything, asshole. You can't touch me."

"Looks to me like you were prowling this car, not to mention what you were planning on doing up there." Tommy nodded toward the dead drop. He and Sophia still held an arm.

"I don't know what you're talking about." The man stiffened. Tommy shoved him against the car. "Don't fucking lie to me."

Sophia grabbed her flashlight from her pocket and shone it on the man. He wore torn flannel shirt under a puffy black jacket. His jeans hung low on his hips and he wore new running shoes.

"Tommy, look." She pointed at the car still parked at the base of the dead drop.That guy's been watching us deal with this dipshit."

The car pulled out and cruised slowly past Sophia and Tommy with the headlights off. The windows were so tinted, she couldn't see inside. As it pulled slightly ahead of them, the driver gunned the engine and spun the tires against the parking lot asphalt.

"Fucking asshole," said the car prowler.

"Did you get the plate?" Sophia yelled to Tommy.

"No."

"I got it," whispered the car prowler.

Tommy and Sophia looked at each other and then at the

man. He was smiling.

"It's yours for a price."

"How about the price is you not going to jail tonight?" Tommy said.

"C'mon man." The man clapped his hands together. "I've got information you need."

"And I have the keys to your freedom," Tommy said, dangling his handcuffs in the man's face.

"146HRT."

Looking at Sophia, the man repeated it slowly as she wrote it down. "146HRT. You should get yourself a better secretary, man."

Tommy looked at Sophia, barely containing a grin.

"What did you call me?"

"Oh, sorry ma'am. I just thought, you know, you two were…"

"Were what?" She'd put her notebook onto the front seat of the car.

He looked at Tommy. "Hey, man."

"You're on your own, buddy. But before I unleash my partner on you, why don't you tell us how you're so sure about the plate.

"Cuz I've seen it before. The car and that guy. He comes by at least once a week."

"Does he always get out or does he stay in the car usually?"

"Sometimes he just stays in the car. Other times he gets out and climbs up there like he did tonight."

"What's he doing up there?"

"Beats the fuck out of me." The man looked at Sophia. "Never bothered to look."

"Can you describe him?"

"Not really. I've never seen him up close. Some white dude. Usually wears that stupid hat and coat. I almost rolled him one time last winter when I was cold. I thought that coat might be nice to have but honestly, he's too creepy even for me to rob."

"Wow, standards." Tommy pulled out a smoke.

"Hey man, can I have one?"

"Jesus Christ. Do I look like a smoke shop to you?" Tommy tossed one in the man's direction. "And keep the matches, I don't want them back."

"Look, I can get you guys some good shit on these guys. I don't know what they're dealing or anything, but this is a busy spot."

"Busy spot for what?" Sophia picked up her notebook again.

"Like I said, I don't know what's going on but there's a lot of nice rides cruising though here, stopping and getting whatever that thing is up there."

"What's your name?" Tommy moved closer to the man.

"Johnny. Johnny Canton, and I got a warrant. I'm being straight with you. It's a little one though. It's for taking a leak in Courthouse park.

"Well, who doesn't piss in that park, huh?"

"Ok, here's the deal, Johnny. We want you to stay away for a while, just until we figure out what's going on up there. You can help us with that, right?"

"It's a deal, Officer. I'm gone. You won't see me again. I promise." Johnny brushed off his coat. "Can I please have my flashlight, though?"

Tommy threw it to him. "Now, get lost."

Sophia climbed into the car. "Well, I hope that plate is good, or we've just fucked ourselves."

CHAPTER EIGHTEEN

Since this was his first kill, Eldon soon realized that doing something so rash was ill-advised. He suspected the amount of alcohol he'd consumed had something to do with it, but normally that meant acting inappropriately at a bar, not killing someone. He felt slightly overwhelmed.

Luckily, no one was going to miss Shirley Townshend. She was almost a ghost. He'd stripped her name off of the utility bills. She had no family or friends, having moved here in the fifties with her husband. She'd lived in a depressing vacuum, a self-imposed cocoon created after her husband's death. Mowed down by a milk truck in a crosswalk on his way home from church, he was dragged two hundred feet before a bug-eyed cabbie flagged the driver over and pointed to the bloody mass of human caught in the axels of his truck.

Eldon was reasonably sure that he was safe for the short term, or at least long enough to get out of town or create a story that was believable enough to keep him out of jail. But in the meantime, he was going to have to dispose of Shirley's body. He wrapped her in a shower curtain he carefully detached from the upstairs bathroom. The seashells and seahorses bathed her in pink as he rolled her up and fastened the open ends with duct tape. He was surprised at his own lack of empathy. He understood he was not a kind man, but even he was taken aback by the ferocity that seized him when he swung the bottle at Shirley. She wasn't an evil woman, just a meddling annoyance. He could have continued living under her floorboards, enduring her occasional requests for assistance. It wouldn't have killed him.

He dragged the body into her bedroom. Pulling back her heavy quilted duvet, he lifted her onto the bed and pulled the top sheet and blanket over her. He tucked in the sheets, just like a son comforting an ailing mother. He placed the duvet and throw pillows on top of her. Before he turned off the lamp on her bedside table, he closed her bible and placed it into the table drawer.

The following morning, after getting no sleep and nursing a major hangover, Eldon reported to work promptly at eight AM.There was a stack of work tickets in his computer queue, a sight that filled him with relief. A busy day was a fast day, and he had lots to clean up at home. He quickly worked through the queue, handling most of the ticket requests remotely. Given his pounding head and cotton mouth, it was just as well. He didn't trust himself now, despite his sobriety. He'd suddenly discovered his aptitude for homicide, and it filled him with a sort of perverse pride.

He got home slightly after four. Careful not to change his patterns, he went in through the basement door. One could never know if one of the neighbors really did watch out for the old lady. He'd have to come up with some excuses should they come to the door during the holidays. He'd make up some family who really gave a shit, send her on long deserved vacation with a church group, put her in the hospital for a spell. Maybe he could make up a dummy dressed like Shirley and prop her in different windows.

Shirley's bedroom was at the back of the house. Cluttered with old clothes, dirty linens and stacks of Life magazines, Eldon could have tossed a match into that room and had the entire house engulfed in a minute. He sat on Shirley's bed, next to the lump that contained her body, and eyed a pair of slippers peeking out from underneath it. It made him think of his mother, who farmed him out to his aunt and uncle in Chehalis, exiling him to a life of threats and beatings. When he was old enough to be on his own, he set out to find his mother, who had remarried and started another family. She'd been so alarmed at seeing him that day in the Safeway a few blocks from her home, that she'd called the police. It was an amusing scene, this socialite trying to explain to some tired, old cop why she didn't want her son to talk to her in public. In fact, it was so pathetic that the cop had escorted Eldon home, buying him a coffee and suggesting he apply to work for the city in the IT department after he learned of his impressive computer skills.

But now Shirley was beginning to smell. She kept the heat up high, like most old folks. Eldon finished a casserole from the fridge and downed a few beers. He couldn't take the chance of getting pulled over for a DUI, so he sat in the living room and watched TV until close to twelve-thirty. Pulling up forest service maps on his computer, he found a service road off of Highway 2 that would take him close to Spada Lake. It was under two hours to drive there. Without any complications, he'd be back in time for work.

The body was heavier than he expected. Grabbing one end, he pulled her down the basement stairs, one thump at a time. At the bottom, he turned out the lights, even the computer monitors.

Eldon backed the Subaru up to the basement door, opened the hatch and lined the interior with plastic garbage bags. He put Shirley's feet in first, straining against rigor mortis to fold her over into the back of the car. He covered the body with a tarp and a shovel, along with four rocks and some polypropylene rope.

Eldon went back in and made a thermos of coffee. He grabbed his laptop and threw it onto the passenger seat.

Traffic on I-5 was light all the way to Highway 2. Headlights drilled him as he drove east but few cars followed him. Driving deeper into the Wenatchee Forest, the darkness was soon complete.

When he reached the end of the county maintained road, he pulled over and waited. Spada Lake was a reservoir with vehicular access near Olney Pass. It wasn't likely to be staffed this time of year and since it was public utility land, no camping was allowed.

With the windows down, he slowly sipped coffee listening for signs of others. The night was only full of the sound of leaves rustling against a languid breeze and the lapping of the lake against the shoreline.

When Eldon was finally convinced he was alone, he calmly opened the hatch and pulled Shirley out. The wind had picked up and it had started to rain. Slinging her over his shoulder, he walked down to the shoreline and dropped her to the ground. He put a small flashlight in his mouth and moved quickly. Fastening a rock to the end of each hand and foot, he took off his shoes and pants and waded out into the lake pulling her body with him. She sunk quickly, which he didn't expect, and he panicked, suddenly terrified he would be tangled in the ropes and drawn to the bottom with her. He dropped the last rock and struggled back to shore

It would be next spring before she was found, if ever. The polypropylene rope was marine grade. Her limbs would give way before the rope would.

On the way home, he tried to calculate how much time he had left in Seattle, how long he might be able to hide her disappearance. His temper had failed him and thrust him into this predicament. His routine was going to be disrupted but his business would have to be re-arranged beyond what he could imagine in an hour and a half drive back to the city.

NCIC and WASIC was down, which always seemed to happened just when the system was needed the most, and Sophia and Tommy were too nervous to request the information on the registered owner belonging to the plate by way of radio. It was late and they were both tired.

"I'm out of here. I need to spend some quality time with my dog." Sophia rubbed her eyes and stared at her computer screen.

"Yep." Tommy sounded like he was out of breath.

"You ok?" She looked over her shoulder at him.

"I'm fine. Just getting too old for this shit."

"Go get some rest. And do it at home, with your wife."

"Didn't I tell you? I'm back with the wife. Things are good now."

"I'm really glad to hear that, Tommy. Evelyn is a good woman."

"Yes, she is. And she should get a frickin' medal for putting up with my ass."

" I guess I can take you off my shit list now," Sophia laughed.

"Leave me on. No doubt I will do something stupid in a day or two."

Sophia turned off her computer and stood up. "So first thing tomorrow, we run that plate, pray it hasn't been flagged and then go from there."

"Don't hold your breath. That kid is probably full of shit. If that plate comes back to a car that even remotely resembles that ride we saw tonight, I'll be surprised."

"Fingers crossed."

Sophia and Bodhi settled down for a late dinner of steak and oven roasted broccoli, Bodhi eating her small piece in one gulp. Sophia opened a good bottle of merlot, making a mental note to stop after two glasses. It was the first time she'd had any alcohol since she'd last seen David alive. Only a few nights had passed but it seemed like months ago.

She glanced at her answering machine. She'd been so busy with work, she hadn't check it in three days. The message light blinked three times, indicating three messages.The first was from her mother, reminding her of her promise to come down to California for the holidays. Her mother didn't care which holiday, just one or all. The second message was from Shelly Torres asking Sophia to call her on an urgent matter. Shelly never called her at home, only on her cell phone.

The third message was from David. She sat upright. He sounded stressed, his voice higher than usual.

"Hey, it's me. I got your message to meet. I'll be there but then I'm gone. I have a feeling I'm being watched and I think it's a cop. Can't say for sure. It's just a hunch." David cleared his throat. "Despite what you think, I still care and I'm so sorry for what I did." The call ended abruptly, as though he was timing it.

Sophia rummaged in her work bag and pulled out her digital recorder. She transferred the message from her voicemail, checked that she had it and then pulled her answering machine out of the wall. She called Tommy's cell. It went to voice mail.

"Damn it, Tommy." She hung up, poured herself another glass of wine and hit the speed dial for Shelly.

"Hey, Shel."

"Dang, girl. Nice of you to call me back two days later."

"I'm a shitty friend. I deserve anything you have to throw at me."

"You've been busy."

"And you know that because…?"

"I watch the news, read the papers. You should try it."

"Yeah, except more often than not, we are the news and the

news doesn't always get it right."

"Look, I was actually calling you to ask you something."

"You can ask, but you know I'm not always going to give you an answer."

"Fair enough." Shelly cleared her throat. "Marcus Burton. What can you tell me about him?"

Sophia took another sip of wine.

"Why are you asking?"

"Can't tell you that."

"Off the record?"

"Off the record."

"What do you want to know?"

"He called the assignment editor and asked for a favor."

"What kind of favor?"

"He wanted us to hold off on a story about the Halifax kid."

"Really."

"Yeah, and I thought it was strange because the story didn't really have legs. You know, she went missing and then suddenly she wasn't missing, she was with her brother, and then these rumors started popping up about her being a victim in some abuse thing…" Shelly was waiting for Sophia to finish the story for her.

"Is there a question in there for me?"

"I want to know what you have to do with all of this."

"Did you hear I was involved?"

"Burton suggested that you and Tommy had been re-assigned to work another case. That you two were officially off the Halifax case, and that it was closed. He said that it had been a huge misunderstanding and the result of a teenager's overly vivid imagination."

"And so what do you want from me, Shel?"

"I want the truth, the real story. I don't trust him. He's a cheese weasel, as far as I'm concerned."

"Again, off the record?"

"At some point I'm going to need something on the record."

"Honestly, Shel I don't know what the hell is going on and what Burton does or doesn't have to do with any of this. I interviewed her teenage brother, and he may be an asshole on some level but he was seriously messed up by what he saw. And I believe him. So, yeah, we're off the case, that's true. But I don't believe for a moment it was a mistake or the result of some kid's vivid imagination."

"That's what I thought. Look, I won't pass this on. I'll try and do an end-run without setting off any alarms. I promise I won't involve you."

Sophia had heard that before. "Do what you have to do, Shel but don't count on me right now. We have some serious attention coming our way. I can't take a pee without someone opening a file on me."

"You got it, my friend. I'll do everything I can. Talk later?"

"Sure. See you soon."

Sophia hung up and finished the bottle.

CHAPTER NINETEEN

Sophia beat Tommy into the office again. Jess, always alarmingly perky first thing in the morning, came over and sat down.

"So, what have you two gotten yourselves into?"

"What do you mean?"

"Well, you and Stinson seem to be geeting a lot of interest from the command staff lately, that's all."

She and Tommy had been out of the office over the last couple of days and apparently had missed some fireworks.

"We were pulled off the Halifax case and it was inactivated. Aside from that…"

"Oh, it wasn't just inactivated, it was closed 'unfounded.'" Jess lowered her voice. "You didn't hear about that little dust up?"

"No"

"Yeah, I guess Pierson went a little ballistic when the order to unfound the case came down from Burton's office. I was in the women's bathroom, and you know what the walls are like in there, and the two of them were going at it like two cats in heat. It wasn't pretty."

"Could you hear what they were saying?"

"Not for the most part, but I did hear Burton say 'call off

your people' and then something about 'no more discussion' and 'friend to the department.' I couldn't make out the rest of it."

"Jesus. This is ridiculous. In all my years on this department, I don't think I have ever seen such a cluster."

"Well, at least not one that wasn't officer initiated." Jess chuckled and then turned somber.

"How are you doing?"

"I'm OK. Just trying to move on to other things." Sophia typed in her password on the computer. "Wouldn't mind knowing if they have any leads on David's case, though."

Jess was good friends with the homicide case detective and had probably asked around.

"Between you and me…" Jess looked over her shoulder. "I don't think they have squat. Almost sounds like a professional job. Slugs dug out of the wall, casings picked up. Only thing the guys at the scene mentioned was the smell of really strong cologne and they didn't find any there."

"I smelled that, too. That means we just missed the suspect. He could have been watching the whole time."

"Who wears that much cologne anyway?"

"Beats me. Maybe something trying to mask the smell of something else when he's around people."

"I suppose. Seems like kind of an old guy thing."

Sophia felt a pang of guilt. She really should pass on the information about the phone message and the fact that Victoria Tilden claimed to have seen David at the dead drop. But she had promised Tommy she'd keep it quiet at least long enough for them to figure out the connection to Grace Halifax.

"Thanks. Keep checking for me, OK? I can't afford to show my face over there at the moment, much as I'd love to."

Tommy walked into the office whistling an indecipherable song. This generally meant one of two things; he had either spent the night with some bimbo he was 'dating' or he'd hit it big at the track. Since neither of those two things was happening with any regularity as Sophia knew, she was puzzled.

"What's with the happy noise?" Sophia swung around in her chair.

Tommy dropped his bag. He looked at Jess.

"Mind if I talk to my partner in private for a moment?"

"Nope. Don't want to be an interloper."

"There you go with the big words," Tommy said.

Tommy leaned over and whispered to Sophia. "We need to go out and do some field work this morning." He had a twinkle in his eye. "I have a name to go with that plate."

"Who is it? Do we know him?"

"Not yet, but we will."

They didn't have to drive very far. Azzo Martins lived on Capitol Hill, a short trip from headquarters. His condo sat above a bank of garages. Brick lined the facade of the units, framed by white columns, and matching window and door frames. Each condo had its own deck that spanned over the garage.The car from the night before was parked in front of a garage door. Tommy felt the hood.

"It's cold."

He peered into the rear passenger window. "And the genius didn't even try and hide this shit." He pointed to a hat and wig laying on the backseat.

"Can I help you with something?" A man popped out onto the balcony. He took a sip from a coffee mug.

Tommy flashed his badge. "Mr. Martins? We need to talk to you about a hit and run accident involving this car."

"Really? Jesus Christ." He put down the cup. "Hang on, I'll come down."

"Works every time," Tommy said leaning against the car. "People love their cars."

Martins wore dark, creased jeans and a crisp white shirt that strained against a bulging stomach. His wet hair was pushed back behind his ears.

"Must be a mistake. I'm the only who drives this car and I haven't been in an accident. As you can see, there isn't a mark on it."

"Actually, I'm surprised you didn't recognize us from last night." Sophia said.

"I don't understand."

"Sure you do." Tommy stepped between him and the front door.

"I, I was home all night." Perspiration formed on his upper lip.

"Really? Because we have a witness who puts you down there all the time."

Martins hung his head and started to cry. "I'm sorry. I didn't think it was illegal."

Tommy stepped closer to Martins until he was face to face.

"You didn't think collecting pictures of men having sex with little kids was illegal?"

Martins looked around. "Can we go inside, please? I don't want my neighbors to see me like this."

"Sure," Tommy said and as they climbed the stairs behind him, he looked over at Sophia with a grin and mouthed 'that was easy.'

The inside of Azzo Martins' condo looked like something out of a design magazine. Every piece of furniture was matched with a complimentary accessory. The walls were covered with original art. The home smelled faintly like vanilla bean.

"Have a seat, sir." Sophia waited for him to sit, then took her place on the edge of an Eames ottoman.

Dark circles of sweat formed on his expensive shirt.

"So Mr. Martins, we know about the dead drop and we are very concerned that you are involved in the distribution of child pornography."

Martins was either going to vehemently deny it or cave. Either way, they were still in a bit of a bind. They hadn't read him his rights, but on the other hand, he could very well be just a witness to something non-criminal.

Martins began to sob. Tommy looked at Sophia and then back at Martins.

"Ok, Azzo. Take it easy now. We have to take care of a couple administrative things before we can go on with this conversation." Sophia pulled out her advisement of rights card and read it to him slowly. "Do you understand these rights as I have explained them to you?"

Martins took a breath and blew his nose.

"Yes."

"It would make it easier for us to talk to you if we didn't have to take notes. Do you mind if we record this?" Tommy placed the recorder on the coffee table.

"That's fine."

"And, just so you know, nothing you tell us here is going to surprise us. We do this every day. And I can't promise you anything, but if you can give us some useful information, it could look really good for you. You see where I'm going?"

"I've tried to fight this. I really have. It's a disease, you know." Martins looked at Sophia and Tommy.

"Sure," Sophia said.

"Yeah, I totally understand. I get off on all sorts of weird shit. If my partner knew the half of it…" Tommy looked out the window.

"Thank you. I appreciate what you are trying to do, really."

"So why don't you tell us what you know about the dead drop." Sophia glanced at the recorder.

"I learned about it on a private board. It's in this place called New World. Are you familiar with that?"

"I know a little bit, but go on."

"Anyway, I met this guy on there. He looked like a kid but I'm not stupid…"

"Ok."

"Well, he said his name was Davey, but I later learned he goes by Gregor in the, uh adult areas."

"So Davey and Gregor are the same person?" Tommy clasped his hands together, knitting the fingers tightly. It was what he did when he wanted to hit something.

"Yes, but their avatars are different. Davey is like a kid and Gregor is, well he looks like some kind of devil with the goatee and slicked back hair. Very creepy."

"And how did you figure out they were the same person?"

"That was an accident. We met up in a private chat and discovered we were both in Seattle, and then somehow the issue of kids came up."

"Kids?"

"Yes, like uh, well, where you could find them in New World. You do know that looking at virtual porn is not against the law, right?"

They didn't, but both Tommy and Sophia nodded.

"Right, so anyway he gave me some instructions and I got into the room and then I met with some other people who eventually told me about the dead drop."

"Nobody vetted you?" Sophia asked.

"Oh, I'm abbreviating the story a bit." Martins ran his hands through his hair and wiped his face with the back of his wrist. "So, yes, there was a bit of a vetting process. I met with this Gregor fellow at a bar up here on Capitol Hill."

He looked at Tommy. "And I know what you're thinking – it was not a gay bar. I'm not gay."

"No judgment here, Azzo. But I gotta say, this is a pretty nifty condo here for a straight guy. I'm just saying…" Tommy looked at Sophia. She rolled her eyes and shook her head.

"What he's saying," Sophia said, "is he really doesn't care what floats your boat."

"Except what floats my boat has to do with children." He started to sob again.

"Look, we need you to come downtown and talk to us some more and maybe meet with a sketch artist. Would you be willing to do that for us?" Sophia stood up.

"Now?"

"Yes, now."

"I thought I could just talk to you here."

"We need to identify this guy, Gregor. Sounds like to me, he's the ringleader."

"It would really help us find the real bad guy here, Azzo." Sophia put her hand on Martins' shoulder.

"I know I have a problem. I've tried to overcome this. I've been in therapy for two years."

Tommy walked over to the window and looked down to the street. He turned back to Martins. "Before we head downtown, did you load anything on that drive the other night?"

"No, it was empty. I didn't leave anything. I put it back."

"So would you recognize this guy, this Gregor, if you saw him again?"

"I think so. I mean it was dark in the bar but he was pretty distinctive looking. Chubby, hairless little man."

"Sounds delightful."

"Let's go down to our office and have a sketch artist come in. We really appreciate all your help."

Martins stood and smoothed out his pants. Sophia and Tommy stood silently while he put on a jacket and stuffed his phone and wallet into his pocket.

"I hope this won't take too long. I've got an appointment with my therapist later this afternoon."

"No problem." Tommy walked behind Martins as Sophia led him down to the car.

They put Martins in the soft interview room with a bottle of water and a candy bar, then returned to the bullpen and met at Sophia's cubicle.

"Ok, so we barely have enough to hold this guy. I have no clue about that virtual porn stuff he was talking about. We've got to create some reason to get a sketch artist here. And I think we both know that we've officially gone back to investigating a case we were told not to investigate. I don't know whether to be happy or freaked out that he's rolling." Sophia spun slowly in her chair.

Tommy sat with his elbows on his knees, rubbing his hands together.

"I don't want to leave him alone for very long and give him a chance to change his mind. Other than admitting to liking to look at virtual naked kids, we've got nothing on him and certainly nothing to hold him here if he decides to leave or lawyer up." Tommy stood and began to pace.

"Why don't you try and find someone to come here and sketch something for us."

Sophia started dialing. "Go keep the pervert busy."

She knew of only a couple of on duty sketch artists, both of whom worked patrol. With her luck, they'd be furloughed and there was no way they were going to get permission for overtime. Otherwise, she'd have to reach out to other departments and she wasn't very excited about extending the reach of information beyond her and Tommy.

Martins sat at the table looking like a beaten dog. He ran the palms of his hands over the top of the table. Tommy pulled out a chair. He left the door ajar to give the two men some air. The usual foot traffic passed up and down the hall. Detectives, administrative specialists and the occasional brass slowed down enough to take a peek into the room. Martins sat silently as Tommy tried to engage him in small talk.

"You like living on the Hill?"

"It's OK. Starting to get a little crazy at night. I don't like going out much by myself." Martins sat back. "You live in the city, detective?"

"No."

"Sorry, I didn't mean to pry."

"Not a big fan of city life."

"I can imagine you see a lot of ugliness."

"Enough to make me not want to live here."

Sophia came to the door and asked Tommy to step out.

"Jesus. I can't keep up the nice guy thing much longer. What do you know?"

"Still working on getting a sketch artist. Not having much luck."

As they stood in the hall, one of the IT guys sauntered toward them. Sophia remembered him from an uncomfortable encounter last spring, when she caught him looking through a case file on her desk while upgrading her desktop. He'd received a stern reprimand from his supervisor and was banned from servicing the computers in the sexual assault unit. The IT guy slowed down to get around Tommy and Sophia. As he did, he looked into the interview room, pausing almost imperceptibly.

Sophia whispered to Tommy. "Did you see that?"

He continued down the hall and then looked back just before turning the corner.

"That was weird."

"What? He's weird."

"No, did you see how he kind of paused when he went by the room? Like he recognized Martins?"

"Go see where he's headed." Tommy walked in and grabbed Martins by the arm.

"Come with me. And stay quiet. I want you to take a look at someone." Tommy led Martins down the hall towards the robbery unit.

Sophia pulled out her phone and acted as if she was on a call. The IT guy kept walking then turned toward the robbery unit. He stopped at the desk of the admin, who pointed to an empty cubicle.

"That's the one," she said. "It's been making some crazy noise all day."

Sophia motioned to Tommy. He led Martins down the hall towards robbery. Tommy put his finger up to his mouth and walked Martins past the desk where the IT guy was working. As he passed the cubicle, Martins glanced at the man typing on the keyboard and then back at Tommy. His eyes widened. Tommy pulled him out of earshot.

"That's him. That's the guy who calls himself Gregor. What the fuck kind of sick joke is this?" Martin headed for the elevator lobby.

Tommy ran up to Martins and caught his arm. "Hey, slow down."

"I can't believe you brought me down here knowing that guy worked here." Martins' eyes darted from one side of the hallway to the other. "Get me out of here."

"Do you really think we're that stupid? Of course we didn't know he worked here." Tommy was out of breath. "I don't even know the guy's name. Do you?" He looked back at Sophia, who was looking up the number for IT.

"Something funky. I can't remember, but I'll know in a minute." She put up her hand as someone answered. "Yeah, can you tell me the name of the IT guy who's up in robbery?" She motioned for Tommy to take Martins back to the interview room.

"What is it?" She pinned the phone to her shoulder so she could write. "Eldon Loveschild? Hey thanks. No, no problem just wanted to ask him something, and I was embarrassed to ask his name. "

Sophia hung up and dialed personnel. She followed a distance behind Tommy as he led Martins back down the hallway.

"Fran, I need a big favor and I need you to keep it quiet. I need an address on an employee as fast as you can get it to me.

Do me a favor, will you? Text it to my phone."

Martins had gone from remorseful to furious.

"I can't fucking believe this. That guy saw me in here."

"Calm down…" Tommy stood next to the door, letting Sophia sit across from Martins.

"Don't tell me to calm down."

"Mr. Martins, we had no idea Gregor or whatever his name is, worked here."

"I don't believe you. This is exactly something you people would do. Get me killed."

"Maybe if you didn't hang out with…" Tommy stopped himself.

"Look, Mr. Martins we're going to figure out what's going on, I promise. How about another water or maybe a coffee or pop?"

"I just want to go home."

"Look, I don't think he saw you. He was too engrossed in the computer. He doesn't have your address or real name, right?" Tommy said.

"I don't think so. He's an admin on that site though, so who knows what he can find out about me."

"Azzo, we need you to work with us. If you want to stay out of jail, we need you to go home and stay off of the computer. Don't go to that site, whatever you called it…"

"New World," Martins said.

"New World. Don't go there until we tell you it's OK."

"I'm never going there again, I swear."

"Stay off the Internet and don't go to the dead drop. Just lie low, got it?" Tommy said.

Sophia stood. "And you have our word on this: We didn't know he worked here."

"I'll drive you home," Tommy said and then looked back at Sophia. "We'll talk when I get back."

CHAPTER TWENTY

Sophia started making notes. She called HR again and talked Fran into giving her Loveschild's home address. She pulled the house up on Google maps and printed out the bird's eye view. A quick bit of research revealed that the home was originally owned by Henry and Shirley Townshend. It was purchased in 1957, and the only legal change on the title was when Henry died in 1972 and the house was placed in Shirley's name as the sole owner. Sophia couldn't find Eldon's name attached to any of the legal documents associated with the home. She ran his name for wants and warrants. He was clear, had a valid driver's license and appeared to have had no contacts with the police, with the exception of a ticket for expired tabs in 2005. She did a Google search on him and came up with a few references on some obscure computer sites. He was a ghost - a man with no apparent history on the Internet, at least not under that name. She then typed in the name Gregor. It came back with over fifty-five million hits.

They could bring Eldon in for questioning but if he was smart enough to be a blank slate on the Internet, and if he was an administrator in New World, he was smart enough to keep his mouth shut. Not to mention that he was quickly looking like a suspect in a child pornography ring case they 'weren't working.'

Sophia's desk phone rang.

"Sophia, it's George Anderson. You got a minute? This is important."

"Sure. What's going on?"

"Someone must have picked up the dead drop last night. I got an alert on the remote software."

"We sat on it for a few hours, and we actually watched a guy pick it up. We snatched him up today and he claimed he didn't leave anything on it or take anything off."

"Well, someone did. Maybe he's lying. There's a newsflash for you."

"Did you get anything from the remote, or whatever it is you do?"

"I got an IP address but without a warrant, I can't get you anymore information. But I can tell you this much. Whoever accessed it dumped a bunch of nasty child porn on it. I was able to use the software to access the sites that were loaded. They're pretty common. We see 'em all the time. This is why these guys use the peer to peer stuff. It's safer for them to share it without getting busted. Somebody got sloppy and didn't wipe the drive."

"So at least we have confirmation that child porn is being accessed and, or, shared. We just don't have an identity."

"Right. But this is enough to get a warrant. I can get one together pretty fast, and get it signed. This company is pretty good about getting stuff to us on an exigency basis. I should have subscriber information before the end of the day." He paused. "Just remember something, they're probably stealing WIFI from a neighbor so we may have to get creative. The subscriber may be some completely innocent person who has no idea his hard earned dollars are paying for more than just a fast connection for Netflix. It would help if you can identify one of the suspects coming and going from the house, and connect him to a prior conviction. That would seal the deal with a judge."

"Thanks, George. Keep me up to date, will you?"

Sophia called Tommy.

"Can you talk?"

"Sort of. I'm still here with Martins. He's suddenly become very talkative."

"Good or bad?"

"Hard to say. I'll have to call you back."

"Ask him again if he put anything on or took anything off that drive. Anderson just called and said he got a remote hit on the device. Someone accessed it. Maybe it happened after we left. He's writing up a warrant now."

"I'll ask. We're just chatting at the moment."

"You're not going to piss him off again are you?"

"Nope. Just making small talk like I do."

Sgt.Pierson suddenly appeared at her cubicle. Sophia hung up on Tommy.

"How are things going?"

"Fine."

"You still working on that homeless case?"

"Just about to get a warrant on it."

"Good to hear." Pierson put his hands in his pockets and looked around the office.

"Anything else going on I should know about?"

"Not really. Just catching up on some old cases."

"Well, if anything changes, you'll keep me in the loop, right?"

"Sure thing, sarge." Sophia gave him her most confident smile.

Sophia headed down the hall to the restroom. As she neared the end of the hall, she nearly ran into Eldon. The two stutter stepped around each other. He said nothing as he passed and headed back down the hall toward the interview room.

Sophia paused at the end of the hall and watched him. Eldon slowed and glanced into the room. He stopped when he realized it was empty and turned to head back. His eyes met Sophia's. A part of her wanted him to know, to challenge her, confront her, but he passed by with only a slight smile and a nod.

It was on.

Eldon went back to his office and sat down at his cubicle. He crossed his arms and stared at the blank monitor on his desk. That detective, the bitch who'd confronted him and ratted him out for looking at some fucking file on her desk, was onto him. And she and that old guy had that shithead from the bar in the interview room. He knew that guy couldn't be trusted. He should have gone with his gut and denied him access.

Eldon walked down 4th Ave to the bus stop. He was confident the guy at police headquarters didn't know the location of the project and hadn't met any of the players. But he knew about the dead drop.

Eldon didn't think the man saw him, but that detective had given him a look. Maybe she was just being a dismissive cop, the kind that looks down on civilians. Maybe he was overreacting.

Getting off the bus in Lake City, Eldon looked around, making sure he wasn't being followed. The old paranoia, the disease that had held him captive for so long, was returning. He felt a rash rising on the back of his neck and around his crotch. He let himself in through the basement door. No one had asked after Shirley, and according to the weather report, her body was under a layer of ice.

He'd thought about moving the servers upstairs now that he had it to himself. It would make it so much easier to run the business where the light was better. He'd begun to feel like a vampire, living in Shirley's basement. But now he was glad he hadn't made the change. If the cops were onto him, it was best that he only needed to worry about making up a story about Shirley, not explaining a wall of servers housing thousands of images of children, taking up the living and dining room. He needed to get them out of the house all together. An exit strategy was in order.

Eldon called Augustine. He was the master admin for the project they called Baby Watch.

"Auggie, it's Eldon. How are things?"

"Hey, boss. Things are busy. Lot's of satisfied customers."

"Any issues at the house?" Eldon rummaged through the medicine cabinet, looking for something to put on his rash.

"Nope. We're good neighbors. The lady next door even brought over some cookies. Came over with her little girl. What a little hottie." He laughed.

"We don't shit where we live, Auggie."

"Don't worry. It's all good. I'm behaving myself. I have lots to keep me busy here. When are you coming by? We've got some really nice stuff coming in from Amsterdam."

"I'm going to stop by later. Do me a favor. Make sure the guys stay inside today. Keep things quiet, OK?"

"Something I should know?"

"Just being cautious. Remember where I work. I hear things. Just want to make sure we are being smart."

"You're in charge."

"I may stop by later tonight. I don't want to talk over the phone. Let's keep things tight."

Eldon hung up and paced. He was in an uncontrollable panic, something he hadn't felt in years. This was a character flaw and he understood it to be a game changer if he didn't get a handle on it. He needed something to take his mind off of things.

Sitting in front of his computer, he took a deep breath and logged in. He needed to visit his angel, needed to see her face.

CHAPTER TWENTY-ONE

Sophia called Tommy back after Pierson left.

"How's it going with Martins?"

"I don't know what to do with this guy, Soph. He's pouring out his guts to me. I'm learning all sorts of sordid shit from this mope. I'm just a little worried he's going to off himself after I leave."

"Is he giving you anything about Loveschild?"

"He's a little hinky on that guy. I can't really tell if he's afraid or holding back. But he's freaking me out a little."

"In what way?"

"He's suggesting, not sure if that's the right word, but what the hell, that there's a group or a ring in Seattle. And I get the impression that he thinks there are people attached to his thing that are," he lowered his voice, "connected." Tommy paused. "At least that's how he puts it. But he won't drop any names. And the more we talk, it's like he's putting two and two together for the first time."

"Anderson reminded me that these guys are pretty much pathological liars."

"Yeah, I know, and believe me, guys like this… well back in the day, I would have beaten the truth out of him. You know, used an enhanced interrogation technique."

"I'm not listening." Sophia said.

"You know it's true. But hey, I'm the new police. I love everyone."

"Are you really worried he's going kill himself?"

"He's wound pretty tight right now. I'm trying to get him to call his shrink, maybe get in earlier to see him. He's in his office making a call."

The connection was starting to break up.

"Hey, I can't hear you."

It sounded as though he'd dropped the phone. Then she heard a single, muffled gunshot.

"Tommy! What the hell is going on? Tommy!"

Sophia called the chief dispatcher.

"This is 664. There's been a shooting at 404 Bolyston Ave. I'm calling from headquarters. I was talking to my partner. He was there with a witness. I don't have a connection anymore."

Jess, Tony and Jimmy gathered around her desk. She picked up her cell phone and screamed into it.

"Tommy!"

There was the sound of scuffling, as though the phone was underfoot.

"Tommy!"

Jess grabbed Sophia's arm. "Let's just go. Bring the phone and keep trying to raise him."

The ride up the hill seemed to take forever. Patrol and fire had already arrived. Yellow crime scene tape was strung across the entrance to the condos. Paramedics descended the stairs, carefully stripping off their light blue protective gowns, stained with blood.

Tommy stood out on the balcony with a patrol sergeant. A cigarette dangled from his mouth. Sophia could see blood on his jacket and shirt. She jumped out of the car.

"Are you ok?"

"Yeah, I'm fine. Havin' a great day." He took a long draw off his cigarette. His face was a peculiar shade of gray with a tinge of fake tan.

Sophia climbed the stairs two at a time. Jess ran after her. A new officer put his hand up to stop her at the top of the stairs but waved her through after she flashed her detective shield.

Azzo Martins lay on his back at the end of a long hallway. His right index finger was still in the trigger guard of a small revolver, next to his head. Brain matter and chunks of hair stuck to a door behind him. Blood streaked the soft pastel blue paint on the wall in a gory waterfall.

Jess stood behind Sophia. "This is why I never want to go to homicide. I couldn't look at this shit day in and day out."

Sophia bent over Martins. Most of the back of his head was missing. His eyes were partially open and there was a strange softness to his features.

"We meet again, Detective." Sgt. Drew Taylor had come up behind her and Jess. Both women jumped.

"Jesus."

"So the two of you once again show up somewhere with a dead body. Is this some kind of joke, Benedetti?"

"I wasn't here when it happened. My partner was." She nodded at Tommy who stood in the living room.

"You weren't there for the other murder either, as I recall." He looked around the condo.

"Much nicer place than that last one where your husband lived."

"He was my ex- husband. And I know how this looks."

"It looks like you enjoy beating us to our scenes and sticking your nose in where it doesn't belong. That's what it looks like.

You didn't get transferred to homicide, and I didn't get the memo, did I?"

"No sir."

"Get out of here unless you have something to contribute. You're contaminating my crime scene."

Sophia and Jess walked into the living room. Tommy was wiping his hands with an antiseptic towelette.

"What the fuck happened?"

"Remember how I said I was afraid he was going to off himself? I was right."

"How did he…"

"He was in the office. I thought he was calling his shrink. I was talking to you. You know the rest, I think. I saw him walk out with the gun. He was holding it to his head. I tried to get to him. I didn't even think about drawing my weapon, which I have to admit was really stupid."

"He could have killed you."

"Point taken."

Tommy's eyes were watery and his jaw was tight.

"I gotta get some air." He brushed past Jess and Sophia.

"He's a mess." Jess spoke softly so no one could hear her.

"Fuck."

Jess pointed to the door. "Let's go."

"There's a line of folks that would love to see a pedophile take one to the skull." Sophia said.

"A pedophile? Ok, I'm confused. Tell me again what Tommy was doing here?"

"Let's get out of here and find Tommy. We need a unit meeting to get everyone up to speed about what's going on."

"No shit."

As she left the condo, Sophia noticed a black unmarked car parked across the street. The window was rolled up and the man's face looked away as she descended the steps. But as she got to Jess' car, she had no problem recognizing the driver. It was Assistant Chief Marcus Burton.

CHAPTER TWENTY-TWO

Jared always sat in the back of English class so he could slouch safely out of view of the teacher. He was bored as usual, not interested in early English literature. He wanted to study steampunk, something edgy and progressive, but Mr. Adams only wanted to shovel shit like Shakespeare at them. At least last semester he'd assigned A Voyage to Arcturus, so Jared and Petra could geek out on a sci-fi book.

He was still flying high from discovering his stepfather was a bonafide pervert. He had plenty of time to devise a plan to out him, but he worried about his mother and her career, and what she would do when she found out. She'd probably believe Ed, who'd protest that it was all a big misunderstanding. That was her job, after all. She spent her days trying to figure out how to keep rapists and murderers out of jail. He was sure that Ed would try and blame him for the porn. He'd act all cool about it, explaining to Shelly that Jared was a teenager, and experimenting, and that it was no big deal. He'd come to Jared's defense, encourage her to forgive him for his indiscretions.

Jared would have to set a trap for Ed and make it idiot proof.

As soon as the bell rang, Jared headed for his locker. Barrett Halifax stood across the hall from him, his arms crossed. He was uncharacteristically alone.

"Hey, I need to talk to you."

Jared ignored him.

"Poppins, I need to talk to you."

Jared turned around. Barrett was standing next to him.

"I have a problem I need solved."

"I thought I was your problem, Halifax. Can't one of your fuck buddies help you?" Jared looked straight ahead. He hated him so much he could hardly stand to share the same air with him.

"I think we have a common problem…"

"You and I? We don't have anything in common."

Barrett hesitated. "Yeah, we do."

Jared grabbed his Chemistry lab book, shoved it into his backpack and shut his locker door.

"You're fucking kidding me, right?" He tried to muscle past Barrett. "I'm gonna be late for class."

Barrett blocked him. The hallway had cleared except for the two boys.

"I saw your step-father, Ed and my father talking the other day."

"What the fuck are you talking about, Halifax?"

"They were sitting in your dad's car and it looked like they were having a fight. An argument."

Jared stared at Barrett.

"He's not my stepfather. He's my mother's husband." He pulled tighter on the strap to his backpack. "And why should I care?"

"You know about my sister, right?"

"I only know what everyone else has heard. Something about pictures."

"Yeah." Barrett cleared his throat. "Really fuckin' bad pictures."

"Where did you see them, anyway?"

"On my dad's computer."

"Shit."

"Look, I know I've been a royal fucker to you…"

"And everyone I know."

"Right." Barrett looked down the hall and then back.

"My dad was really angry. He was all up in Ed's face."

"Where were they?"

"Here, at the school, in the parking lot. I was here late working out."

"So they were arguing. I don't get it. What do you want me to do about it?"

"I need you to get into Ed's computer and see, see if there's a connection," Barrett looked over his shoulder, "a connection to my dad. I just thought since we both have this thing…"

"Halifax, you and I? We don't have a thing. She's your sister, not mine. And Ed's a piece of shit who fucks my mother and beats me up. Why don't you just go to the cops?"

"I can't turn in my father. No one will believe me."

"What about your sister?"

"Dude, she's autistic. She can barely even talk."

"What about your mother?"

"She's clueless."

"Or maybe not."

"Let's keep my mother out of it for the moment."

"That's cool. But I still don't know what you want from me."

"Fuck it. Never mind. I should have known…" Barrett put up his hands.

"Look, let me think about it. I can hack, but I'm not sure I have the skills to make it happen."

"Let me know, ok?" Barrett turned and jogged down the hall and around the corner toward the lunchroom.

Jared headed to class. Now he had even more incentive to screw with Ed.

Jess hugged the center line with the Crown Vic trying not to run over several bicyclists as she drove back to headquarters.

Sophia pulled her phone off her hip and answered.

"Benedetti, it's Anderson. I've got a name and address for you."

"Hang on." Sophia grabbed a notebook out of her pocket. "So, 23rd and E. Spruce? That's in the central district, isn't it?"

"On Google it looks like it's one of those houses that's been condemned. Kids squat in them all the time. I guess they're still inhabitable. At least someone appears to be paying the utility bills."

"Listen, we just lost a witness. Guy shot himself. Tommy was there. It's a mess. And we're about to have brass all up in our ass shortly. Can you get some guys to set up on the house until I can try and get a search warrant?"

"You guys handle your end. I'll get a warrant. And we'll pull in some folks from narcs."

"George, you should know something about this case."

"You mean about some of the players? Yeah, I know."

"How do…"

"Take care of your partner. I'll be in touch." George hung up.

"Sounds like this case has just gotten a lot more complicated." Jess pulled into the garage entrance and swiped the prox card to open the gate.

"You have no idea," Sophia said.

Tommy had changed into his spare court suit, the one that seldom saw the light of day. He sat in front of a blank monitor screen, hands on the keyboard but motionless.

Sophia put her hand on his shoulder. "You ok?"

"I'm fine. Just have to go over and talk to homicide. That

should be fun."

"We have a name and an address."

"No shit. George came through, huh?" He smoothed down his tie and ran a comb through his hair then tossed the comb into the top drawer of his desk.

"They're getting some bodies to sit on the house until he can get a warrant. I'm heading up there. You can join us later."

"Sure, you bet." Tommy stood and stretched.

"I'll call you when I'm done." He turned around. "Be careful. And you need to get Pierson on board. We're hanging out there with this, Soph. Tell him to grow a pair." He disappeared around the corner.

Pierson was staring at his computer screen. He looked up when Sophia knocked on the door.

"What's up? You ok?"

"Just wanted to check in. I figured we owed you an explanation."

"Oh, you mean you thought I should know why you two are apparently following up on a case we closed at the request of our chief? You mean that explanation? Can't wait to hear it."

She closed the door and sat down. "This is a real clusterfuck."

"I'm not sure I want to know."

"ICAC is in the process of getting a warrant for a house where we think a child porn ring is set up, and we think a current city IT guy may be involved. And yes, it all stems from the Halifax case. But it's also about my ex-husband…"

"Whoa. Back the hell up, Benedetti. You're going way too fast for me."

"David Montero, my ex…"

"I know who he is, or was."

"He called me a week ago and told me he had some information on the Halifax case, and on the day we were supposed to meet, he ended up dead."

"What was it he was going to tell you?"

"I don't know but we've since learned from our rape victim, Victoria Tilden that David was at the dead drop…"

"The dead what? I'm totally confused here." He leaned back and rubbed his temples.

"I guess we've left you more out of the loop than I realized."

"Tommy should know better. He's got more time in this unit than anyone. Not to mention time on the job."

"We're in this together. Have been since the beginning. He's not going to take the heat alone."

"That's to be decided at another time." Pierson sat up. "So get me up to speed and do it fast."

"There's a place under the freeway where these child porn guys are doing something called peer to peer sharing. Victoria said she saw David."

"Ok, so Montero was involved somehow…"

"I don't know. Maybe." Sophia stood up. "She also saw Marcus Burton with Stewart Halifax."

Pierson remained silent.

"David wasn't with Burton and Halifax.Victoria is a little off, but she puts Burton and Halifax at the scene. And she said there was another person there, but she couldn't say whether it was a man or a woman. I think David stumbled onto something. I think he was trying to confirm his suspicions by going to the dead drop. And I believe someone recognized him and made the connection, maybe to me, maybe not."

"So where are we on this mess?"

"We asked for some help from ICAC, since technically this case was better suited for their expertise."

"Ok, I'm liking this." He sat up straighter. "I'm still not happy with the two of you, but at least you've gotten it out of our bureau."

"Then there's the problem of Burton," Sophia said.

Pierson stood and looked out of the window.

"I've got two years left at this place. I've got a great life planned for me and my wife. We've got a place over on Lake Chelan."

"Look, we didn't mean to go behind your back."

"And I know why you did." He brushed down his mustache with his thumb and forefinger. "So what are you in here for, Benedetti?"

"I want us, all of us, to sit on a house that George Anderson has identified as possibly the source for this ring, and then I want us to assist on the warrant. And I want to take these monsters out."

"Be careful of what you wish for, Sophia." Pierson looked out the window again and then waved his hand toward the bullpen. "You and Tommy can take Jess. Let ICAC supply the rest of the bodies. And don't do a damn thing without calling me. You need to be 100% sure you have the right place."

"Yes, sir."

"And close the door."

Sophia looked back as she closed the door. Pierson stood at the window, looking down at the street in the rain.

"I said, close the door."

Jess was just ending a phone call. Jimmy and Anthony tapped away at their computers.

Sophia peered over Jess' cubicle and lowered her voice. "I need you to assist me with something. Bring your go bag."

Jess grabbed her bag, strapped on her gun and followed.

CHAPTER TWENTY-THREE

Sophia and Jess cruised slowly by the house. It was snuggled between two new condo complexes that loomed over the block. Dark except for a dim light in the back, most of the windows were covered with graffiti-decorated plywood. The grass was at least eighteen inches high and a golden shade of brown.The neighborhood was in the center of the latest gentrification craze. Big developers were quickly buying out generations of families and constructing 'green' apodments and ultra-modern single family homes for white urbanites. But there were enough run-down houses left on the block to make the neighborhood sketchy.

A Chevy Caprice, favored by drug dealers, slowly circled the block. This was going to be a difficult location to surveil. The dealers were going to assume they were the targets, so they'd be scarce, or worse, they'd confront undercover detectives as they sat in their cars. The trick was not to tip off whoever was in the house. Surveillance savvy criminals studied patterns, just like cops. If the neighborhood suddenly became quiet, they'd be screwed. Thankfully, the narcs were good at setting up in these areas, blending in with their forfeiture seized Hondas and old SUV's.

Sophia and Jess parked several blocks away in a shopping

center parking lot. They were dead giveaways in their pool car with a radio antenna sticking out of the roof and their exempt license plates.

"We won't be able to stay here for very long." Jess looked out the window at the cliental hanging out in front of Starbucks. Groups of four to five young males clustered together, watching the parking lot and streets with more scrutiny than they did of each other. As soon as Sophia and Jess pulled in, heads were on a swivel.

"We can't get too close to the house." Sophia checked the rearview mirror.

"I know that, but Jesus, we'll be lucky if we don't on-view a drive-by."

"We can't get sidetracked. Put your blinders up." Sophia needed some time to shift gears. She was worried about Tommy. She dialed him up.

"Hey, where are you?"

"On my way." The radio blared in the background.

"We're at 23 and Jack. Meet us up here and I'll brief you."

"Almost there."

Sophia called Candy and arranged for Bodhi to spend the next couple of days with her. She asked her to give the mutt a few extra scratches.

Sophia was shocked by Tommy's appearance despite the fact she'd seen him only a couple of hours ago. His face was drawn and pale and when he got out of the car, he moved like an old man.

"What the hell is happening to him?" Sophia said.

Jess sighed. "He looks exhausted."

The spark was gone, as was the fight. It happened on the

job. She'd seen it before with guys who stayed too long.

She knew this would be his last case, and she made a promise to herself that it would be the best.

"So what's the plan?" Tommy lit a cigarette, leaned against the car and looked out into the parking lot.

"Narcs are up on the house as well as some intel guys. I just want to put lots of eyes on the place, see if anyone is coming and going."

"And hopefully see our friend from IT." Tommy took a long pull from the cigarette like he was smoking a joint, and then let it out in a thin stream.

"Take a look at the surveillance logs for me, will you? I haven't read the latest." Jess pulled out Sophia's computer and logged in.

"Looks like two men either stay at the house or visit. They seemed to be putting in shifts at the residence. They've tailed them back to other houses and apartments, so I'm guessing they don't live there. Looks like this may just be where they're running the servers."

"Or maybe it's just a little clubhouse where they hang out, and one of them just shared his stash on that drive. More likely that Loveschild freak is running things at his crib." Tommy flicked his cigarette to the asphalt.

"These guys are driving, right?"

"So far all of the plates are coming back with reports of sale on them. Tony and Jimmy are trying to run down the old owners to see if they have anything on the new buyers. We don't know who these guys are."

"How about a good old fashioned traffic stop?" Jess said.

"Can't afford to spook them before we can get a warrant. If there's evidence in that house, it'll be gone like a fart in the wind."

"We've got to get something for George to put in front of a judge, prove there's enough to get a warrant." Sophia slid her hands around the steering wheel.

A man shouted from across the parking lot. Two men fisted bumped a greeting and glanced in the direction of the three detectives. One of the men nodded to Tommy.

"Jesus, it's like old home week up here. Every shit bird I ever arrested is camped out in this place." Tommy lit another smoke.

"Take a break from the cancer sticks."

"Today's not a good day to give 'em up, Soph." He climbed into his car. "Let's head over there. We're gonna get shot or shoot someone if we stay here any longer. I'll set up around back."

"Sure thing. But why don't you leave in an hour, Tommy. We can sit a couple of blocks out. There's already a few cars close and someone has the eye." Sophia started the car.

Tommy nodded and rolled out of the parking lot.

Sophia parked the car in front of an apartment building two blocks from the house and turned off the engine. She and Jess mulled over several scenarios as they sat in the car. If some guys were using the house without permission, that made things a little less complicated, because it would be hard for anyone to claim residency and might make it easier to get a warrant. But without more evidence that the house was headquarters to a child porn ring, most judges wouldn't give them the green light to search the place.

"We need to identify these guys."

"We will. They'll make a mistake."

Sophia released the seat as far back as it would go and stretched her legs. "You don't have to stay all night. I just want to touch base with a couple of guys out here. Between you and me, I don't trust everyone to track on this with the same level of dedication. A lot of these guys are just cashing in on the money train."

"I'll hang for a while. Nothing else going on for me right now." Jess shifted in the seat. "Can I ask you a question?"

"Yep."

"What's the deal with Tommy?"

"What do you mean?"

"I haven't been here very long, but in the last few weeks, he's been really, I don't know, really bi-polar."

Sophia laughed. "That's just Tommy. He'd like people to think he's a complicated guy, but he isn't really. He's just a typical cop who's nearing the end of his run. I don't think he's handling it very well, but what do I know?"

"I just hope he's going to be OK."

"You know something I don't?"

"Guys were just talking about the dude who shot himself."

"Are you saying people think Tommy shot him?"

"That's the inference, I guess."

"Well, that's fucked up. Tommy is many things, but he's not a killer." Sophia looked Jess in the eye.

"Hey, I'm just repeating what I've heard. Not saying I agree with it. I just wanted to get your take on things, since he's your his partner."

"He's got a lot going on, but killing some child molester? I don't think so."

Sophia squinted through the windshield at a man walking toward them with his head down. Heavyset, he wore a dark hoody and tan pants.

As the figure passed their car, he looked up in her direction and then quickly looked away.

Sophia turned on the car and pulled into the street.

"Who was that?"

"Our best evidence for a warrant. That, my friend, is Eldon Loveschild."

Sophia jumped on the radio. "Guys, the male who's walking up to the house is our main suspect. I don't want him to make any of you, so stay low or out of the area."

"Roger that," came the replies.

"Yes, fucking, yes." Sophia hit the side of steering wheel.

"Let's drive around and take down some plates. He probably drove here." Jess said.

Jess pulled out a note pad and started scribbling plates of parked cars.

"Hey, sorry. I shouldn't have said anything earlier about Tommy."

Sophia slowed the car to a crawl. "No big deal. Forget about it."

The radio crackled. It was Vince Turbin, one of newer Narcotics sergeants. "We'll stay out here until we get relief. You want us to follow that last guy home if he leaves?"

"Yeah, bed him down. I just want to confirm what I already have." She hesitated. "But someone was supposed to be sitting on him. I'd like to know how he slipped past your guys."

"I'll take care of it. Won't happen again." Turbin said.

Sophia called George and gave him the information about Eldon. They'd have a warrant by the next afternoon.

Back at the office, she and Jess ran fifty plates, all parked within a two block radius of the house. Nothing showed up registered to Eldon Loveschild. But a battered old Subaru came back to a familiar name: Shirley Townsend.

Sophia had her man.

The following afternoon, Pierson call Tommy and Sophia into his office.

"Burton is supposedly out of town at a conference. He gets back in two days. I don't know whether or not he has someone on the inside sniffing around, but if he does, I can guarantee we'll all be back in patrol if this doesn't pan out. Where are you on getting this warrant?"

"We'll have it in a couple of hours," Sophia said. Two guys are coming and going pretty consistently, and the main suspect showed up at the house last night. We've identified all of them. Mostly minor stuff on their records, but with the identification from Mr. Martins of Loveschild, we're good."

"The late Mr. Martins," Pierson said and looked at Tommy.

"Hey, I didn't shoot the guy."

Pierson laughed. "So you say."

"Look, I'm checking out when this whole thing is over, so you can insinuate all you want, Sarg. I wouldn't waste lead on that piece of shit, even if the city bought it for me." Tommy stood up and walked to the door.

"Put this thing on me if Burton starts squawking. Besides, what the hell is he going to say if we get in that place and we find a child porn ring? Let's pretend it doesn't exist? I don't know if he's just protecting a friend, or his own ass and if it's the latter, I want to be the one who puts the bracelets on him."

"Don't fuck this up." Pierson said. "And keep me in the loop. No more surprises."

"I'll ask Turbin to keep the narcs on the detail while we get an ops order in place. We'll hit the house in the morning."

"I want to be there. Get Anthony and Jimmy on the ops order and have them run it by me."

Sophia followed Tommy out of Pierson's office.

"And make sure Jess gets a piece of this," Pierson yelled.

"Yes sir."

Sophia met Tommy at his desk.

"Tommy."

"Yes."

"Go home and get some rest. You stayed out there all night, didn't you?"

"I'm fine. I'll meet up with George, get the warrant and coordinate with Jess and the guys."

"Are you sure?" The idea of getting a run in with Bodhi and a good night's sleep was so appealing.

"Yeah, partner I'm sure." He looked at her, his eyes settling gently on her face. "You know, I've done this a time or two. Piece of cake." Tommy turned back to his computer. "Take the rest of the day off."

"I'm going to take you up on the offer." Sophia picked up her bag and slung it over her shoulder. "And I should probably take advantage of an evening off. When you check out, I'll have to actually work for a living."

Tommy laughed. "Get out of here."

Sophia swung by the Metropolitan Market and picked up some fresh vegetables and a chicken breast. While she was in the check out line, Shelly called. Sophia let the call go to voicemail.

In the car, Sophia listened to the voicemail.

"Hey Soph it's me. Uh, I just got a really strange call from a blocked number with a tip about an investigation that might involve some prominent folks in the city. And the caller mentioned you. Call me."

Son of a bitch. If Tommy called her, I'll kill him.

She was so glad to see Bodhi's face at the door that she forgot about Shelly's voicemail. The pup's tail and butt moved in unison.

"Hey girl, mama's home." She leaned down and let Bodhi slurp at her face. Changing into running clothes, she grabbed Bodhi's leash and headed down to Alki.

The sun was deep in the sky, just about to settle on the Olympic mountain range. Sophia ran without her iPod, listening to her breath syncopate with the sound of her shoes again the pavement. Dodging people, dogs and bikes, she rounded the point, passed the Coast Guard station and lighthouse and headed for Beach Drive. She pushed herself up Admiral Way, willing her legs to stride longer. When she reached her house, she was soaked in sweat.

After a quick dinner, Sophia cuddled with Bodhi on the couch and tried not to think about David and the image of Azzo Martins lying in his own blood and brain matter in his beautifully appointed condo. But most of all, she wondered about Grace Halifax, a little girl she'd never even seen.

Bodhi watched Sophia, her deep brown eyes rarely wavering.

"I promise you a trip to the mountains or the beach or both. You're such a good and patient girl." Sophia leaned in to kiss Bodhi and laid her head against the dog's chest.

At four AM, Sophia went straight to the briefing location, a church parking lot a half a mile from the target, to meet with the outgoing surveillance detectives. It was dark except for the lights of several vehicles, their engines softly churning. The air was unusually humid, and thick with the smell of damp plant life.

"Nothing new overnight," Turbin reported, sipping from a venti Starbucks.

"Thanks. Can you keep a couple of guys on the house until we hit it?" Sophia said.

"The Gonzalez twins are sitting on it now," Turbin said.

Sophia walked over to where Tommy, Jess, Jimmy and Anthony were huddled.

"I'm missing some serious beauty sleep right now," Jess said.

"Me, too." Jimmy took a long pull from a silver thermos cup.

"Too late for you, Paulson. No amount of sleep is going to improve that mug." Tommy leaned against his car and tap a brand new pack of cigarettes. There was a soft breeze coming from behind Tommy.

"Jesus, Stinson. What the hell are you wearing? Some kind

of chick perfume?" Jimmy fanned his face.

Sophia caught the scent and froze.

It was the same cologne she'd smelled at David's apartment.

Sophia looked at Jess who seemed oblivious. Maybe she hadn't noticed it at the scene. After all, she didn't go all the way into the apartment, choosing to wait outside.

"Nah, just something my wife got for me. It's one of those metrosexual colognes. Something men with good self-esteem can wear. You know, something you wouldn't be able to pull off Jimmy."

Sophia's heart raced. She started gulping air.

Jess pulled her aside. "You OK?"

"I'm fine," she murmured.

She walked back to the group, avoiding Tommy's gaze. Maybe it was a coincidence but this was not the time to confront him.

"We're going to hit the house this morning as planned." Sophia pulled out a briefing packet.

"Yes m'am." Tommy said.

Sophia ignored him and continued. "We also have guys set up on the other dipshits so SWAT will be taking them out at the same time we are taking the house."

Jess piped up. "Pierson's not insisting we have SWAT serve the warrant at the house?" She looked around the parking lot. "Where is he, anyway?"

"Fuck SWAT," Tommy said. "We don't need them for this. We know the house is empty. Narcs bedded them all down last night. I'd rather do this with our guys. At least I recognize them all. Half the guys in SWAT look fifteen years old."

"We've got two robbery detectives sitting on the Halifax house. Those kids aren't going anywhere without our guys on them. If it looks like he's taking them somewhere…" Tommy spit. "We'll take him out."

CHAPTER TWENTY-FOUR

Sophia used to think she was a very lucky person. Usually that took the form of not taking chances, not setting herself up to fail. There was no explanation for her good fortune. Without a doubt, a day didn't go by when she wondered when it would all end.

And then it did.

The detectives who sat on the house overnight reported no movement between midnight and three AM. They'd been up on the house for three days and the suspects had established a routine; the first suspect usually didn't show up until after noon. All things remaining equal, the house would be vacant.

Pierson rolled in during the briefing. He waited for Sophia to finish.

"Everyone vest up. We don't know what's in there," he said.

"Tommy, you and your partner will be point." Pierson addressed each detective directly as he spoke. "Jess, Anthony, Jimmy and I will bring up the rear. Narcotics and ACT detectives will hold the corners and the backyard. Galloway from the South anti-crime team is gonna breach the door. It's boarded up pretty tight so it's bound to be as dark as the inside of Stinson's ass in there. Make sure you have a light."

Pierson looked at Sophia and then back at the rest. "And for fuck's sake, be careful. I don't want anyone getting hurt. Let's mount up and go."

Everyone climbed into a few cars and drove the three blocks to the house.

"God, I love this part of the job," Jimmy said, pulling the velcro tighter on his kevlar vest.

"Kids." Tommy gunned the car as they left the parking lot.

"Old man," Anthony said.

The street in front of the house was quiet. Two blocks away, a dog walker headed toward them. Sophia got on the radio.

"See that woman with the dog? Turn her off."

The squad headed up the walkway in a single line behind Galloway. Sophia held him by the back of his belt.

"On my count." Sophia said. She took one last look behind, making sure that everyone was there. Tommy patted her on the shoulder.

"Let's do this."

The ram hit the door with a crack that could have been mistaken for a gun shot. She and Tommy rushed in. She moved to the right, Tommy to the left.

"Seattle Police!" Tommy said it quickly and then repeated himself. The conical beams of their flashlights danced around the room as everyone tried to get their bearing.

"Clear," Tommy yelled. He and Sophia moved forward slightly, allowing the rest of the team to enter and take position.

It was probably a lovely living room thirty years ago. But now it was mostly empty and littered with newspaper and plastic cups. Most likely, it had been a haven for squatters off and on for years.

Pierson and Anthony moved into the hallway and to the back of the house. Jess and Jimmy split off into the kitchen.

Sophia's flashlight landed on a recessed door in the ceiling of a narrow hallway. A leather handle was attached to one end. She motioned to Tommy.

"Tommy, look up there when I turn off my light."

Soft blue light leaked from the corners of the opening.

"Somethings up there. I can hear fans running."

Tommy got on the radio."Clear the house and then stay out of the hallway."

Tommy and Sophia trained their weapons up to the ceiling. A shadow dipped into the light on one edge.

"Someone's up there," Sophia whispered.

"Not for long." Tommy grabbed a chair and slid it to the opening.

"Tommy, what the hell are you doing?"

"My job." He stood on the chair with one leg and then jumped back as a staircase landed against the floor with a loud 'thud.' Tommy toppled against the wall.

"Shit!"

All Sophia remembered seeing was the muzzle flash from the suspect's gun as he dipped down from the opening. She fired three shots in rapid succession. Tommy flattened himself against the wall.

The suspect didn't drop right away, momentum pitching him toward Sophia as she pedaled back, until he landed head first, two feet away. She stepped on his hand, still gripping a Sig Sauer P226 and then kicked it out of range.

"Motherfucker," Tommy said. He sat up and scrambled toward Sophia.

"I could have killed you, asshole."

Jimmy, Anthony and Jess ran into the hallway.

Jess jumped on the radio. "Shots fired." Three tones went out over the air, alerting officers citywide to a major incident as the chief dispatcher echoed the information with the address.

"Is everyone ok? Anyone hit?" Pierson yelled from the living room.

Sophia looked at the suspect, trying to discern a face. There was little left of his skull.

"I'm fine," she said.

Tommy shouted again. "Seattle Police." His flashlight and gun were aimed up at the opening in the attic.

"Where the hell did he come from?" Jess sounded out of breath. "I thought the place was empty."

Sophia looked at Tommy, his arm shaking slightly from holding his pistol up to the attic opening, and caught his eye.

He whispered. "I'll bet a month's salary there's another one up there."

"Stinson, Benedetti. Drag him out of here. I'll cover you," Pierson said.

Blue lights flickered from above them, the sweet smell of old wood and rock wool insulation drifted from the opening.

Stinson leaned over just as Sophia grabbed the suspect's right wrist and started pulling him across the floor.

"Wait for me, Beni." He picked up the man's other arm.

"Shit, this guy is heavy."

"And he's ten pounds down without most of his head," Stinson said.

'Yeah, I see that. Pull."

They dragged the body through the narrow front door and onto the porch.

A dozen squad cars had arrived and were spread across the entire block. Patrol officers bolted toward the front door.

"Set up a perimeter. We've got enough in here."

"Wish I could remember being that happy to wear the uniform," Stinson said. He tapped her arm. "Incoming dipshit."

Marcus Burton jogged up the front porch stairs in his dress blues, unusual for a man who generally shunned a uniform for expensive Italian suits. Stinson turned and went back into the house.

Jesus Christ. He's supposed to be out of town.

"The house isn't clear yet, sir." Sophia moved in front of Burton. He smelled like aftershave, cigarettes and expensive Scotch. "We don't know if there are any more suspects up there. This guy dropped out of the attic."

Burton ignored her and grabbed her arm as she turned to walk through the doorway.

"I'm still a cop, detective. I can take care of myself."

"Sir, we need to let the medics get to this guy." She waved at the three EMT's standing at the end of the walkway.

Burton looked down at the body and then at her.

"I think you and I both know there's nothing that can be done for this man. He's missing his head for chrissakes. Who is he?"

"No idea, sir. A surveillance team has been sitting on this house for a couple of days. We believed it was empty."

"Well, clearly there this was an operational failure. Who's in charge of this mess?"

"My sergeant's inside."

"That didn't answer my question, detective."

"I'm the lead detective, sir. Sgt. Pierson is my supervisor."

Jerry Filson walked up onto the porch, pulling down the ID panels on his raid jacket so the word POLICE was visible.

"Can I tell these patrol guys to stand down? I'm worried they're gonna shoot one of us." He looked down at the suspect.

"Nice shootin'. This your handiwork, Benedetti?"

From inside the house Stinson yelled.

"Show me your hands! Show me your hands!"

There was a loud thump and a scream.

Sophia ran inside. Dressed in cargo shorts and a sleeveless white shirt, a man lay on his stomach, one arm awkwardly pinned under him, the other stretched out to his side.

"Get that hand out, now!" Stinson peered down through the attic opening, his gun aimed at the man on the floor.

Anthony pulled the suspect's arm from underneath him and handcuffed him. When the detective rolled him over the man screamed in pain.

"My arm! It's broken. That motherfucker pushed me."

The man's stomach cascaded over his belt as he lay on his side. Sophia pulled him over onto his back.

"Hey there, Eldon." Sophia grabbed him and with assistance of Anthony and Jess, got him on his feet.

"This is harassment. You fucking bitch. I know you." Eldon turned back to Sophia. "You and your fucking piece of shit husband."

"What did you say?" Sophia walked over and took his jaw in her hand.

"Nothin.' I want my lawyer."

She shoved his head back, nearly hitting Anthony.

"Slow your roll, Beni. We got this asshole." Anthony pushed Eldon out the front door and led him to a waiting patrol car.

Sophia lowered her voice. "Did you hear that?"

"Yes," Jess said.

"I need you to go with Anthony. See if you can get Eldon to talk, even small talk. Get him to mention David again. I want to make sure I know where this is headed."

"Are you sure? We haven't cleared the attic yet."

"Speaking of that, where's Tommy?"

"Last I saw him, he was headed up there." Jess pointed to the hallway ceiling.

"Holy shit," Tommy said from above them.

"Are you ok, Stinson?"

A single set of footsteps creaked above her.

"I'm fine. It's all clear."

"I'm coming up." Sophia grabbed the highest rung she could reach and pulled herself up until her foot landed on something solid.

"You gotta see this."

It was a short climb. In the dark, she could make out hundreds of blue lights, blinking incessantly like fire flies. She pulled herself up the rest of the way. Stinson had holstered his gun. The attic wasn't small, but with all of the machinery crammed into the space only a few full-sized men could fit up there without having to double over under the rafters.

Sophia scanned the room.

Row after row of servers lined every square inch of wall in the room. Two desktops sat near the opening. A couple of folding chairs were scattered up against the wall, most likely a product of the two men scrambling to react to the entry team. Even with several fans running on high, the heat was stifling. It was a wonder that anything actually worked. Sophia walked over to a piece of plywood hanging over a vent and pulled at it until it fell off. The dim light of dawn filtered into the space. It was larger than she had originally thought, one of those houses with an attic that would have been easy for a second story build-out.

"I need some air."

"This is the fricken' mother lode. This is where these shit heads have been running their enterprise. We got the bastards." Stinson leaned down and grabbed a computer mouse and moved the curser over the monitor screen.

"Don't touch anything, Tommy. We're going to have to get an addendum to the search warrant. We need CSI and the forensic guys out here to handle all of these computers. I don't want to lose anything."

The adrenalin was still pumping. Rivulets of perspiration ran down her back under her Kevlar vest.

"I've got to get out of here." She looked over at Stinson who was double clicking on various files on one of the desktops.

"Seriously, Stinson. Stop it. Leave the damn computer alone."

"I know what I'm doing. I just want to see one little naked girl so I can go down there and pound the shit out of that freak." Stinson's face was blue from the light of the computer screen. His eyes darted around the files, thousands of them listed in blank, unnamed folders set against a desktop of daisies.

She pulled Stinson's hand away from the mouse. "Stop."

"Well, what have we here?" Marcus Burton squeezed through the opening, crawling into the attic.

"Warm up here, eh?" Burton bent over and brushed dust off of his knees.

"I think we have the heart of the operation right here. We need to tweak the search warrant before we start looking at this stuff."

Sophia followed Burton's eyes as they scanned the room. The muscles in his jaw tightened. She moved over and stood in front of him.

"We really don't want to mess this up, Chief."

Burton stepped around her and walked over to one of the computers. He leaned over and then pointed to a folder on the screen.

"What's this?" He grabbed the mouse and started to double click on the icon. A cascade of folders bounced out onto the screen, but before Sophia could turn off the monitor, Burton clicked on another folder. A picture of a naked woman straddling what looked like an enormous zucchini filled the screen.

"Damn!" Burton moved closer to the screen. "Isn't that, uh, shit what's her name, what's her name?" He closed his eyes. "I got it right on the tip of my tongue. Oh, you know who I'm talking about. Stinson, come over here and take a look."

"Yeah, Chief I don't really wanna see anything that's on these computers," he said.

"This doesn't look like a child to me, detective," Burton said. "I hope you didn't shoot that man for nothing."

"Stinson, why don't you get a couple of uniforms to keep people from coming up here. Post them in the living room. I'm going to head back to the office and bang out the addendum." Sophia reached for the mouse and then turned off the monitor.

"We really need to get out of here, Chief. At least until the warrant is updated."

"I get it, Ms. Benedetti.

"It's Detective Benedetti, sir."

"Yes, I get it, Detective Benedetti. You two go ahead. I'll ensure this scene is secure until you get the uniforms in place."

She looked at Stinson. He shrugged his shoulders and walked toward the attic opening. She caught up with him as soon as they hit the floor.

"Jesus Christ. Why is he here? Pierson said he was going to be out of town."

Stinson adjusted his holster and wiped his forehead. "Because he's up to his ass in this case."

"Which is exactly why we can't leave him up there alone."

"Send one of the uni's up."

Sophia pulled out her shirt and let the sweat run down her abdomen. Stinson's cell phone played the opening bars from Shaft. He pulled it from his belt holster and answered.

"Hey, baby." Sophia knew he wasn't talking to his wife. Now more than ever, she needed him to have her back, and from the smile on his face, she knew her welfare was the furthest thing from his mind.

CHAPTER TWENTY-FIVE

Despite the warmth of the day, stepping out of the front door felt like a blast of air conditioning. There were still a couple of patrol cars parked on the street in front of the house, their occupants busily running names and plates on their mobile data computers. She scrolled through her contacts on her phone, trying to locate George Anderson's number.

"Looking good, Benedetti."

Sophia looked up. Sergeant Daryl Parker stepped from his patrol car, his eight-point hat tipped back on his head. In the academy, he'd been fit and lean, a newly discharged Marine. Now, he was a member of the 'blue button' club, his belly so large it protruded over his belt exposing the blue buttons on his uniform shirt meant to be neatly hidden in a pair of dark blue wool pants.

"Not now, Daryl." Sophia looked up and gave him a weak smile.

"If not now, when?" He stood up and straightened his hat. "You know I like a woman who sweats. And I especially like one who's a good shot."

"You want to go through the next several months of bullshit with me?" She knew from watching other officers go through the scrutiny in the aftermath of an on-duty shooting, the second guessing was going to be fierce. Then there was the press, always ready to find a reason to make a good shooting look bad.

"If you were my girl, you bet I would." He smiled. "I'll be there in spirit, baby."

"Jesus, Daryl. You're always just shy of an EEO complaint every time you open your mouth."

"Damn, girl. Why do you have to come at a brother like that?" He smiled, leaned closer and lowered his voice, "Besides, how bad can it be? You killed a kiddie diddler. You did us all a favor. They'll be parading you all over the news."

"Thanks." She paused. "I think."

Sophia looked back at the house. "Hey, I need you to do me a really big favor."

Parker tucked in the back of his shirt.

"Anything. What do you need?"

"That asshole Burton is up in my scene. I need you to grab one your guys and post him up there with Burton until I get back."

"Happily. I hate that fucker." Parker locked his cruiser.

"Do your best to stay civil."

Parker chuckled and adjusted his duty belt.

Sophia forced a smile and put her hand on his arm. "Make him uncomfortable. Keep an eye on him. I need some time to get the addendum to my warrant signed and then get back in there. I have a bad feeling about this one."

Parker smiled. "For you, I'll do it." He turned on his heel and yelled at a rookie busy getting crime scene tape out of his trunk. "Foster, come with me."

The officer dropped the tape back into the trunk and walked over to Sophia and Daryl.

Out of the corner of Sophia's eye, she noticed a mass of cheap suit headed toward her. Sgt. Glenn Mullins was moving like a marionette. His legs were long and spindly. His left arm swung as his right hand cradled a phone to his ear. As he got closer, he held up a finger.

"Don't tell them anything. Nothing. We'll release a statement later. In the meantime, stall 'em with some bullshit about getting child molesters off the street blah, blah, blah." He winked at Sophia. "Yeah, that's it."

He hung up and reached out his hand. "Glenn Mullins. I'm your guild rep. You did the shooting, yes? You haven't made any statements, have you?" He grabbed her hand and squeezed it hard, the way insecure men always did. She'd forgotten that one of the first calls an officer made after a shooting was to ask for a Guild representative, someone who would walk the officer through the maze of administrative protocol.

"No one's asked me anything. Well, Burton walked all over my scene but he didn't ask me about the shooting."

"Burton? I thought he was out on personal leave. Hell, what do I know. I can barely keep up with my own schedule, much less the comings and goings of an assistant chief." Mullins looked at his phone. A call was coming in but he put the phone in a holster on his hip.

"Good. I'm glad you've kept your mouth shut. You wouldn't believe some of the stuff I've heard guys say after a shooting." He looked past her at the house. "It's normal, you know, what you're feeling right now."

"I'm not sure you do," Sophia said.

Mullins pulled his shirt cuffs out from his jacket sleeves. He still moved and twitched as if he wore a bullet proof vest and wool class A uniform pants.

"We're going to have to head downtown, give a statement to homicide. I'll be there the whole time, you know, to help you out in case it gets tricky."

"Tricky?"

"Muddled. It happens."

"There's nothing muddled in this for me, Glenn."

"Good girl. That's what I like to hear. Still, I need to be in there for the interview."

"Good girl? Are you looking at me? I want to make sure you can actually see my eyes rolling back into my head, Mullins."

"No offense, Benedetti."

"Sure."

Sophia looked up at the attic. Burton was up there, doing God knows what, and the rest of her crew were waiting to process the scene. Pierson stood by himself, lost in a conversation on his phone, his face downcast and weary.

Sophia eyed Stinson who leaned back against a department pool car, a cigarette dangling from his mouth. He looked at her and then glanced over at the medical examiner's assistant as he pulled a gurney from the back of the ME's van.

She walked to the house, Mullins following her. "Can't I just go up to homicide first thing in the morning? I've got to get another warrant."

"Yeah, I'd love to help you out, Benedetti, but you've got to come downtown and talk to those guys today, like now preferably." Mullins said. "I'll be there with you the whole way. You'll lose a lot of details if you put it off. Can't avoid it, I'm afraid." He pointed toward the house. "Have one of the other guys in the squad get the warrant."

Sophia sighed and looked at her watch. "I've got to go back in for a minute and talk to Daryl Parker. We're going to have to impound the scene until I can get back here."

"Make it quick. The faster we get down there, the sooner it'll be over. Still got your weapon?"

She touched her Glock with the underside of her arm. "Yes. Why?"

"Your Captain should have taken it from you and given you a replacement."

Mullins adjusted his tie and looked in the side mirror of his pool car. "Technically, the homicide detectives are supposed to take your duty weapon. No worries. We'll figure it out. Hang on to it for now."

"I haven't seen Captain Laramount out here. The only brass

I've seen is Burton." She broke into a jog and ran up the front stairs.

Mullins yelled after her. "Make it quick, Benedetti. I got a tee time for a round at the Home Course."

Sophia paused at the front door. The medical examiner, a young guy named Evan Browning, had the suspect's body on its side while he examined the exit wound. Evan wore a black Megadeath t-shirt over running shorts.

"I was in the middle of a run," Browning said, as if he'd read Sophia's mind. "I can't get shit done anymore, you know what I mean? I was up all last night at that multiple down south, and all I wanted to do was run off some of the stench from that scene, but then I catch this mess." He made a note on his clipboard.

"It's not like we planned it," Sophia said.

Browning looked up at her. "I'm being an asshole. Don't mind me." He patted the back of the man's pants. "Doesn't appear to have any ID on him. We may have to run his prints if we don't find it somewhere in the house."

Browning's assistant rolled the gurney to the bottom of the stairs.

"Just leave it there for now," Browning said.

He turned his attention back to the suspect. An oddly symmetrical blood stain covered most of the suspect's shirt and pants. He was lean – not like Eldon. This one had taken care of his body. Her first thought was that he was a runner or bicyclist - his calves were thin, taut and shaved. It wasn't uncommon for a more sophisticated criminal to shave his body to avoid leaving trace evidence behind at crime scenes. This guy was more than just a virtual geek. He was a predator.

What was left of the suspect's face was sunken and shriveled, but he appeared to be white and in his early 40's. The sun peaked over the roof line of the house next door and directly into her eyes, making it difficult to see. She crouched next to Browning.

"Is his whole body hairless?"

"I haven't looked everywhere but so far, it looks like just the legs." The ME pulled up the shirt, "Check that. His chest is shaved nice and pretty, although not recently. He's got a good level of stubble going on here." Sophia leaned over Browning's shoulder to get a better look.

"Benedetti, get the fuck in there," Mullins yelled from his car.

Sophia leaned down and patted Browning on the shoulder. "Thanks."

He picked up a large bowie knife from the porch deck "And by the way, he had this down the back of his pants."

"Nice." Although the suspect had come down from the attic gun in hand and had managed to get off one shot, it was nice to know that he'd been armed with a knife, too. Just a little extra icing on the cake when it came to the firearms review board.

Sophia stepped into the living room. The adrenaline dump from the shooting was starting to wear off and fatigue was beginning to set in.

"Hey, I thought you were heading downtown?" Parker and the rookie stood at the end of the hallway at the entrance to the living room.

"Is he still up there?"

"Yes, ma'm." The rookie shuffled uncomfortably. "Well, I think so."

"Parker." Sophia lowered her voice. "I thought I asked you to get him out of there."

"I had the rookie call him out but he didn't answer. I didn't want to contaminate your scene by going up there."

"He probably heard you down here and decided to hide."

"Chief!" Sophia hollered into the hole at the top of the ladder.

There was no answer.

"Have you heard anything? Are you sure he's still not up

there?" she said. Parker and the rookie looked at each other and shrugged.

"It's been pretty quiet, ma'm."

Someone had pushed the attic ladder partially up. The rookie pulled it down for Sophia who yanked on the rope handle.

"I've got it, thanks." She looked at the rookie and suddenly felt old. His face was so smooth, she wondered if he'd even started shaving.

Parker laughed. "She don't need any help from you, boy."

The rookie looked sheepishly at Sophia. "Sorry, I was just trying…"

Sophia pulled herself up the first two rungs and then hooked her foot on the bottom rung.

The attic was still dark, and it took a moment for her eyes to adjust, despite the warm glow of the computer monitors. The dull whir of the fans sounded surprisingly loud.

"Chief?"

Sophia didn't see him at first. He was standing at the far end of the attic with his back to her.

"Chief?" Sophia cocked her head to get a better look. He was swaying side to side. She moved closer.

"Oh, shit." She turned him to her. Burton's face was purple, his tongue protruded from his mouth. A thick extension cord was wrapped around a roof beam and then around his neck. His hands were closed into fists, turned tightly at the wrists. She fumbled to pull out her knife from her kevlar vest pocket, and started sawing at the cord with one hand, while trying to support his weight with the other. With one last swipe, his two hundred and forty pounds thumped to the floor.

"Parker, call medics," she screamed, as she tore open Burton's shirt and pulled at his tie.

"Come on, come on. I need help up here." She couldn't find a pulse at his carotid artery. His chest was flat and deflated.

Parker pulled himself through the opening. He knelt down

beside her and started pumping Burton's chest.

"This is a fucking waste of time, Beni."

"We have to try." She pulled Parker away and started doing compressions.

"Jesus, how long was he up here hanging?" She put two fingers on the side of his neck. "Still no pulse."

"He's dead, Beni." Parked pulled her away.

Sophia stood up. Her vision narrowed and a rushing sound filled her ears. Her breath slid in and out unevenly, captured by the stifling heat. She bent over, hands on her knees.

"Unfuckingbelievable."

CHAPTER TWENTY-SIX

Mullins drove Sophia back to headquarters.

"Well that was an unexpected surprise, huh?"

"Can we just not talk right now?" Sophia said.

"Sure but you gotta be prepared to talk later. Have to explain why you shot that guy."

Sophia turned to Mullins. "He dropped from the fucking ceiling and shot at me. Is that good enough for you?"

"Calm down…"

"Don't tell me to calm down."

"Ok, just try and relax. I'm trying to help you here." Mullins ignored his phone as it vibrated in the center console.

"I need to talk to my partner."

"I don't know where Stinson is but it'd be best if you didn't."

"What is your role here, Mullins? Because I'm getting the distinct impression that you're more interested in your tee time than helping me out. And I don't appreciate the tact you're taking - like I did something wrong. This was a good shoot."

"Of course. It's just a little more complicated with the Chief offing himself and all."

"Fuck him."

"Ok, then."

They rode in silence the rest of the way.

Sgt. Taylor met them just inside the entrance to the seventh floor.

"Detective Benedetti. What a surprise."

He'd just hit her last nerve.

"Just get me to an interview room, Mullins."

Mullins escorted her past Taylor and down the narrow hall.

"Your captain is waiting for you."

"Great. Can't wait." Sophia glanced at Mullins. He shook his head.

"Keep it together, Benedetti. He's on your side."

Captain Benjamin Laramount sat in the small interview room with his back to the door. His suit jacket hung over the back of the chair. He looked over his shoulder as Sophia walked in the room but didn't stand or acknowledge her.

"Captain, I'm going to get some water and then come back. I'd appreciate it if you wouldn't talk to Benedetti until I'm back in the room," Mullins said.

Laramount said nothing.

Mullins looked at Sophia. She nodded for him to go.

Sophia sat in the hard plastic chair and looked at Laramount. He stood and closed the door, then sat on the edge of the table, leaning over her.

"This is not good, Benedetti."

"What part? The part where I killed the child molesting piece of shit or the part where his accomplice killed himself?"

"What are you talking about?"

"The chief."

Laramount stood up and smoothed back his hair. "And you know this how?"

"I know it because of the evidence."

"What evidence do you have exactly, detective?"

The door opened and Mullins walked in with two waters. Behind him, Drew Taylor stood in the hallway.

"We need to do this interview. And you can't be in here Captain." Taylor walked in and dropped a legal pad onto the table.

Laramount put his jacket on, headed for the door and then turned. "We'll revisit this conversation, Detective."

"Not if it's about this event, you won't." Taylor shut the door and sat across from Sophia. "I hate that asshole."

Sophia took the water and cracked the top open. "What do you want to know?"

"Just start from the beginning, Detective."

Her interview with Taylor over, Sophia went back to the office. She called Pierson.

"I'm officially on administrative leave."

"Lucky you. How're you doing?"

"Fine, I guess. Tired."

"We're just finishing up here. Jess got additional warrants for the house and the computers. Anderson wrangled some help from a task force officer with the Secret Service's financial crimes squad to collect computers and the servers. "We've got another hour or so left."

"Is Tommy there?"

"He was here for a while and then said he had some personal business to deal with. Pissed me off. This place was a real dump and we could have used the help."

"He didn't mention it to me."

"That's Stinson." Pierson said.

"I'll be at home if you need me."

"Of course. I'll ask Jess to work with Tommy on this. You just take care of yourself, ok?"

Bodhi was startled but happy to see Sophia in the middle of the day. Candy had dropped her off earlier. Dog toys littered the living room, and several couch pillows lay on the floor. The smell of dog was heavy and comforting.

Sophia's cell phone vibrated on her hip.

"Hey, it's Jess." Her voice was hoarse.

"You sound terrible. Are you getting sick?"

"No, it happens when I get really tired. Weak-ass vocal cords, I guess." She cleared her throat. "So how are you doing? They kind of swept you out of the scene pretty fast."

"I'm fine." Sophia sat at her kitchen table and poured herself a glass of wine.

"Glad to hear it. I was worried, I mean, it's hard enough to shoot someone but then the whole Burton thing…" Jess' voice cut out.

"I'm really still in shock, I think. And I can't talk about it, you know?"

"Yeah, no problem. I was just worried about you."

A few sips of wine began the unraveling. "I need to go."

"Call if you need anything."

Shortly before ten o'clock, she tried Tommy's phone but it went to voicemail. She left two messages, asking him to call her as soon as he could. She thought about calling her mom and dad but decided it would be better to tell them the story in person when they were all actually speaking to one another.

She'd never felt so alone.

Sophia sat on the couch with a cup of Sleepy Time tea and Bodhi. She put the TV on low, only to provide white noise for her racing mind. She couldn't stop thinking about the possibility that Tommy had killed David. Why would he sacrifice himself, his pension, his career? She had to be wrong.

Her body soon relaxed under a heavy fleece blanket, Bodhi curled hard up against her legs. The dog's rhythmic breathing lulled Sophia to sleep.

Her phone startled her, hurling the empty coffee cup wedged between her hand and thigh to the floor. It was one AM.

She answered it in a haze.

"Hey, it's me." Tommy's said almost in a whisper.

"Where have you been? I've tried calling you for hours."

"I was at the scene for most of the day and then I needed to go clear my head." A woman's voice was in the background.

"You alone?"

"No, I'm home."

She couldn't tell if he sounded resigned or relieved.

"We've gotta talk."

"I can't come over. I promised Evelyn I'd stay home." He lowered his voice. "Did they tell you to not talk to anyone about the shooting?"

"Yes, but screw them. I need to talk to you."

"We're gonna have to lie low for a few days. We did good, you know."

"I know." She cleared her throat. "What the hell happened today?"

"Let's talk later. I'm dead tired." Evelyn said something to him in the background.

"I'll be there in a moment, babe."

"I'm glad you're home with Evelyn."

"Don't let them get to you, OK?"

There was an uncomfortable silence, one that she hadn't felt since the first days they worked together, when Tommy felt he was being punished by being saddled with a rookie detective.

"Any idea how long I'm going to be out on admin leave?" She was trying to keep him on the phone.

"It varies. Depends on how complicated they try and make it. Maybe a couple of weeks. I'm not sure. My last shooting was twenty-five years ago. They do things differently now, as you might guess. Enjoy the time off."

"Take care of yourself, Tommy."

"You, too."

She hung up feeling so disconnected from Tommy. It surprised her how attached she'd become to him. It wasn't romantic, she was sure of that. But he'd changed in the last couple of months, become more detached. She worried that he'd started drinking again. More importantly, she worried that he'd become a stone cold killer.

CHAPTER TWENTY-SEVEN

After three hours of fitful sleep, Sophia made herself a cup of coffee and wandered out to the garage. She'd left her Jeep parked in the driveway, allowing her to get to the covered Moto Guzzi Le Mans resting tightly against the wall. She pulled off the cover and tossed it in the corner. The bright green tank needed a touch of wax but aside from that, the bike was pristine. She rolled it out into the driveway, straddled the seat and pulled in the clutch. Kicking it into neutral, she turned the key and the monster roared to life. It was the perfect bike for her - Italian, sexy and fast as hell, but with classic stylings.

She sat back on her haunches and admired the bike's profile, the way it reminded her of a feline predator. It was seven years old with only twenty-five thousand miles on it and she'd put over half of them on just jetting around the city. Bodhi wandered over and sat on her foot.

"I need to go for a ride, girl. You understand, right?" Sophia scratched Bodhi behind both ears, grabbed her collar and escorted her into the house.

She called Candy and arranged for her to watch Bodhi for a few days.

"I need to go see my folks," she lied.

It was a calculated risk leaving town after a shooting. Sophia called Jess and told her she was headed to San Fransisco for a quick visit but asked her to keep it on the down low.

"I just need to clear my head. I won't be gone long."

"Are you letting Pierson know?" Jess said.

"I'll only be a phone call away."

"That wasn't my question."

"I'll call you when I get there. How's that for a compromise?"

Jess laughed. "That's not a compromise, that's a promise. And not a very convincing one."

"I promise."

"How about I come with you, provide some moral support?"

"Unless you want to ride on the back of a bike on a seat not meant for sitting, you're welcome."

"I have my own bike," Jess said.

"I'm impressed, but I need to go alone."

By noon, she was on the road, the Le Mans' transverse v-twin winding up and down as she put it through the drill. Her earbuds sank into her ears, holding back the roar of the engine and the wind battering her full faced helmet. Live's 'I Alone' crashed between her ears as she deftly leaned the beast in and out of turns. It was a little over twelve hours to Tiburon. Opting for I-5 instead of 101, she made sure she had her badge, gun and ID in the event she was pulled over by State Patrol. The troopers were notorious for citing city cops. There was no professional courtesy extended generally, but Sophia hoped she could use her sex to an advantage and talk her way out of a speeding ticket.

Once past Portland, she cranked up the engine and pushed it over eighty. It still wasn't fast enough, the memories of the last few weeks coming in torrents. It wasn't until she'd traveled over four hundred miles, that she realized the inside of her helmet was soaked with sweat.

She arrived in Tiburon shortly before one am and pulled

onto Beach Road, where she could see her parents' home perched on Corinthian Island across Belvedere Cove. The lights were on in the living room, a sure sign that her father was still up, reading. The front porch light glowed as though it was powered by a thousand fireflies. Sophia took off her helmet and balanced it on her thigh.

Not only had her father hated that she was a cop, but he despised David. Perhaps he saw something in David that she didn't. Sophia was certain it took all of his will power to not say 'I told you so' when David nearly killed her.

She started the bike and put on her helmet. It was only a matter of time before someone would call the police and she'd have to badge her way out.

She sat until her father turned out the light. He stood at the window as though he was trying to make out the figure sitting on the motorcycle, then slowly pulled the curtains closed. As he did, Sophia fought the temptation to wave, to let him know she was home.

Sophia gunned the engine and headed onto the 101, over the Golden Gate Bridge and into the Mission district. The streets were busy with scores of people straggling out of bars. She navigated slowly.

Sophia pulled over on San Carlos at 18th and parked the bike between two trucks. Leaning it over and on to the kickstand, she stepped to the curb and took out her phone.

"Hello?" The voice was smokey with sleep.

"Gideon, it's Sophia."

"Jesus Christ, Beni. What time is it?"

"It's really late. I'm sorry. I'm outside your apartment and I need a place to crash for a few hours."

"Hang on."

Muffled voices rose and fell in the background.

"Hey, if this isn't a good time, I totally understand."

"No it's fine. Let me get the door."

Sophia grabbed her helmet and pulled off her jacket. Her

soaked t-shirt hung over her jeans hiding her Glock model 27.

"Try the door. It should be open."

Despite the darkness, Sophia could tell the lines of the building had changed little. The soft beige exterior of the Victorian inspired apartment building, blended into the background of the neighborhood. From the high-end European cars parked on the street, the Mission was no longer a haven for the down and out.

The lobby smelled as it always had, flooding her with bursts of memory. It had been ten years since she'd been back to this place. The carpet was new, but already worn in places. The light fixtures had been updated, as had the wallpaper and furnishings, but the smell of the place hadn't been affected. Cedar, offset by gusts of patchouli, lingered everywhere.

Sophia climbed a flight of stairs where Gideon stood in the doorway of his apartment.

"Hey"

"It's good to see you." Sophia wrapped her arms around his lean frame before he had a chance to close the door.

"Come sit down. You look terrible. What's going on?"

Sophia sat on the couch and laid her head back. "I'm sorry to put this on you."

"Like I said, forget about it. How come you didn't go to your parents' place?"

"We're still not talking much."

"Don't hang on to that shit for very long, girl. It's not worth it."

"I just can't deal with it right now."

Gideon sat down and put his arm around her. Sophia leaned against him.

There was a thump and a terse 'fuck' from the bedroom.

"You ok in there?"

"Yep," a deep male voice replied.

Sophia laughed. "So you're back to men, I see."

"Women are just too much work. You know that…"

Sophia shifted on the couch. "I don't know about that. After all, it was a man who tried to kill me. That's pretty high maintenance."

"You do have me on that one." Gideon smiled. "You want some coffee, or do you want to try and sleep?"

"Can I just crash here for a few hours? I'll stay out of your hair. Go back in and entertain your gentleman friend." Sophia curled up in a ball to fit on the small couch and planted her head on a throw pillow.

"All right. I can go in a little late tomorrow. We'll talk in a few."

Gideon covered Sophia with a blanket. She was out before he closed the bedroom door behind him.

The sound of the front door clicking shut woke her. Disoriented, she sat up and scanned the room. Gideon had upgraded the furniture. Gone were the brick and board bookcases, stuffed with books on the coming revolution. In their stead, were tasteful cherry built-ins filled with art books and hand thrown pottery. The couch was paired with two leather chairs and a large wooden coffee table, covered a few days worth of the New York Times. The sun poured through the kitchen window, sending splinters of light into the room.

"Good morning." Gideon appeared, his hair wet from a shower. "How about some coffee?"

"Sure." Sophia's head pounded from dehydration. She swore she'd sweated out half her body weight on the ride down. She shuffled into the kitchen and hugged Gideon from behind. "I hope I didn't ruin a romantic night."

"No you didn't. This isn't a new thing. Parker still likes his apartment and his freedom and frankly, so do I."

"Good for you. For the both of you." She looked around. "Did he leave already?"

"He has a cat, so he has to get home pretty early to deal with that."

"A cat, wow. You're dating a guy with a cat." Sophia rubbed his back.

"Hey, I remember you getting pretty tight with the house cat back in the day."

They had shared a house with three others during their days at San Fransisco State. It was the best time in her life. Away from home, she was able to stretch and experiment. She and Gideon had a fling that lasted exactly three and a half weeks, until they both realized they were about as wrong for each other as two people could be.

"So are you going to tell me what's going on?" He set a large mug of coffee down in front of Sophia.

"I shot someone."

"Someone who deserved it, I hope."

"He shot at me first." Sophia was struck by the fact that was incredibly lucky to be eight hundred miles away, drinking coffee on a good friend's couch.

"Did anyone else get hurt?" He'd stopped mid sip.

"No, I mean none of our guys. Another suspect broke his arm."

"Good, good." Gideon leaned back in his chair. "So, what else is going on?"

"David is dead."

"I'm sorry, I guess."

"He was murdered."

"Not by you, I hope."

She smiled.

"Well it's easy for me to say this, but that's your job, to kill bad guys if they try and kill you. What was this guy doing that made him want to shoot you, anyway?"

"Distributing child porn."

Gideon clapped his hands. "As a citizen of this great country, I salute you and thank you for your service. Fuck him."

"I wish I shared your enthusiasm."

"David wasn't involved, was he?" He stopped and looked at Sophia.

"I don't think so but I'm pretty sure his death is related somehow."

"That blows." Gideon finished his coffee and stood up. "Another cup?"

"No, I'm good." Sophia nursed the lukewarm liquid left in her cup."Hey what time does Jason's shop open?"

"Which shop? He has a couple now."

"Whichever one he works at."

"Let me check." Gideon grabbed his laptop and started to surf. "Thinking of getting work to commemorate your shooting?"

"Not funny, dude."

"Sorry. If it were me, I'd totally tattoo the date and time on my arm to remind me that I managed to take a child molester off the streets."

"Can I take a quick shower?"

"Of course. Clean towels are under the sink. Want me to call and make an appointment?"

"Would you? Ask Jason if he can do a quick job this morning."

"Got it."

Sophia headed to the bathroom, passing Gideon's rumpled bedroom. Sheets were jumbled across the bed and floor. The shades were open to the view of the building across the street.

Her body ached from the trip, the battering from the wind and the vibration of the engine and the road. She closed her eyes and let the water wash over her face and neck, back and legs.

Gideon knocked on the door. "He can do you first thing, but you've got to get there in a half an hour. Don't spend too much time getting pretty in there."

"Thanks."

She hugged Gideon good-bye on the street, straddled her bike and secured her helmet.

"Don't be such a stranger. You don't have to wait until you shoot someone else to come see me, you know."

Sophia hit him on the chest. "Stop it. I know. I won't make it so long next time."

"And Soph," Gideon took her hand. "Don't freeze out your parents for much longer. They've already lost one kid."

She smiled and kicked the bike into gear.

Jason greeted her with a wide smile and a bear hug. "What brings you down here?"

"Need some work. Just one on each wrist. Nothing fancy."

He was six foot four, with a bald head and arms the size of Sophia's thighs. His tight black tee shirt hugged his muscled frame. Colorful tattoos burst from his short sleeves and traveled to his knuckles.

"You still copping?" His question was part small talk and part professional curiosity. Sophia suspected he dabbled in weed sales on the side. They'd developed a respectful detente over the years. She brought him business, he looked the other way when it came to doing ink for a cop.

"Yep"

"Let me give us some privacy." He turned the 'open' sign around and led her to the back room.

"I appreciate it."

Jason pulled out his tattoo machine and lined up his ink cups. "What'll it be today?"

He turned the music up so high, Sophia had to shout.

When she was done, she sat on her bike and let the sun play

on her face. She was careful to pull her leather gloves over the protective clear tape that covered her new art. On the inside of her left wrist, the word 'lucky' on her right, 'survivor.'

It was time to head home.

CHAPTER TWENTY-EIGHT

Over the course of the next two weeks, Sophia took the opportunity to catch up on the little details in her life that she had disregarded for a year. She started a yoga class up in the Junction, and even found time to meditate for a few minutes every day. She and Bodhi went for runs at Lincoln Park and down at Alki, capping every one off with a cookie and a latte.

Jess called a couple of times just to check in, uncomfortably aware of the elephant in the room - the fact that she couldn't discuss the shooting with Sophia. But she was able to fill Sophia in on the current gossip on the department, including the persistent rumor that Tommy wasn't coming back, that this was his swan song.

The case was coming along, but Anderson hadn't found any images of Grace on the hard drives. Despite her best efforts, Jess hadn't been able to pull the little girl out of the Halifax home.

"I wish I had better news for you," Jess said, leaning against her desk, the phone wedged between her ear and shoulder.

"Stewart Halifax is involved somehow," Sophia said to Jess, scrubbing her kitchen countertop for the fifth time that week.

"There's nothing there. At least not yet." Jess sounded tired. She'd been putting in double shifts trying to link together

Sophia's case and stay on top of her own caseload. "By the way, have you talked to Tommy?"

"Nope. If he wants to talk, he can call me."

"That sounds a little harsh, like you're breaking up with him," Jess laughed. "But seriously, no one's seen him since the shooting. Did he retire and forget to tell anyone?"

"I just need some space right now. And he needs to figure out what he's going to do. I hope he's spending time with this wife and talking over his options." Sophia stopped cleaning.

"Jess?"

"Yes."

"The day we went to David's. Do you remember smelling anything out of the ordinary?"

"I didn't go into the apartment. I just looked in through the door. I don't recall anything particularly pungent. Why do you ask?" Jess said.

"No reason." Sophia stepped out onto her back deck. "I miss everyone."

"We miss you, too," Jess said. "I'll check in with you in a couple of days, OK? Maybe come by in person, have a glass of wine or a cup."

"Sure."

"Detective Benedetti?" The woman said.

"Yes." Sophia paused and pulled the phone away again to double-check the caller ID, a blocked number.

"Can you talk?"

"Who is this?"

"Isabel Proust."

"Like the writer?"

"Yes, but no relation. I wish." The woman laughed softly. "I was David's…" She paused as if to assemble the perfect words. "I was a close friend."

"How did you get this number?"

"I'm sorry to call you on your cell. I found your number in David's things, and you were the only other person who seemed to know him. He was a bit of a blank slate when I met him."

"Why are you calling me?"

"Frankly, I'm not sure. I, I guess I thought it might help me find some closure. Everything happened so fast. I didn't get to say good-bye." Isabel's voice cracked. "He spoke about you often. Would you be willing to meet for coffee."

Her curiosity piqued, Sophia said, "How about this afternoon? At the Starbucks around the corner from David's place?"

"I can be there at two. I'll be the tall blonde," she laughed.

"See you then." Sophia hung up and sat on the front porch with Bodhi. Her home faced west and the sun just peaked over the roofline to the southwest. She stretched her legs down the stairs. The neighborhood was quiet, with most folks working during the day. Bodhi put her head in Sophia's lap and closed her eyes.

Isabel sounded pretty normal. For all she knew, the woman was a raving lunatic or a witness in David's death. *Christ, she could be a suspect.*

She reconsidered the meeting. But there were too many unanswered questions and it was quite possible that Isabel Proust might be the last link to the mystery that was David's life for the last two years.

Sophia arrived at Starbucks early. It was busier than she expected, full of moms and babies. At the tables near outlets, sat a few folks, their heads deep in thought in front of laptops. Baristas busily prepared drinks. The roar of the milk steamer filled the room every few minutes.

Sophia was dressed in Seattle casual - jeans and a loose white t-shirt, under a lightweight jacket. She ordered an Americano and took a seat in the back so she could watch the door.

The door opened and a woman dressed in a pair of Ann Taylor pants and a Burberry coat walked in. She was on the phone, but scanned the room as she spoke. Seeing Sophia, she nodded but continued to talk on the phone. As she walked up to the table, she ended the conversation abruptly.

"I'm Isabel. I recognize you from photos David showed me."

"I'm surprised," Sophia said.

"Surprised at what?"

"That David ever talked about me."

"All the time."

Isabel excused herself to get a drink. She was an exquisitely beautiful woman. Her hair was combed back into a loose bun while tendrils of wispy blond hair framed her face. When Isabel sat down across from her, Sophia was transfixed.

Isabel reached into her purse and pulled out an envelope. She slid it across the table.

"I found this in David's things. It had your name on it."

It was another travel drive, this time in the shape of a mini-sized Snickers bar.

"Well this beats the last one."

"Pardon me?"

"Nothing. I was thinking about something else I saw recently."

"It's a computer thing, right?"

"It's a portable storage device. Makes it easy for people to share data from one computer to another." Sophia put the envelope in her pocket, dreading the idea of opening anything on the drive.

Sophia stared into her coffee cup. "So tell me again, why did you call me?"

"I guess I wanted to meet you, see you in person. David had a lot of guilt and grief over what he did to you." Isabel took a sip of her drink. She looked at the scar on Sophia's throat. "Do you know if they've identified a suspect in his murder?"

"I don't know. I've been off work for a little while."

"Hopefully for a vacation." Isabel sat back in her chair and swept back a wisp of hair from her face.

"As you probably know, I was a prime suspect for a short time." She glanced at the front door as it opened, startled at the noise. "And then when I was cleared, the detective didn't seem to want to take my calls."

"That's pretty standard. Unless you're family or…"

"Of course." Isabel looked at her watch. "I'm sure you're curious about my relationship with David."

Sophia shifted in her seat. She wasn't convinced she wanted to know everything.

"I'll tell you what I told the homicide detectives - David and I met at a hospital." Isabel sipped her coffee slowly and deliberately. "Actually, it was an inpatient treatment center over on the Eastside. We became friends and occasionally," she blushed, "occasionally more."

Sophia expected to have more of a reaction. She was glad David wasn't alone for the last days of his life. Isabel didn't strike her as David's type, though. But what did she know? She wasn't his type either.

"You know our history?"

"Yes, I heard a lot in group."

"Group?"

"In therapy. Like I said, we were both in a treatment program. I guess, technically I'm violating the rules by talking about it but since he's…" Isabel set down her coffee cup and glanced out the window.

It felt like such a violation. Her marriage to David was no one's business.

"Were you in love with him?"

Isabel smiled and traced her finger along the edge of a small napkin.

"David was damaged." Looking at Sophia as though she hoped for a glimmer of recognition, she continued. "He was really, really hard to love." She pulled her chair closer to the table. "And I've been in enough therapy to know when someone's not a good choice. But he had his moments." She paused. "I'm sure you remember that."

Sophia tried to read Isabel, but she was either out of practice or the woman was doing a good job of hiding her true feelings. There was something there that Sophia couldn't tease out, something rueful or spiteful. Or maybe Isabel was just confused.

"I remember a lot, most of it not pleasant, to be honest."

Isabel looked down and took the last sip of her latte. "I don't know. Life goes on. I have to continue working on myself, my recovery. This is a dangerous time for people like me."

"What do you mean, 'dangerous time.?'"

"It would be easy to relapse, with all that I'm feeling." Isabel looked at Sophia. "I've never had to deal with something like this. I have a lot of guilt about what happened to David."

"I can't imagine why. Did you know he was trying to contact me?" Sophia was beginning to get the feeling Isabel wasn't telling her everything.

Isabel folded her hands neatly on the table. "David and I shared some of the same demons. That's all I'm prepared to say. He was very agitated and restless over the last two weeks of his life. He was very obsessed with something." She brushed down the cuffs of her coat. "He never stopped trying to be a cop. I just assumed it was one of his little 'projects.'"

"Projects?"

"He was fixated on someone in the police department. Frankly, I assumed it was you."

"If it was, I wasn't aware of it. Did he ever mention any names?"

"No, he didn't talk to me about that part of his life."

There was an awkward silence, and then Sophia stuffed her napkin into her cup and stood up. "I should get going. I'm back to work in a couple of days, and you'd think I would have gotten all of my errands out of the way with my time off, but I still have a few loose ends to tie off."

"Thank you for meeting with me. I'd like to do it again."

Sophia had that feeling, the one that when she didn't heed it, there was always trouble to follow.

"I need some time. It's not personal. I'm sure you are a very nice person but…" She tried to find the right words. "I'm a little uncomfortable forging a friendship under these circumstances. I hope you understand."

Isabel stood up and tossed her cup into the garbage. "No problem. I get it." She walked off without a good-bye.

Isabel was out the door and around the corner before Sophia could finish putting on her coat.

CHAPTER TWENTY-NINE

The lobby to Headquarters was made of glass and stone. A small public counter separated records staff from citizens coming in from the street to request an accident or incident report. A desk officer was stationed to the north of the bay of windows behind a small desk. He or she was the last line of defense between un-credentialed visitors and the floors of detectives and brass. To the left of the desk was where people applied for concealed weapons permits or got their fingerprints taken for sensitive jobs requiring a background check. One side of the lobby contained the names of fallen officers, set into a stone facade built with the hope that no more names would be added. But since Sophia had been hired, there'd already been more metal plaques sealed into the wall.

When Sophia walked in, Sergeant Janice Bowerman was chatting with the desk officer.

"Benedetti." Bowerman waved her over. "I'm with you today."

"What happened to Mullins? Did he have a tee time again today?"

"He's a good guy, just a little rough around the edges. I think he's on vacation."

"I just want this to be over with."

"You didn't bring a lawyer, did you?"

"Why would I need a lawyer"

"You don't. Well, not normally. Didn't your Captain call you?"

"No."

"That's a little unusual. Your Captain should have touched base at least. I mean, this is a little different than your average OIS."

"Only because that asshole Burton killed himself at my scene…"

"Hang on." Bowerman took Sophia by the elbow and led her to the elevators. "Let's go somewhere more private."

Bowerman closed the door to the interview room.

"It's not you."

"What?"

"It's Tommy Stinson. They're trying to hang him out."

"Tommy didn't even fire his weapon," Sophia said. "I don't get it."

"Someone has it out for him. Word is they're going to say that Tommy's action, his pulling open that attic door, was what put you in danger."

"What the fuck is going on around here? That guy was going to shoot someone regardless. He wasn't coming out to surrender while simultaneously fired his gun. Maybe Tommy could have waited a little…"

"That right there? That's what they're hoping for, just so you know. Don't say it if you don't want your partner taking the fall here."

"Maybe he should," Sophia said under her breath. Tommy hadn't returned any of her calls after that night they talked. Maybe he'd skipped town.

"What did you say"

"Jesus, nothing."

There was a knock on the door before it opened. Drew Taylor popped his head in.

"We're ready for you, Benedetti."

As she stepped out into the hall, Tommy, Jimmy, Jess and Anthony gave her a thumbs up. Tommy walked over and whispered into her ear.

"Tell the truth, exactly like it happened, Soph."

Sophia smelled alcohol on his breath.

"Have you been…" Sophia stepped back.

Taylor pushed Tommy away. "Stand off, Stinson."

"Fuck you, Taylor," Tommy said.

The firearms review board consisted of members of the homicide squad, a captain, an assistant chief and a civilian observer who didn't have any voting power. There was a Powerpoint presentation by the investigating team of detectives and then an opportunity for board members to ask questions. Drew Taylor sat in the back of the room, arms crossed. On the other side of the room, a clean cut man in an expensive suit sat by himself.

"Who's that?" Sophia whispered to Bowerman.

"Based on the suit, I'd say he's a Fed."

"Why would the Feds be here?" Sophia studied the man's face.

"Maybe they're looking at taking your child porn case federally. I don't know."

The first question came from Captain Ray Allen, a former SWAT commander.

"Detective Benedetti, could you tell me why you didn't have SWAT serve this warrant?"

"My squad has done dozens of warrants without SWAT. We didn't think this was going to be any different."

"But it was. And as a result, a man died. Perhaps it would have happened anyway but perhaps not."

Sophia looked at Bowerman.

"It's a dangerous job, Captain. You should know that. Sometimes shit happens."

"And your partner, Detective Stinson. Was that a planned

tactic, him pulling down the attic door? Were you ready for that?"

"Of course."

Sophia looked at Taylor. A slight smile crept across his face.

"I see. So, the fact that your partner nearly got you killed doesn't bother you?"

"I thought this was about what happened at the house, not what didn't," Sophia said.

"Fair enough, Detective." The Captain shuffled a few pages. "What can you tell us about Chief Burton's connection to this matter?"

Sgt. Taylor spoke up. "That's part of a separate investigation."

"He killed himself at her scene, Sergeant Taylor."

"Still not relevant."

Sophia spoke up. "I don't know his connection but I guess it's safe to say, he had one."

Bowerman shook her head at Sophia. "Again, not part of this review. Let's keep going."

"Detective Benedetti, is it common for your partner to come to work drunk?"

"Who are you talking about?"

"Your partner, Detective Stinson. He was drunk on the day of the shooting."

"No he wasn't."

"Really? So you don't know that he was ordered to take a breathalyzer at the scene?"

Sophia looked at Taylor and then at Bowerman. "I don't know anything about that."

Sophia felt a surge of adrenaline. How was it that this was the first time she'd heard about this? She didn't want to betray a confidence, speak up about him being in AA and being sober for over twenty years. There had to be a mistake.

"You fired how many times, Detective?"

"Three."

"And only one round struck the victim."

"He wasn't a victim. He was a suspect."

"Fair enough. But only one round hit him."

"I haven't been privy to the investigation. I know I made the head shot."

"Did you try and aim at center mass or just go for the fatal shot?"

Drew Taylor tapped the side of his head.

"It was dark, he was armed. He came down so fast, I didn't have time…"

"Thanks to your partner."

Sophia stood up. "I'm done here. You'll have to ask Stinson."

"You're not free to leave, Detective."

"Yes she is. We have all we need," said Drew Taylor.

Sophia pushed opened the door. It slammed against the wall. She walked past the squad, their eyes wide with surprise.

As she reached Tommy, she stopped. "I hope it was worth it."

Sophia walked out on the parking deck with Bowerman closely behind her.

"Hold up, Benedetti."

"I have nothing to say to you or anyone. That was complete bullshit."

"They're desperate. The Captain and Burton were friends."

"Why let him run the FRB then? He can't be neutral. He's going to crucify me."

"He's going to crucify Stinson."

"If anyone gets to crucify Stinson, it should be me."

"You're going back to work tomorrow. Do yourself a favor and keep the chatter about this to a minimum. There's still a lot of speculation about what happened in that house. And the press is sniffing around. They think there's a big story in this and maybe there is, but trust me, you don't want to be at the center of it."

Sophia got into her car and sped out of the garage leaving Bowerman standing alone on the parking deck.

She poured herself a tumbler of wine and inserted the thumb drive Isabel had given to her into her laptop. This was probably what David had been trying to get to her when she'd been too busy trying to ignore him. Or maybe it was evidence in his homicide. But she wanted to make sure it wasn't something personal; pictures or writings of their time together.

A series of files popped up, and soon her screen was populated with thumbnails of photos of the dead drop location. She double clicked on the first photo and a dark image materialized. Using the zoom tool, she enlarged the photo and recognized Stewart Halifax standing alone near a car.

The next photo was a sharper resolution. Stewart was talking to someone but, his back was to the camera. Sophia scanned the thumbnails, looking for the mystery man's face.

She clicked on one near the end. Her heart tumbled. There were two images in the photo, but the only one she recognized was Marcus Burton. The third person never stepped out of the shadows.

Sophia stood up to catch her breath. Pacing her living room, she downed the remaining wine and poured some more. So David somehow got these photos implicating Burton and Halifax, and that was what he was trying to tell her. But who was the stranger who appeared smart enough to stay in the dark?

She tried to use the zoom tool to segregate the image, but it only pixelated the image more. Flipping through another dozen, she stopped at one where a car's headlights had illuminated the bottom half of the mystery man.

Only those legs and shoes didn't belong to a man.

Her mind raced. The wine was jacking her up.

She pulled out her cell phone. Jess answered on the first ring.

"I need to talk to you," Sophia said.

"Ok."

"I need to show you something."

Jess laughed. "Is this work related or fashion related?"

"What it is, is really fucked up."

"You sound like shit."

"I feel like shit, and I'm a little drunk so I shouldn't drive. Can you come over here?"

"Are you home?"

"Yes. I just really don't know what to do here. I need some advice."

"I'll be there as soon as I can."

CHAPTER THIRTY

Sophia made herself a cup of coffee, then changed out of her sweatpants and t-shirt into a pair of jeans and a pressed blouse. Bodhi stayed at her heel until she sat back down at her computer.

Sophia printed the photos, then copied the thumb drive and put it back into the envelope.

Jess arrived a half an hour later, knocking softly. Bodhi barked and pawed at the door until Sophia opened it. She butted Jess' knees.

"Well, hello to you too, Bodhi." Jess squatted and gave the dog a solid rub.

"Thanks for coming."

"Sure." Jess wore faded jeans and a red t-shirt. Her badge was tucked into her pocket. Her Glock sat in a holster in the small of her back.

"So what the hell is going on? Did something go wrong during the FRB? Whatever you said to Tommy sure didn't sit well."

"That's a whole other issue I don't want to talk about right now."

"I guess. But the guys are pretty confused right now. You and Tommy OK?"

Sophia shrugged and offered Jess some coffee. "Or would you prefer a glass of wine."

"I'll take one glass but that's it."

Sophia sunk into the couch. "You know the dead drop, the one under the freeway, right?

"Of course. Victoria Tilden put Stewart Halifax and Burton at the scene." Jess sat next to Sophia. "But no one's been able to confirm that Halifax is a part of this. I mean, I sure as hell believe he is, but there's nothing solid linking him…"

Jess reached over and touched Sophia's arm. "I've been working the case in your absence, Beni. I know all of this. What's going on?"

"Sophia stood up and walked over to the laptop. "So the other day, I guess it was Tuesday of last week actually, I met with a woman named Isabel Proust. She gave me this." She handed the thumb drive to Jess.

Jess flipped the thumb drive over. "Who's Isabel Proust?"

"She was David's girlfriend, I guess."

"Jesus, Beni. You should have called me or Tommy. You know better than that."

Sophia exposed the USB stick. "David had this at the house. I think it was what he was trying to get to me before he was killed."

"And…"

"And this is what was on it." Sophia pulled up the copies she'd made.

"Is that Burton?"

"Yep."

" And Stewart Halifax?" Jess picked up one of the photos. "Who's the other guy standing to the side?"

"It's not a guy."

"You're right. Those are definitely a woman's legs…"

She looked at Jess. "I can't fucking believe it. I feel like a complete fool."

"Whoa, slow down, Beni. Do you think the woman in the

photo is Proust?"

"I don't know." Sophia took a deep breath. "She shows up out of nowhere, hands me this envelope and acts like she wants to be my friend. She even said she wanted to meet again. And she starts asking a bunch of questions about David's murder and the status of the investigation."

"You didn't tell her anything, did you?" Jess rubbed her eyes and pushed back her hair. She stood up and walked to the window.

"Of course not. Give me some credit."

"Sorry."

"Well that makes two of us."

"Have you talked to Tommy?"

"No."

"Look, it makes no sense for her to turn over something that would implicate her. I mean, she must have looked at what was on the drive, right?" Jess finished the rest of her wine.

"Who knows? Maybe she didn't see this one." Sophia picked up the photo and looked at the image. "Maybe she's making amends. I ran her up. There is nothing in the system under that name. She's a ghost."

"Maybe Halifax was there to confront Burton. Could this be Mrs. Halifax?"

It hadn't dawned on Sophia that Ginny Halifax might have come along with her husband. But that was a stretch. That woman seemed to care only about her white carpet and her pristine furniture.

The coffee wasn't doing its job. Sophia felt like someone had covered her in a warm, wet blanket. She laid her head back against the couch and called Bodhi up. The dog jumped into her lap, making both women laugh.

"Lap dog, huh?" Jess leaned against the windowsill. She had a softness to her that Sophia had never noticed. When she first came to the unit, Sophia thought Jess was more interested in looking good than doing good. For the first time, she felt a kinship with her, as though she was the only person she could trust.

"Ok, we've got to think this through." Jess sat next to Sophia and scratched Bodhi under the neck in the sweet spot. The pup's tail wagged.

"We have to get this to Anderson in ICAC. I think they're out from under the late Chief Burton's sphere of influence, you know, just in case there are others…" Jess sat up. "There's nothing on here that's evidence in David's homicide, right?"

"Not that I can see, but who the hell knows? I mean, what if they're all involved? What if this," she shook the envelope containing the drive, "what if this is what got David killed?"

"Look, George Anderson and those guys have got to have more information by now. They took a ton of stuff, computers, drives, all sorts of evidence from that house, and from those other guys, when they served the warrant. We need to talk to him first."

"And then we'll deal with homicide?"

"Yes, and then we'll deal with homicide. We'll have to finesse that conversation. But let's deal with this thing first." Jess pointed at the envelope.

"Well, they're the last people I want to piss off. I might as well withdraw my name from consideration, take it off the eligibility list. They won't touch me with a ten foot pole." Sophia closed her eyes."Have you heard anything about how the homicide investigation is going?"

"I've tried to get an answer out of my contact, but he's being pretty tightlipped. But there's something going on with Stinson. I walked over there the other day and heard one of the guys say his name and when he saw me, they all clammed up."

"Let's get this over to George in the morning," Jess said. "Do you feel OK to be alone?"

"I've got the mutt."

"You know what I'm talking about." Jess smiled.

Sophia took Jess' hand and squeezed it. "I'm good, really."

Jess held onto Sophia's hand. "I can stay. I'd like to stay."

Sophia let her hand remain in Jess' grasp. She closed her eyes.

Jess kissed her, pulling her toward her.

"I can't…"

"Not now or never?" Jess let go of her hand and leaned against the armrest.

"I'm a little drunk."

"And?"

"And I'm not ready for this."

"I shouldn't have."

Sophia stood and walked to the door. "I'm sorry."

"I get it." Jess slipped out the front door and jogged to her car.

CHAPTER THIRTY-ONE

A cold front moved into the Pacific Northwest shortly after midnight, and a frigid breeze snuck though the old double-hung windows in Sophia's bedroom. She nearly fell out of bed reaching for the heavy wool blanket that was draped over the chair next to the bed. Exhaustion and Bodhi's warm body kept her sound asleep until the alarm clock went off.

She rolled onto her side and scratched Bodhi behind the ears. She closed her eyes and thought about Jess. The kiss had come out of left field. She'd been unprepared but not unwilling.

After a hot shower, she got dressed in a pressed pair of dark pants and a crisp white blouse she purchased during her amnesty from work.

Sophia parked her car in her usual stall and walked into the building. Her desk was covered with case files and new intakes. Tommy's desk was clean. His chair was pushed in up against the desk and there was no sign of his briefcase. She cracked open one of the bins above his desk. It was empty. He was either getting ready to retire or getting ready to be fired.

Sophia heard footsteps down the hall. She expected to see Tommy but it was Jess who gave her a quick nod, and headed to her desk.

Sophia walked over and leaned on the cubical wall.

"Sorry about how I left things last night."

"I shouldn't have…" She paused and looked over the cubicles. She lowered her voice. "I shouldn't have kissed you. I don't want this to be weird."

"I'm not sure how I feel about it."

Jess laughed. "So there's hope then?"

"Maybe. I don't know."

"I'll take that as a yes." Jess pulled off her gun and put it in her top drawer.

Sophia pulled out the stack of photos and spread them across her desk. "We need to go down to ICAC and talk to George Anderson. He needs to see this stuff. Plus, I want to know where they are on the case."

"Sounds good. I don't have anything on my plate today, unless you want to wait for Tommy."

"Let's go. I don't even know if he works here anymore."

When Sophia and Jess walked into ICAC, several people started clapping.

George peeked out of his office.

"Hey, welcome back. You did the world a great service by taking out Augustine Verbeck. He was a frequent flyer down here."

"I guess I should say thanks but I honestly don't know how I feel about it."

"Take it while you can. No doubt it won't last." George waved the two women into his office and asked them to take a seat. He got up and shut the door.

"I'm really glad to see you, Sophia." He looked at Jess. "I don't believe we've met."

"I thought you knew Jess. She's been in SAU for a couple

of years," Sophia said.

Jess shook George's hand. She sat back down and George leaned up against his desk.

"So this child porn ring is incredibly extensive. We're talking worldwide. This is huge, Sophia."

"You're kidding me." Sophia said.

Jess smiled.

"No, I'm not kidding. We're still trying to confirm how widespread. Obviously we believe Marcus Burton played some role or at the very least, he enabled them to operate without much scrutiny." He stroked his beard. "Although, maybe his ex-wife might be able to add…"

"How about David Montero," Sophia said. "Was he involved in this?"

"We found nothing to link anyone by that name. But I have to tell you, it's still pretty early in the investigation. We have a ton of information we still need to get from the computers. Who's he again?"

Sophia pulled the file folder from her case and spread the pictures from David's thumb drive on George's desk. "He was my ex-husband."

"I didn't know that." George looked at the photos. "But I haven't seen his name on any hard drives."

"How about the name Isabel Proust?"

George looked at her and frowned. "No, can't say it does. Should it?" He looked at the photos one by one.

"Where did you get these?"

"They came from David."

"When?"

"Actually, I got them from this Proust woman. She met me for coffee a couple of days ago and handed me an envelope with this thumb drive in it. She said she found it in David's things when she was cleaning up." Sophia pulled out the envelope and handed it to George. "I think this now is evidence in the case." She glanced over at Jess and then back to

George.

"Ok, I recognize Burton, and I'm assuming that's Stewart Halifax. Who's this?" He leaned in to get a better look.

"Well, that's the complicating factor here. I think it's Proust."

"So she dumps off evidence implicating herself to you and disappears into thin air?"

"That's what I said," Jess said.

"Do you have a location for Ms. Proust?"

"Nope. I met her for coffee not for an interrogation. And don't bother, I already ran her through all of the databases. She doesn't exist. And her phone number, which I might add, worked just fine the other day, is disconnected."

"She was probably spoofing her number anyway, if she knows what she's doing. Odd that she would even want to meet with you. Why not just drop this in the mail?"

"I have no idea."

"So have you been able to connect Stewart Halifax to this case?" Jess said.

George scratched his head. "We've got his daughter Grace identified in several of the photos now. We didn't have him on film until these pictures you brought in today." He sat down at his desk. "But none of the suspects picked him out from a photo montage."

"That won't matter now. I mean, this is clearly Halifax in these photos."

George held up his hands. "Well, there's some pressure being brought to bear about how we go forward."

Jess stood up and started to pace. "From where?"

"From the prosecutor's office. They're very nervous about going up against Stewart Halifax and his fleet of lawyers."

"Well, that's bullshit. We need the evidence on those computers that links Halifax to this ring. Now we have a photo of him at the scene of the dead drop with Marcus Burton, who presumably killed himself because of all of this. I'm not asking you to manufacture it George, but I know it's on there, and I know he's guilty. As far as I'm concerned, there's at least a couple of deaths directly related to this investigation. I'm not going to sleep knowing that that little girl is still living under the same roof as that monster. And who knows what's happened to those other kids?"

Sophia's cell phone rang. It was Tommy. She stepped out of George's office, leaving Jess and George in silence.

"Hey what's up?"

"Sophia, I need to talk to you right away."

"Meet me at George Anderson's office."

"Ok, I'll be there in fifteen."

The first thing that Tommy saw were the pictures spread across the desk. Jess stood in the corner, and Sophia in front of the desk.

"What's this?" asked Tommy.

"Photos of Stewart Halifax and Marcus Burton and a woman who's probably in the wind."

He slowly moved his hand over the prints and then pushed them away. "Who's the woman?"

"I don't know for sure." Sophia stood in front of Tommy. "Where the hell have you been, by the way?"

There was an uncomfortable silence. Tommy's face was bright red, and sweat ran down his temple.

"I took some time off." He looked down and then at Sophia. "Where did you get these photographs?"

"It was on another thumb drive that David was trying to get to me."

"How did he know about the drop?"

"I don't know, Tommy. Somehow he stumbled on the photos, put two and two together and figured out it was related to the case we were working.."

"That's a little thin."

Sophia looked over at George. "This is your case. How do you want to proceed?"

"You've brought new evidence to me which I am obligated to investigate. We probably should let my sergeant know about these photographs, and let it play out."

"So who's the woman in the photos, assuming it's a woman?" Tommy picked up the photo.

"Not really sure, but I think it's someone named Isabel Proust."

"And I don't know this name because…?" Tommy looked at Sophia.

"I tried to call you. She wanted to meet with me and I agreed."

"And now she's a suspect in this whole thing and you didn't think it was important to try a little harder to reach me?" Tommy walked out of George's office, slamming the door behind him.

Tommy climbed into his car and quickly drove from the parking lot.

"Jesus, I thought shooting someone would feel bad. I swear to god, it almost feels worse knowing I may have been played by that woman, and now I feel guilty about keeping Tommy in the dark and treating him like he's some child. What is wrong with me?" Sophia and Jess walked out to their car.

"Nothing's wrong with you. And if you want my opinion, Tommy's being an asshole. He's been AWOL, not on leave. He wasn't taking anyone's calls."

"I need to ask you something."

Jess looked at Sophia.

"Did you think Tommy was drunk at the shooting?"

"Of course not. Who said he was?"

"At the FRB, the captain asked me about it. Said Tommy was drunk and had to leave the scene."

"That's crazy. He was there…"

"Jess?"

"He left early but I was under the impression he had a medical thing."

"But he wasn't drunk."

"I didn't smell anything other than that god-awful cologne he was wearing. Besides, he doesn't drink, right?"

"Right."

As they pulled into the parking lot, Sophia noticed Tommy's car already parked and empty.

Sophia and Jess walked into the office. The door to Pierson's office was closed.

Julie was at her desk prepping the weeklies for the commanders. She didn't look up.

"Who's in there?" Sophia asked.

"Stinson." Julie said as she turned and answered the phone.

Jimmy stood up and peered over his cubicle.

"Hey Benedetti, your phone's been ringing off the hook since you left. Answer the goddamned thing."

"Well, whoever it is hasn't left a message. Are you sure it was my phone and not Tommy's?"

"Yeah, I'm sure it was your phone. I got up and looked. It was a blocked number.

Sophia picked up her cell phone. She had four missed calls. The first message was from Victoria Tilden, informing her that she had some 'fabulously interesting news.' The last three messages were hangup calls. As she listened to her voicemail, another call came in.

"Hello?"

"Detective, it's Barrett Halifax."

"How can I help you, Barrett?"

"I need to see you." It sounded as though he'd been crying.

"See me about what?"

"About my sister."

"Barrett, I'm probably not the right person for you to talk to. I can put you in contact with the current case detective."

"I don't want to talk to anyone else. It's really important."

Sophia looked around the room. Jess watched her out of the corner of her eye.

"Where do you want to meet?"

Jess walked over and leaned on the corner of the cubicle.

"We could meet at the coffee shop on 10th Ave. How about in 20 minutes?" His voice began to fade as if he had moved away from the phone.

"Barrett, are you okay?"

"Just please hurry." Sophia heard a muffled cry.

"You know you should really call George and let him deal with this," Jess said.

"Barrett doesn't know George. He may be our final chance to get to Stewart Halifax."

Jess frowned. "If you get me kicked out of this unit and sent to first watch south, you're coming with me."

"Don't worry, I'll have your back. That is, if I still have a job when this is done."

CHAPTER THIRTY-TWO

Barrett sat at a small table in a darkened corner of the coffee shop. As Sophia neared the table, she saw the little girl who was at the center of one of the most convoluted investigations Sophia had ever known. Grace was an apt name for the cherubic little girl sitting quietly next to her brother. Dressed in a beautiful blue jacket and patent leather shoes, her blond hair lay softly in ringlets against her cheeks. She made no eye contact with Sophia.

Then Sophia saw Barrett's face.

Both of his eyes were ringed with bruises, and a fresh scratch traveled from the middle of his forehead down the ridge of his nose. His hair looked as though it hadn't been washed in several days. Sophia smiled at Grace and then looked at Barrett.

"What happened to your face?" She reached out and touched the side of his cheek. He flinched and looked down.

"I got in a fight at school. It's nothing."

Sophia looked back at Jess, who pulled out an alcohol tissue from her bag.

"Here, why don't you wipe the blood off your nose," Jess said.

"Who're you?"

"This is my partner, Detective Vance." For the first time in three years, she was introducing someone other than Tommy as her partner.

"What happened to the old guy?" Barrett asked.

"He's working on something else right now."

"I kinda liked him, even though he was sort of a prick to me that last time."

"Detective Stinson can be that way sometimes. You need to tell me what happened to you. I don't believe this was a result of a fight at school."

Barrett looked down at his sister. "You okay Gracie?" The little girl stared at Sophia, and then at Jess.

"How about I take Grace for a cup of hot chocolate?" Jess reached out her hand to the little girl who grabbed it. Grace jumped off the chair and followed Jess to the coffee bar.

Sophia sat next to Barrett and put her hand on his shoulder. "What happened?"

Barrett hung his head and began to sob.

"Barrett it's okay."

He sobbed again.

"She's my baby sister. I couldn't protect her." He covered his face with his hands.

Sophia grabbed a napkin and pressed it into his hand.

Jess walked over with Grace.

"We're going to sit over there and play with my phone." She took the little girl by the hand and sat her at a small table near a window.

Sophia turned to Barrett. "None of this is your fault."

"I used to take a lot of pictures of my sister on my camera phone. She loved to dance around the room in her underwear. I uploaded the photos to my dad's computer because my laptop wasn't working. One day he found the photos and just started yelling at me. I didn't understand why he was so angry. He told me to take the photos off my phone and called me a pervert."

"Were they the same photos you saw on that website?"

"They looked like the same, but in those photos, Gracie was naked." He looked at Sophia, eyes brimming with tears. "I swear to you, I never took any photos of her naked."

"Does your Dad still have that computer?"

"The police took it away, but I think he got it back." He wiped his nose with the back of his hand. "I'm sure he still has it."

He had the computer all right. Returned to him with best wishes from Marcus Burton.

"How about photoshop? Anything like that on the laptop?"

Barrett stopped crying. "Yeah, he does. But…"

"Who else uses that computer?"

"No one really. It's sort of the one anyone could use."

"What about your mother? Does she use it?"

"She has her own computer. Why are you asking me about my mother?"

Jess and Grace were having what looked like a very animated, if one way, conversation.

"It's my job to ask the questions."

"My mom is seriously clueless. She and my dad rarely see each other. He's either at work or out at his various clubs or charity events. I know he blamed my mother for Gracie's condition. You know she's autistic, right?"

"Yes."

"So she's pretty much incapable of communicating like you and me. I know you wanted to interview her early on in the case, but my mom was afraid to tell you about her autism and also afraid of how it would impact Gracie."

"Barrett, did your dad ever take your sister with him when he went out at night?"

"Sometimes."

"And do you know where he went?"

"He told me and my mom that he was taking her to see a specialist, someone who might be able to help her with the autism. I thought it was a little weird that he only saw the therapist during evening hours, but he said this guy was doing him a professional favor. My mom and dad fought about it all the time."

"Fought about what?"

"About taking her to a specialist. My mom didn't want Grace having some kind of breakthrough without being there, I guess."

"She could have gone with your father."

He looked up at Sophia. "You think he was taking her somewhere and letting those fucking assholes take photos of her?"

"I don't know, Barrett. We have to get that computer from your father. Are you sure he still has it?"

"I think so. My mom was on it the other day."

Sophia weighed her options. If she asked Barrett to go back to the house and take the computer, he'd be acting as an agent of the state, and it might look to a judge as though she was trying to seize evidence without a warrant. She supposed it would be okay if he simply took the computer into his room and hid it under his bed.

"Stay here for a minute."

She sat next to Jess. Grace poked at Jess's phone, staring intently at the colors filling the screen.

"What do you think about Barrett trying to get the old man's computer and holding it until we can get a search warrant? Unless he knows what he's doing, and he was able to completely scrub it, that computer may still have evidence on it."

"You're probably on thin ice, Sophia."

"Don't you think we have enough to get another warrant and seize the laptop? It seems to me that Barrett can testify that he saw his photos on the laptop and if he can identify them as being the same ones he saw online, minus the naked factor, it could implicate Stewart Halifax, right?" Sophia said.

"And guess what the Dad's going to say? He didn't post those photos, his son did. He can say that his teenage son was experiencing some misguided sexual confusion and took advantage of his sister. Both of them had access to the computer, right?"

"Barrett had talked about meeting some guy online when he'd stumbled upon the photos. He claimed it was an accident. What if we could lure that guy into meeting with Barrett?"

The barista leaned over the table next to them to retrieve a cup. Sophia stopped talking until he walked away.

"I'm going to call George and run this by him. Keep her busy, will you?" Sophia motioned to Barrett.

"Why don't you hang out here with your sister. I need to make a call."

Barrett pulled out a chair and sat down. Grace pushed the phone across the table to him.

"Pretty colors, Gracie."

Sophia walked outside. The sun was between clouds, its rays reflecting off the windows of the Starbucks. Sophia pulled out her sunglasses.

She dialed George Anderson.

"I have an interesting question for you."

"Go ahead. I'm all ears."

"First off, is virtual child pornography illegal?"

"Generally, no. The court has gone back and forth on the issue. It's constantly evolving because computer aided animation is so realistic. But if the 'children' aren't real people, it's hard to get a conviction."

"What if the face is based on a real person but the rest of the body is not? Or at least it's animated with the help of a computer?"

"There was plenty of real child porn on the servers at that house."

"Barrett took photos of his sister with his phone. She was in her underwear. I think his father took the photos, uploaded them to the server and provided his sick fucking friends with virtual porn."

"I can almost guarantee that he's erased everything on that lap top. However, unless he's a really sophisticated computer nerd, those deleted files are still hidden on the hard drive. I could recover them with forensic software."

"I'm going to need your expertise to try and lure whoever is out there into a meeting with Barrett Halifax. But, we won't actually use Barrett. We'll use you. You guys do this all the time, right?"

"Sure, that's no problem. However, given all the media attention this case has gotten, it's not likely that any of these guys are still lurking in the same rooms.

George exhaled deeply. "Look, Sophia, there are thousand and thousands of these guys out there. You're not going to get them all. Keep it simple. Let's concentrate on what we have. Setting up another drop will be far too complicated. They're not going to fall for it."

"I know you're right. I just can't wrap my brain around this shit."

"One foot in front of the other for now, Detective."

Sophia hung up and went back inside. Jess stood up and nodded for Sophia to follow her to the back. Business had picked up and people were waiting for tables.

"Barrett just told me his father beat him up last night." Jess said. "We have to get these two kids out of the house. And you mentioned that there's another child too, right?"

"The kid brother, George. I'm not sure I trust Ginny Halifax to side with the kids on this one. She's going to be a real problem for us. I don't think there's any amount of evidence that's going to convince her that her husband is involved in something this horrible. We're going to have to come up with a Plan B." Sophia glanced over at Barrett and Grace.

Jess tapped the tabletop. "What if we created some ruse and

convinced Stuart Halifax that his children and wife were in danger. Make him think that we don't have all the bad guys in custody yet. Hell, we can tell him that one of the suspects made threats to kill his family. He's a doctor, so he's not likely to cancel a bunch of appointments and lose all that money."

"Great. And he can keep working while we keep an eye on the kids." Sophia said.

"Maybe it can buy us some time. In the meantime, we can arrange for the kids to stay at a hotel and we'll put a uniform outside the door. If his Dad did this to him, we can't in good conscience leave them with that bastard."

"We can give it a try. I'm thinking Halifax is laying low, being on his best behavior. We're way too close for comfort."

Sophia walked over and sat down next to Barrett.

"I have an idea about how we can make this whole situation better Barrett. But I'm going to need your help."

"Okay." His eyes were puffy and wet.

"We're going to try and get you, your brother and sister and your mom separated from your dad."

"He's never going to let you do that."

"Well, we're going to try and see if we can convince your dad that the family is in danger. It's not the truth mind you, but it may be enough for him to let us take you into protective custody. That will give us enough time to try and figure out whether or not he's involved."

Barrett looked at Grace. "I know he's involved. I just feel it in my gut. I want this whole thing to be over, and I want my sister to be okay."

"We want that too, Barrett. But it's going to take a little more work before we can be sure. Do you have somewhere you can go for the afternoon?"

"I'm supposed to pick up George from school today. I could take them to a movie or something."

"Perfect. Keep your cell phone on. I'll call you when I know whether this is going to work." Sophia put her hand on

Barrett's shoulder. "And if we can't convince him to let us take you into protective custody, I want you to call 911 if he even looks at you funny. Do you understand?"

"I'm not afraid for me."

"I know, Barrett."

Sophia and Jess walked Barrett and Grace out of the coffee shop. Barrett took his little sister's hand as the two of them walked away. A fine drizzle had started to descend on the city, and as the two kids rounded the corner, Grace looked back and waved. Her blond curls bounced on the back of the collar of her coat.

CHAPTER THIRTY-THREE

The phone rang three times.

"Dr. Halifax, this is Detective Benedetti."

"What do you want, Detective?"

"Look, I don't have very much time. We have reason to believe your family might be in danger."

"From whom?"

"We don't believe we have all of the suspects related to your daughter's case in custody. There is a concern for her safety."

"Detective, I can protect my children. In fact, we're all here in the living room about to play a board game."

He was lying. There was complete silence in the background.

"I'm not handing my children over to the police. Not now, not ever. And I think you of all people should understand my commitment to my family."

"Sir, I saw your son today." This was a desperate move and she knew it.

"Then you saw what happened to him."

"Yes."

"What exactly did Barrett tell you?"

"He told me you hit him."

Halifax laughed. "Is that so?"

"I can arrest you right now for assaulting your son."

"You're right detective, you could. But I didn't assault Barrett. I just got home from a conference in Dallas two hours ago. I can refer you to a very nice TSA agent who practically gave me a cavity search over some medical supplies I had in my carry-on. Would you like his number, because his supervisor will be hearing from my lawyer in the morning."

It would be easy enough for her to check his alibi and he knew it.

"Barrett took a beating on the soccer field yesterday. Face planted as a matter of fact. The boy's lucky he still has his teeth. Well, at least that's the story he told me this afternoon when I called him from Dallas."

"I'll be more than happy to call TSA but in the meantime, we still need for Grace to come in for an interview with a specialist."

"Detective, I think I'm done accommodating you."

The phone went dead.

Jess stood over her. "Did he just hang up on you?"

"Yep."

"I say we go hook him on the assault."

"We can't. He didn't do it."

"What? You saw Barrett's face."

"Barrett lied to me. But those injuries didn't come from a fall in a soccer game. They were caused by a fist."

Jess walked around the cubicle. "For what reason? Why would he tell you his father hit him?"

"I have no idea."

Sophia looked at Jess and rubbed her temples. She was exhausted. The strain of the past few months was sprinting quickly up on her. She felt as though she was losing control of her case, her partner, and her life.

Jared tapped furiously on Ed's computer, trying every possible combination of words, letters, or dates to hack his password.

Ed would be home soon and there'd be hell to pay. He was pretty sure that his mother had taken Ed to task for being such an asshole. But then again, Sherry Poppins had changed drastically since marrying Ed and Jared was feeling less like her precious little boy and more of an interloper.

The slow mechanical whir of the garage door opening startled Jared. Ed drove a piece of shit Honda Accord with a flow master muffler, and as it rumbled into the garage, Jared thought how easy it would be to trap Ed in the garage with the car running. Except no one would ever believe Ed would kill himself. He was a human cockroach.

Jared quickly backed out of the computer's browser and cleared the recent history. If Ed noticed it was taking longer to access his porn sites and decided to check the browsing history, he'd see that someone had cleared his cache. Jared cursed himself for being so careless but it was too late. He slammed the computer shut, grabbed his backpack and sprinted up the stairs to his room.

Jared gently closed the door to his room. It was a wreck, worse than usual. Someone had tossed it. Clothes were hanging out of drawers and his closet had been emptied into the middle of the room. His mattress lay halfway off of the box spring.

Dropping his backpack on the floor, he stood near the heater vent and listened for Ed. He reached into his dresser, and pulled out a small baggie of pot secured behind a heap of unfolded underwear, and shoved it into his backpack. Shutting the drawer, he scanned the room.

Footsteps paused outside his door. Jared quickly flipped the lock.

"I know you're in there, you fucker."

"Leave me alone."

"Listen here, you little shit. You've got your mother so pissed about our little dust up the other night, she won't even give me a hand job."

“Jesus Christ.”

Jared grabbed his backpack and secured it to his back with both straps. He stood on the other side of the mattress to give himself a buffer. He looked out the window. It was a twenty foot drop, not one he’d survive without some broken bones. Ed slammed his shoulder against the door. It blew open and Ed flew into the room.

"Where the hell do you think you're going?"

Ed looked huge. His eyes were wide, his mouth was open, revealing yellow teeth. Both hands were clenched in front of him. Jared steadied himself for a blow.

"Take off that fucking stupid little pussy backpack and fight me like a man."

“If you hit me, you know my mom will go ballistic. Just get the fuck out of my room and leave me alone."

"If you think your mother’s gonna side with you over me, you’ve got another thing coming.”

Jared inched back toward the window.

“She would have before you poisoned her, turned her into a worthless whore.”

Ed bobbed like a prizefighter. He clenched and unclenched his hands, staring at Jared as if to dare him to make a move. He slowly inched around the mattress.

“You've been nothing but trouble since the fucking day you were born. I'm the best thing that's ever happened to her."

“You’re the worst thing to happen to this family. Fucking loser.”

Ed lurched forward, swinging madly. Jared ducked. He hurled himself over the mattress and through the doorway, grabbing what remained of the door and slamming it behind him. Ed flung open the door and surged after Jared as he took the stairs three at a time. When he hit the landing, he lunged for the front door but Ed grabbed his backpack and pulled him backwards, slamming him into the hardwood floor.

"I told you you're not leaving this house.” Ed pushed up his sleeves. Sweat covered his face and soaked his shirt. He was panting.

Jared scrambled to his feet and surveyed the living room. It was full of his mom's books, dirty plates and a few empty beer bottles. On the floor underneath the living room window was Ed's collection of garden gnomes, lined up according to size, tallest to shortest.

Jared lunged for the line of gnomes and grabbed the largest one. He turned towards Ed and held the heavy clay figurine over his head.

"Put that down. It's priceless."

"Back the fuck up or I'll bust it."

"Don't, don't."

Ed ran at Jared, reaching out to grab the gnome. Jared raised the gnome over his head, slamming it into Ed's skull as he crashed toward him. Jared dodged him like a toreador, and Ed fell forward into the fireplace façade, knocking over the gold plated fireplace tools. He slumped to the floor, his lower body resting against the fireplace grate.

Jared dropped the figurine. His heart raced.

There was a large gash on Ed's head where the gnome had landed, and his eyes were half open. His head rested awkwardly on the floor. Sitting on the couch, Jared waited warily for Ed to get up. He glanced at the telephone. Ed's body twitched.

He felt nothing.

Jared slipped into the dining room and unhooked Ed's computer. He pulled a cell phone out of Ed's pocket and put it in his own.

Wiping his face and mouth with the back of his coat, he walked out the front door.

Petra's house was out of the question. His mother would call as soon as she couldn't reach him on his cell. He couldn't ride the bus all night – the transit cops would kick him off eventually.

In between the street lights, it was dark. A car crept down the street and pulled into the driveway next door. Jared broke into a jog.

When he got to the bus stop, he dialed up Adrian. A hoarse and barely audible voice answered the phone.

"Adrian, it's J."

"What's up little man? What the fuck time is it?"

"Sorry it's late. Hey, I got into it with the nazi and I need a place to crash. Can I come by?"

"Hey, bro, normally I'd say yeah but I got some company tonight. You feel me?"

"Yeah, yeah. That's cool. I'm not gonna spoil your night."

"Some other time, 'k bro?" Adrian hung up without waiting for an answer.

Jared tried to unzip his jacket but the tab wouldn't move. It was only then that he noticed the dried blood in the teeth of his zipper. He peered inside the jacket. His shirt, which clung to his sunken chest, was saturated with Ed's blood.

The bus rumbled to a stop. Jared pulled the jacket around him just enough to hide the blood. He flashed his bus pass and walked to the back, taking a seat in the corner and out of sight of the driver's rear view mirror.

By midnight, he'd managed to stay on the same line for over two hours. The bus driver had traded shifts with a heavyset black woman who eyeballed him every five minutes. He knew his time was about up and she was going to call the transit cops. Shivering from fear and exhaustion, he stumbled off the bus at 4th and Virginia.

Panic was beginning to settle in. He couldn't understand why his mother hadn't tried to call. She must have found Ed's body by now. He wanted to tell her what a vulture and asshole Ed was to him. His phone chirped and a text message popped onto the screen.

"Hi, hon. I'm working late tonight. Tried to call Ed but no answer. Is he home?"

Jared texted back. "Don't know im out."

"Where r u"

"With friends."

"K. See u later."

She was working late again. It was eerily reminiscent of the late nights she started working when she was representing that bastard Ed. Working wasn't what was happening, though. Wouldn't it be ironic if he'd killed Ed for nothing.

For reasons he couldn't begin to understand, Jared found himself texting Barrett Halifax.

"R u up?"

Several minutes passed and then the cryptic response came.

"Who this?"

"Poppins."

A minute passed. Jared imagined Halifax texting his friends alerting them to the fact that he was being invaded by one of the nerd squad.

"What's up."

"Need to talk."

"Now?"

"Y"

"Where are u?"

"Downtown. Cant go home."

Another long pause.

"Can u call? I can't leave."

"Can u talk now?"

Something was better than nothing. He'd already made the step forward. Barrett wanted something from him the other day. Now he was in the position to broker a deal.

His phone vibrated. Looking down, he expected to see Barrett's number but it was one he was more than familiar with. It was Ed's cell phone number. He fumbled with the phone he'd placed in his pocket, the one he thought belonged to Ed. It looked dead, but when he tapped the screen, it bounced to life.

CHAPTER THIRTY-FOUR

Jared froze. Maybe it was his mom, calling from the house, from Ed's phone, panicked at the sight of her dead husband.

Or maybe he wasn't dead.

But he had Ed's phone. Or at least he thought he did.

The ringing stopped.

Jared huddled in the doorway of Macy's and stared at his phone trying to calculate his next move. He turned off the ringer and set it to vibrate.

The phone shuddered.

"Fuck," he yelled.

He recognized Barrett's number.

"Hey."

"Yeah. What's up?"

"You know how you said you needed me to help you with something the other day?"

"You mean the day you basically blew me off? Yeah, I remember."

Barrett got out of bed and looked out his window. His mother was headed out to the garage with Grace. The street light shone just enough for him to see she was carrying her oversized purse and had a computer bag slung over her shoulder. She glanced at her watch as she opened the door to the garage, pushed Grace toward the car and then gingerly closed it behind her. He pulled his phone away from his ear and looked at the time. It was half past midnight.

"That's weird." Barrett said.

"What? I need help. I've really fucked up big time."

"Why don't you call your dork squad friends, dude?"

"You know those cops you were talking to the other day? The one's that came out to the school?"

"What about 'em?"

"Do you trust them?"

"The chick was OK." Barrett watched his mother's car slowly move down the alley, her headlights off.

"Why?"

"I need to talk to the police."

"So call 911."

"I can't."

"Look, dude. I'm not going to play fuckin' twenty questions here. Why do you need to talk to the cops?"

Jared paused. "I killed my stepfather."

"What do you mean you killed him?" It sounded like such a stupid question. "When?"

"A couple of hours ago."

"Are you sure you killed him?" Barrett stood up and paced.

"His fuckin' brains were all over the living room."

Barrett sat on the edge of his bed. "I don't…"

"Look, your old man's connected right? Isn't he tight with some police chief of something?"

"I don't know. I don't pay much attention to his friends. What about your mom? She's a lawyer, right? Doesn't she defend people like…"

"Like me."

"Yeah, like you."

"I'm not sure she's gonna want to help me out this time."

"What happened?"

"You know this whole thing with your sister?"

"What does my sister have to do with this?" Barrett's face flushed and he pulled his shirt over his head.

"I found some stuff on Ed's computer. On his laptop. It was…Shit, it's his phone again."

"Whose phone?"

"Ed's."

"I thought you said you killed him."

"I'm pretty sure I did, but I keep getting calls from his cell number." Jared's heart was pounding in his ears now. He could barely hear Barrett.

"Where are you?"

"I'm downtown."

"Where downtown?"

"I'm near the bus station, over by that one precinct."

"So go in there and tell them what happened. You're a juvenile. They can't do much to you. But I still don't know what Grace has to do with all of this."

"Her picture. It was on Ed's laptop. I hacked into his profile on New World and traced his history on the site. I saw her. I saw your sister. She was…"

"Fuck it, Poppins. Don't say it."

"You asked."

"I don't want to hear it."

"That's why I did it."

"Why you killed him?"

"That was part of it. That, and the fact that he was beating the shit out of me."

"There you have it. You've got a defense, right? It was self-defense."

"I fucking caved in his skull, dude. I need to talk to a cop I can trust. Someone who will believe me."

"Why are you asking me for this?" Barrett fished around in the pockets of his jeans and khakis for Sophia's card.

"I know you know."

Barrett stopped his search. "What do you think I know?"

"The stuff about your sister. What's happened to her. The shit's that been going on with your old man."

"I don't know what you're talking about."

"Fuck that, Halifax. I saw it on that site. I saw your sister, and she was with some guy they called the doctor."

"So? That could be anyone."

"Ed had your home number on his phone."

"What the fuck are you talking about? This is insane." Barrett picked up a paperback and threw it against the wall.

"I'll text you that cop's number if I find it. Text me the number you saw on Ed's phone."

"I don't have the number memorized. I just saw your old man's name in Ed's contacts. Maybe it wasn't your dad's number. Maybe he just used your dad's name with someone else's number. I don't know."

"I have to go.."

"Yeah. Send the number, OK? I've gotta do something here soon."

Barrett hung up and texted Sophia's number to Jared.

And then he called 911.

Sophia was sound asleep and didn't recognize the number on her phone.

"Detective, it's Barrett Halifax."

She paused. "Is everything OK? I don't recognize this number."

"Yeah, I'm calling from home. I'm actually calling for a…" Barrett took a deep breath. "A friend who's in trouble. He wants to talk to the police but he's afraid."

"What kind of trouble, Barrett?"

"I don't want to say. It would be better if it came from him. Can you meet with him?"

"Meet where?"

"I'll call you with the information. I don't know exactly where he is at the moment."

Sophia looked at her watch. It was almost one AM. Bodhi was on the bed, firmly behind her knees.

"Call your friend and find out where he is and then call me back." She sat up and turned on the light. "And you need to tell him I want to know a little more before I meet with him."

"I'll do my best." Barrett hung up abruptly.

Sophia let Bodhi out and gave her some fresh water.

Her phone rang.

"Hey, it's me," Barrett said.

"Did you talk to your friend?"

"The cops just picked him up. They're taking him to your headquarters."

"For what?"

"He killed his stepfather."

Sophia pulled on a pair of pants and took a pressed shirt out of the closet. She slid on some loafers.

"Who is this kid?"

"Jared Poppins. He goes to my school and he," Barrett hesitated, "he may know something about my sister's thing."

"He's not related to Sherry Poppins is he?"

"Yeah, he's her kid."

"Barrett?"

"Yeah?"

"Is your Dad home?"

"I think so, why?"

"I called him today. He didn't want to let you guys go into

protective custody."

"I told you he wouldn't."

"Where's your mom?"

"I saw her leave with Grace earlier tonight. About the time Jared called me, twelve-thirty."

"Where was she going so late?"

"No idea."

"And with Grace?"

"I know. It's weird. But that's my mother."

"All right. Keep your phone with you. We're working things out on this end."

"I will."

Now wasn't the time to ask him why he lied to her about his father. He had to know she could check his father's alibi. Why would he be so careless?

Sophia turned on the coffee maker and brewed enough for a large cup. Bodhi sat in the kitchen door, her eyes half open and sleepy.

She called the homicide unit.

Drew Taylor answered the phone.

"I understand patrol picked up some kid on a homicide," Sophia said.

"I can't wait to hear what you're going to tell me, Benedetti. Get your butt down here. Kid's asking for you by name."

Sophia got to the office in twelve minutes. Taylor was on his phone in the hallway outside the holding cells on the seventh floor. The cells were in the center of the building, in an area that ran perpendicular to the rest of the offices. They were hardened to prevent escape and a camera feed monitored all of them. Doors at either end could seal the space from the rest of the floor. Outside the four cells, was a hallway, a bathroom and an elevator that went down to an underground tunnel to the jail.

Taylor put up his hand.

"Yeah, she's right here. I'm going to talk to her. Stand by." He put the phone back in his belt holster.

"So what is it with you, Benedetti?"

"Sorry?"

He shook his head. "Well, follow me."

Taylor walked into the camera room where all of the holding cells could be monitored.Through the two way glass, Sophia saw a boy slumped over the table. His hair fell forward onto the surface. His shirt rode up above his pants to expose an alarmingly white lower back. His legs were so long, his black biker boots lay at an angle on the floor. He was a portrait in goth, framed by the white walls of the room.

Taylor pounded on the window as Ron Dillingham, a new homicide detective, walked into the holding cell. The kid jumped and then returned his head to the table.

"Recognize him? He one of your victims or something?" Taylor continued to stare at the kid in the cell.

Sophia moved close to the glass.

"I don't know him."

"Are you sure about that? Because in addition to asking for you by name, he had your name and number written down on a piece of paper in his pocket." Taylor glared at her from the reflection in the glass.

"I don't know him. But…"

"But what, detective?"

"I got a call right before I called you, from another kid in a case I'm working, and I think the two of them may be friends."

"And, what did this kid tell you?" Dillingham had locked the boy in the holding cell and walked into the camera room.

"He told me he had a friend who was in trouble and needed to talk to someone, but he wouldn't tell me anything else."

"Well, he's in some trouble, all right. He's a fuckin' homicide suspect."

Sophia looked at Dillingham and then back at the kid. "That

scrawny thing?"

"Yeah, that scrawny thing bashed in his stepfather's head with a garden gnome."

Sophia started to laugh but then thought better of it.

"So he had your number so he could confess to you?"

"I have no idea. Barrett wanted to help him."

"Jesus Christ, Benedetti. And who's Barrett?" Taylor said.

"His sister Grace…"

"Oh yeah, the rich kid with the special sister."

Sophia looked at Taylor.

"I'm kidding. Lighten up." Taylor took his phone out, looked at it and then put it back into his pocket.

"Benedetti, I want you to sit in on this interview with Dillingham."

Dillingham cleared his throat. "Hey Sarge, I think I can handle this…"

"Of course you can, but how many juvie's have you worked?"

"A killer's a killer. It doesn't matter to me."

"Well, this kid was probably going to call Detective Benedetti so I'm thinking it would behoove you to have someone in there who's used to talking to kids."

Sophia hated talking to kids. She'd never developed the comfort that people do after they have children. The only kids she didn't struggle with were her nephews.

"I'm sure Dillingham can handle this, sarge."

"You want to come to homicide? I suggest you get in there. Dazzle me with your brilliant technique. I'll clear it with your chain."

Taylor turned and walked out .

"I have no intention of participating, Ron. I'll just sit in the back and keep my mouth shut."

"It's not you, Benedetti. Don't worry about it." Dillingham walked out of the room. "I'll meet you in there in 5."

Sophia ran back to her office one floor below, and grabbed a legal pad. This was her chance to audition for Taylor.

The holding cell area was as clinical and brightly lit as an emergency room. The white walls were peppered with scuff marks. Cameras announced with stiff formality by signs in the hallway, that all conversations were recorded.

Dillingham was waiting for her along with his partner, Marty Kilhanny. Kilhanny nodded to her.

"Everyone ready?"

Sophia noticed a backpack and a paper bag outside of the cell. This was where suspect's property stayed until they were headed to jail.

"Let's see if you can help us break him, huh?" Kilhanny said. He chuckled and pressed the electronic lock button that released the door.

Sophia was the last to step in. She dragged a chair in from the hallway and positioned it so she could see the young man's face.

"Jared, I'm Detective Dillingham. This is Detective Kilhanny and over there is Detective Benedetti. We'd like to talk to you for a bit."

Jared looked at the two men and then at Sophia.

"I'll talk to her."

Dillingham looked at Sophia.

"For safety reasons, we're not going to let you talk to her alone. One of us is going to have to remain in the room."

"Then I'm not talking and I'll ask for a lawyer."

Sophia had never encountered a kid who'd brought up an attorney. She guessed that having a defense lawyer for a mother helped.

"It's in your best interest to talk to us, Jared. This is a big deal, not some fucking video game."

"I fully understand what's going on. I'm not retarded."

"No one is suggesting you are, but Detective Benedetti here, she doesn't do these kinds of investigations normally."

"How do you know what kind of investigation you'll be doing?" Jared sat back and looked at his hands settled in his lap.

"Well, we have a lot of questions for you, so maybe during the course of our conversation we can better understand what all we're looking at here."

Kilhanny stood up and leaned over the boy. "We're more than willing to consider this in the context of self-defense, but we can't look at that without your cooperation. You understand?"

Sophia had heard Kilhanny could sell ice to a penguin, but seeing his mojo up close was impressive.

"Fuck you. I'll talk to her."

"Big man." Kilhanny slapped the table so hard, it moved.

Dillingham pulled on Kilhanny's arm and motioned for Sophia to open the door.

"Let's step out for a minute and see what we can do here."

In the hallway, Kilhanny wouldn't look at her or Dillingham.

"Look, we've got a neighbor putting him there around the time of the murder and leaving in a hurry. We've got his fingerprints on the weapon, and we've got a motive. The neighbor said the stepdad was a real asshole."

"The fingerprints don't mean a thing," Sophia said."He lives there."

Kilhanny shot her a look.

"She's right, and I want a confession anyway." Dillingham turned to Sophia. "How do you feel about it?"

"I'm not afraid of him, if that's what you're asking."

"So you're good with doing the interview alone? I don't mean to be disrespectful, but we do things a little differently around here."

"Well, he's either going to talk to me or not at all. I don't see any downside here."

A woman spoke angrily in the hallway, outside of the

holding cell area.

Sgt. Taylor walked ahead of the woman.

"Is my son in there?" Her eyes darted between the three detectives and then back to the sergeant. She stepped toward the detectives, evading the outstretched hand of the sergeant.

Slapping the closed holding cell door, she screamed, "Jared. Don't say a word to these bastards. Nothing. Do you understand?"

Dillingham and Kilhanny each grabbed an elbow and escorted her out of the holding cell area and down the hall. Sophia waited until they were out of sight. She opened the door to the holding cell and peered in.

"Still want to talk?"

"Sure. I hate that bitch. Besides, she can't invoke for me. I'm seventeen." Jared smiled and stretched his legs under the table. "Let's do this."

CHAPTER THIRTY-FIVE

Sophia sat across from Jared and noted the time and date on her note pad. "I have to advise you that you're being video and audio recorded."

"Yeah, I can read."

She read him his Miranda rights and had him sign the form including the extra language that applied to juveniles.

"So, why did you have my name and number with you."

"I got it from Halifax. He said I could trust you."

"Ok."

"And I know, from stuff I've heard, that you're involved in that thing with his sister."

"But you're here for something else, right? Are you telling me there's a connection between your stepfather and what happened to Barrett's sister?" She looked up from her notepad where she begun to make notes in the margin about questions to ask.

"There's a connection between Ed and Barrett's dad, I guess. Yeah."

"Who's Ed?"

"He's my stepfather. Or was, I guess."

"Got it."

Jared looked up at the ceiling. "Can we just get this over

with? I mean, I know I'm supposed to ask for a lawyer…"

"Sure. Tell me what happened."

"I don't know exactly how they were doing it, but I know that Ed and Barrett's dad knew each other, and I also know that Ed was into some fucked up shit involving kids. At least that's what it looked like on his computer."

"Where is that computer?"

"It's in my backpack. One of the cops took it when they picked me up."

"And how do you know Ed and Stewart Halifax know each other?"

"I saw them arguing in a car at school. Halifax was really hot. He looked like he was going to pound Ed."

"You don't know what they were arguing about?"

"No." Jared yawned.

"You know what Jared, I'm going to step out for a moment and make sure that computer is still in the backpack. I'll be right back."

"Whatever." Jared leaned forward and rested his head on the table.

Sophia stepped outside. Kilhanny gave her a sideways glance and then looked at the brown paper bag on the floor outside the door. A cell phone rang, beeped and vibrated from inside the bag.

"I just want to make sure that computer is in his back pack." She reached into the backpack and turned off the laptop.

"Is that his phone?" She pointed to the bag.

"It's been going off non-stop. " Dillingham put his hands in his pocket and leaned against the wall. "You better get back in there if you're gonna keep him talking. Don't give him time to change his mind." He walked out into the hall.

Sophia looked at Kilhanney. "What's his problem?"

"He really doesn't like it when other detectives horn in on his investigations."Kilhanney said.

"I'm not horning in on anything. I don't control this kid."

"Yeah, well this is a homicide case, and you're not homicide."

"So what do you suggest?"

"I suggest you go in there and get a confession, detective. I'll smooth things out with Dillingham."

A young, lanky patrol officer peered into the holding cell hall. His radio crackled with chatter.

"Sorry to interrupt, but I don't think my partner told anyone about the second phone."

"I don't know anything about a second phone," Sophia said.

"The kid tried to slough it as we drove up. We found it in between a bush and the bus station. I'd be careful how you handle it. Looks like it's got some blood on it."

Sophia looked into the paper bag. A second phone sat at the bottom. She grabbed a pair of latex gloves from a box next to the jail elevator and pulled the phone out, marrying it up with the one from the bag on the floor.

"What do you think you're going to do with those?" Kilhanney asked.

"I'm going to ask him about them."

Jared lifted his head off of the table as Sophia entered the room. She sat down and put the phones in front of him.

"So, is this your phone?"

"Never seen it before."

"Really? Well, let's take a look." Sophia navigated to the contacts and scrolled to Jared's name. "This is really a strange coincidence." She turned the phone so Jared could see his name. "This is you, right?"

"I don't know."

Sophia put the phone down and looked at Jared. "Look, you said you'd talk to me and I took that to mean that you'd be straight with me about what happened. And that includes what's been happening, because I'm guessing that this guy," she pulled open a file and ran her finger down the sheet, "this guy Ed, wasn't exactly in the running for father of the year."

Jared smiled. "Are you trying to get me to admit I did this?"

"Did what, Jared?"

"Whatever it is you have me in here for." He shifted in is chair and ran his hand through his hair.

"You know why you're here."

A text message popped up on the face of the phone. Sophia flipped the phone around to see it. It read 'full of grace.'

"Who's this?"

"Don't know."

"But we're in agreement that this is Ed's phone?"

"Sure"

"And that you had it on you when the cops stopped you."

"I guess so."

"I'll take that as a yes."

"Yes."

Sophia scrolled to the beginning of the text conversation. It was several screens long. The first line read, 'Ecc 3:1, the season is now.'

She showed the screen to Jared. "This mean anything to you?"

"Nope."

At the top of the conversation was a phone number and the name, 'Mary.'

"Who's Mary?"

"I don't know. Some chick from church, maybe?"

"Church?"

"Ed was involved in some church down south. I don't know the name of it. Something Redeemer."

"So this is Ed's phone and you don't know who Mary is?"

"Yep."

Sophia noticed that during older text conversations, Ed had replied 'Hail Mary' every time 'Mary' texted 'full of grace.'

The phone shuddered again. "I ned to tlk. Call asap."

Sophia set aside the phone and sat back in the chair. She

knew at least a couple of guys were watching her through the one-way glass.

"Tell me what happened."

Jared looked up. "Starting when? When my mother met and married the prick, or today?"

"Start whenever you want."

"From the day she brought him home, you know, to… well… basically to let him fuck her…" Jared looked up at Sophia. "He treated me like shit. Like I was in the way. He was a total freak from his gnome collection to his weird friends, his fucked up car, all of it. A while back I got onto his laptop and I found some stuff…" He shifted in his chair and looked at the glass.

"What kind of stuff?"

"Kids."

"I'm not following you, Jared."

"Naked kids doing stuff…"

"Stuff?"

"Sex stuff. I found these sites, online sites, in his browser history on his laptop, and then I found a bunch of hidden files that had thousands of images just like it." Jared put his head in his hands. "And I found pictures that look like they were taken at the church."

"Have you ever seen Grace Halifax, Jared?"

Jared hung his head. Tears started to drop into his lap.

"I saw her on there. "

"On the laptop?"

"And on the internet. At that New World site."

"Let me get you some Kleenex, ok?" Sophia reached out and touched his hand.

As she stepped out of the room, Tommy met her.

"You're doing great, kid." One of the homicide guys must have called him at home.

"We need to get a search warrant for that phone, Tommy." She handed him a torn piece of paper from her legal pad.

"Here's the number. It's him. It's Stewart Halifax texting him."

Tommy took the sheet of paper and headed to the office. He almost broke into a run getting to the stairs.

"And get someone from the U. S. Marshal's service to start pinging that phone. I want that bastard." Dillingham and Kilhanny came out of the video room.

"He's gonna give it up, but get to the homicide. I don't want him getting all hinkey after discussing the kiddie diddling stuff. He really did a number on the vic. His head looks like someone drove over it with a hummer." Dillingham chuckled. "Sounds like he did the rest of us a favor."

There were still pieces of the case that weren't fitting together. Where did the rest of the assholes fit in? Loveschild, Martins, David and most importantly, Marcus Burton.

Sophia dialed George. It went to voicemail.

She glanced at her watch. It was a little after six AM. The early guys were starting to trickle into homicide. Her guys on the sixth floor would hear the rumors soon and make their way upstairs to eavesdrop or offer to help.

Jess popped her head into the hallway.

"Hey, can you take Paulson up to Dr. Halifax's house and sit on him?" Sophia said. "If he leaves, tail him. I have a feeling we're going to hook him up today.

"Sure. How's it going?" Jess said. She glanced into the camera room to get a look at Jared.

"He's doing ok. We haven't gotten around to the murder yet. He's pretty emotional." Sophia looked down the hallway. "Where did they take his mother, do you know?"

"I think she's back in homicide. I saw Turner and Wayne interviewing her. She was pretty calm. Think she could have killed the victim?"

It had dawned on Sophia for a moment, but she could see a lot of blood on Jared's t-shirt, there was blood on Ed's phone and the cuffs of Jared's jacket were ringed in red.

"He did it. But I think he's got a decent case for this, if you ask me. Maybe the mom will back him up, maybe not. In any event, he's a juvie, and Ed was a monster."

Jess started down the hall. "I'm going to grab Paulson and get up there."

Sophia was about to go back in with Jared after she grabbed him a Coke and some chips, when Dillingham stopped her in the hall.

"We ran up the victim. This church he belongs to is pretty popular. There's a few of them, but according to the wife, the one he went to was downtown. But there is one south of here and one on Queen Anne."

"Ok, thanks." Sophia started to turn but Dillingham stopped her.

"You know who else was a member, according to the kid's mother?"

"Who?"

"Burton."

"Chief Burton?"

"Yep. I guess he left them hanging." Dillingham chuckled at his own joke.

"Let's talk about what happened at home."

Jared tucked his hair behind his ears and looked at his hands. He scraped dried blood from underneath his fingernails onto the table and then swept it onto the floor.

"I hacked into his account and saw a bunch of pictures of kids."

"Including Grace?"

"Yes."

"Can you describe the pictures, Jared?"

Jared looked at Sophia. Tears welled in his eyes. "I'd rather not."

"But they were disturbing, illegal?"

"Yes."

"Go on."

"Ed beat me, he burned me with a lighter." Jared pulled back his jacket sleeves to reveal small, melted patches of skin.

"What else did he do?"

"He didn't rape me, if that's what you're asking."

"Ok."

"Mostly, he smacked me around when my mom wasn't home."

"Did you tell your mom?"

Jared smiled. "Sure."

"And?"

"And she didn't believe me. She's a lawyer. Everybody lies to her. She lies for a living."

"But you're her son, Jared."

Jared looked at the floor.

"What happened today?"

"He came home, started beating me. I tried to fight him but he's too strong."

"You couldn't get out of the house, get away?"

"I shouldn't have to leave my home."

"Fair enough. But you fought him anyway?"

"He attacked me. I hit him with one of those fucking gnome things."

"Gnome things?"

"Those ceramic trolls he collects. I picked it up and smashed his head in with it." Jared pushed his chair back from the table and stood up. "Is that good enough for you?"

"Sit down."

He pulled down his tee shirt and leaned against the wall. "I'm done. I did it. Get me a fucking lawyer."

Tommy was at his desk. She was spent, as though she'd run a marathon.

"Any luck?"

"Oh, you're gonna love this, Beni." Tommy was smiling. "Subscriber comes back to Stewart Halifax on that incoming number."

"You're kidding me."

"Yep. He's got two phones on the account. I'm waiting for the paperwork to come in via email. I think you better start writing up a warrant for the Halifax house and his computer."

Sophia sat down. "Barrett, George and Grace are in danger."

"As long as he doesn't know we're onto to him, they're ok. He's not going to hurt his own kids, especially not Grace. Fuck, she's been his bread and butter." Tommy leaned back. "God, I'd love to crush his skull."

"Me too. But we won't, right?"

Tommy laughed, stood up and tried to flatten out the creases in his pants. "Nope. I'm done."

"Good." Sophia picked up her phone.

"Hey, Soph. What was that phrase on the phone that got your attention?" Tommy was sitting rigid, staring at his monitor.

"'Full of Grace'. And then there was a text that answered 'Hail Mary' a couple of times like it was a greeting or something."

"Well, I'll be goddamned…" Tommy stood up and pointed

to his computer screen. "Look at this. It's the billing information from the phone company."

Sophia leaned over.

Billing info: Stewart L. Halifax and Mary G. Halifax.

"Mary. Her first name is Mary." Sophia sat at her desk and pulled up the screen to run WASIC and DOL. She flipped through her file to get Ginny Halifax's date of birth and typed it in.

The Department of Licensing screen popped up as Sophia scrolled through and deleted the information she didn't need and that's when she saw it - Mary Ginnifer Halifax.

Ginny Halifax was Hail Mary. She was pimping her own child.

CHAPTER THIRTY-SIX

Sophia called Barrett's cell phone. He answered on the second ring.

"Barrett, it's Detective Benedetti."

"Hey."

"I need you to listen very carefully to what I'm about to say."

"Is something wrong?"

"Is anyone at home with you?"

"Grace and George are downstairs. And my mother is glued to her fucking iPhone texting away like always. She's in a shitty mood."

"How about your Dad?"

"At work, I guess. I don't know. Why?"

"You need to get George and Grace out of the house right now."

"Why? What's going on? Is it my Dad?"

"No, Barrett, it's not."

"That's good then, right? I was wrong about him."

Sophia held back. "That's right. You were wrong about your Dad. I need you to get out of there. Take the kids to Volunteer Park. I'll meet you there."

"I can't tell my Mom?"

"No. Just go. Now."

Grace and George scrambled to their feet as soon as Barrett announced a trip to the park.

"Grab your stuff. We're going on an adventure," Barrett said.

He peered over the railing from upstairs as he led George and Gracie to the front door. There was no sign of his mother.

As they made the landing, George cried out. "Mommy, we're going on an adventure."

"Shh, George. It's a surprise."

"What's a surprise?" Ginny Halifax stood at the end of the hallway.

"We're going to the park. No big deal. Won't be gone long."

Ginny walked slowly toward them. "It's raining."

"I'll grab their raincoats." Barrett rummaged in the front hall closet, pulling out two yellow slickers. "Here we go."

"I'd rather you stayed home."

Barrett put the coats on Grace and George.

Ginny stood in front of the door.

"Mom, quit being so weird. We're just going to the park," Barrett said.

"Adventure," George shouted.

Barrett held his phone in his hand. Ginny reached out and grabbed it from him. She looked at the screen.

"Why is that detective calling you?" She gripped the phone and shook it at him.

"Because of Grace. This case."

"What has she told you?"

"Jesus, mom. Nothing." He pushed passed his mother and opened the door. "We'll be back soon."

"I'll keep Grace here."

"She wants to come with us." Barrett took Grace's hand.

"Go without her." Ginny picked up the little girl and shoved Barrett out the door and turned the lock.

"Where's Grace?" Sophia stepped from the car.

"My mom wouldn't let me take her with me. What's going on?" Barrett looked back at George sitting in his car.

"I can't tell you right now."

"My mom was acting like a psycho."

"Stay here with George. I'll call you."

Sophia got back in the car and called Pierson.

"We have to stand down. Grace is in the house with the mom. She wouldn't let Barrett take her."

"SWAT's already set up on the house. I'll call you back."

Sophia drove as fast as she could to the Halifax house, stopping at the road block traffic had set up. She parked the car, flashed her badge and jogged to the SWAT command vehicle sitting in the middle of the road.

"Who let you in?" The SWAT lieutenant, a young guy with only a few years more than Sophia, blocked her. He was six four and an easy two hundred pounds of solid muscle.

"I'm the lead on this case."

"You're not the lead here." He was dressed all in black, a large tactical vest covering his upper body.

"Did Pierson call you?"

"I'm a little busy."

"The little girl is still in the house." Sophia looked over his shoulder. "I'm Benedetti, by the way."

"Bloom. Dave Bloom. I don't want to be an asshole, but you really can't be here." He pulled out his phone. "I missed his call."

"The child is autistic," Sophia said.

"I guess this is about to become a hostage negotiation then."

"Let me talk to the mom."

"We have negotiators for that. Unless, you're qualified to do that, too." Bloom tilted his head to this radio mic. Sophia listened.

"The mother says she's going to kill herself and the kid if we don't back off." The transmission broke up but Sophia heard enough.

"Copy," Bloom said. He walked to the Bearcat, an armored vehicle used by SWAT in high risk entries.

"I've been in the house, Lieutenant. I've talked to the mom and the little girl."

A helicopter hovered overhead.

"Fuckin' media." Bloom spoke into his mic. "Someone call our media unit and tell them to get those assholes out of the sky over my scene. I can't hear a goddamned thing."

Bloom turned and walked back to her. "You're not going in, detective. We'll wait her out."

Even from a half a block away, the sound was distinct. One gunshot, then another.

The lieutenant gave the command for officers to make entry. Sophia listened to the radio as SWAT officers went from room to room looking for Ginny and Grace. Sophia closed her eyes and said the only prayer she remembered from Catholic school - the one to St. Anthony, asking him to find missing pets.

"We've got 'em. The girl is alive. Mother's in custody. Looks like she fired the gun to get us in here. Don't know what her plan was after that, but Stafford rushed her and took her down."

"Can I go get Grace? She knows me." Sophia said.

"Get over there. I'll let them know you're coming."

Sophia jogged to the house. The all clear order had been given and the perimeter was coming down.

In the doorway, an officer appeared holding Grace. The little girl smiled when she saw Sophia. Sophia walked up and reached for her.

"She's in shock, I think," the officer said as he passed her to Sophia.

"I've got you, Grace," Sophia said as she took the girl in her arms and walked her back to the car.

Before Sophia turned, Ginny appeared around a corner, her hands cuffed behind her. "Take good care of my girl, detective. I'll be coming for her."

"Over my dead body," Sophia said, pulling Grace closer.

Ginny laughed. "There's far more of us out there than you."

Pulling out her phone, she called Tommy. "It's over."

"So she's in custody?"

Grace was in the backseat. Sophia stepped from the car.

"Grace is with me. Ginny's headed downtown."

"You did good."

"I need someone to bring a car seat up here. See if Jess is free. I have to go tell Barrett and George. Get Stewart to the office."

"Are you all right, Soph?"

"Right as rain."

CHAPTER THIRTY-SEVEN

Tommy put his feet up on the desk and took a sip of coffee.

"So let me get this straight. Ginny Halifax was the ringmaster, Ed Sanderson was her right hand man and Loveschild managed the computer end of things. And they were recruiting kids from the church."

Sophia sifted through the dozen new files generated from the investigation. She'd be working this case until the new year.

"And Marcus Burton was their muscle. He gave them a heads up if cops got too close."

"That's about it." Sophia threw a file onto Tommy's desk. "Remind me again when you're pulling the plug?"

"Soon."

"So you'll be completely useless to me in the meantime."

"Pretty much. But you've got Jess. She's a workhorse."

"I resent that remark, Stinson." Jess said. She stood up and walked over to Sophia and Stinson's cubicles.

"More than happy to help, Sophia," Jess said.

Tommy smiled and looked at Sophia.

"What?"

"Nothing."

Jess laughed and walked over to the copy machine.

"So…"

"Stay out of it, Tommy."

"I'm just sensing a little chemistry between the two of you."

"Like I said."

"Back to our original discussion. So fill me in. Halifax figured things out and started taking the kid to a shrink? He had no idea his wife was some fucking kingpin of a child porn ring? That's pretty hard to believe."

"People will see what they can bear sometimes, I guess."

"And the woman in the photo was Ginny."

"Why were she and Stewart meeting Burton?"

"They weren't. They parked there for a Mariners' game. Ran into him. Burton was probably checking on the dead drop. Nothing related to the ring. Purely coincidental. David was in the wrong place at the wrong time. He thought he had the right bad guys but he only captured two of them in those photos."

"Poor bastard." Tommy put his feet down and stood up. "Killed for nothin'."

"Really? I think he was killed for a reason, don't you? Probably by some drunken loser with an ax to grind. What do you think, Tommy?"

"Why would I know?"

She was waiting for a sign.

Tommy turned away from her and fiddled with his pen. "He worked in the computer field, right? Maybe one of this geeky friends tipped him off. Maybe he was stalking you from across the street and happened upon it. Who knows? The guy's dead."

"It still doesn't feel right."

"Sophia, you're talking about people who rape kids and take pictures of it. And speaking of a drunken loser…"

"Jesus, Tommy."

"Hey, I'm just telling you like it is. He's out of your life and he's never going to be a threat to you again. That's a win, as far as I'm concerned." He put on his coat. "I'm taking the rest of the day off."

Theresa Blunt guided the Washington Audubon Society members closer to the shore of Spada Lake.

"The lake is just exquisite today, isn't it?"

The six women and four men, looked out across the lake and at the mountains surrounding them. All of them had binoculars of varying sizes hanging around their necks. Birdwatching guides tucked in their coat pockets, they excitedly waited for further instruction.

"Hey, is that an otter?" Henry Kadson stared intently into his binoculars.

"Not likely, Henry." Theresa pulled out her binoculars and looked out to the middle of the lake. Something bobbed in the water.

"Looks like someone lost a coat." Theresa looked again.

The object moved closer, rising and falling with the gentle tide of the lake. A soft pink nightgown was wrapped around the torso. A sheet of plastic, dotted with starfish, followed the body in the water.

"Oh dear," Theresa said. "Someone call the police. That's a body."

Bodhi jerked against Sophia, snorting a muffled bark. The tapping on the door was barely audible but the dog jumped from the bed and ran toward the front room barking frantically. Sophia looked at the clock. It was two AM.

She grabbed her gun from the nightstand and pulled back the slide to make sure a round was chambered. Maybe Ginny wasn't bluffing and she'd already outsourced the job to take Sophia out.

The house was dark except for the faint illumination from the streetlight out front. Sophia pulled back the blind and saw the tall figure standing on the porch, the hood of a ski jacket pulled up over his head. The figure knocked louder as though he knew she was home and couldn't hear him above the cacophony of barking.

Sophia tapped the butt of her gun against the window. The figure whipped his head around and pulled back his hood. It was Stinson.

"What the hell, Tommy? You couldn't have called me?" She opened the door. Tommy stood motionless on the porch. His eyes were bloodshot and watery, a sure sign he'd been drinking. The strong smell of cologne, the same one she remembered from David's crime scene rushed at her.

"What are you waiting for?"

"An invitation."

She turned from the door and leaned against the arm of the couch. Tommy closed the door and bent down to greet Bodhi.

"Hey girl," he said, patting her on the back and scratching her behind the ears.

He stood up. "I'm not going to insult you and ask you if you know why I'm here," Tommy said, shedding his jacket onto a chair.

"Go ahead and give it a try. I'd love to hear it."

Tommy sat across from her and rubbed his eyes.

"Just how drunk are you?"

"Not enough to not know what I'm doing."

"Which is what exactly?"

"I need to get some things in order."

"I'm not holding you back, Tommy."

"But you know. I could tell today. Actually, I could tell the other day."

"Did you wear the same cologne tonight to seal the deal?"

"I was drinking that day too."

"When you killed David."

"Yes."

Sophia picked up the Glock and put it in her waistband. The last thing she wanted was for Tommy to use her gun to do something stupid.

"So basically, you don't have the balls to turn yourself in?"

"I went to Montero's apartment to try and talk to him. To get him to leave you alone."

"What made you think I needed you to do that?"

"He called me a few weeks ago. Told me he'd been working a case on behalf of some woman." Tommy smirked. "Like he was some fuckin' super sleuth. It was a case I'd worked on back in the day. A rape that ended up a homicide. Perp beat the shit out of some poor college girl. Left her in a coma. She died three years later."

"I remember that case. The victim was Julia Proust. No wonder that name sounded familiar."

"And we knew who did it. Some piece of shit on the football team. But we didn't have enough."

"Why does this matter?"

"'Cause David talked to an old friend of mine who was suffering a pang of conscience and he decided to share with him that I might have assisted in getting the perp to confess by less than legal means."

"Jesus, Tommy. I don't want to hear anymore."

"That guy was guilty, Soph. He caved in that poor girl's face. He raped her with a broken beer bottle. He was a fuckin' animal."

Sophia stood up and paced.

"David wanted access to you. When I went over to talk to him he brought up the Proust thing. He told me he was going to leak it and take me down. He said he thought I was in love with you."

Sophia looked over at Tommy. "Was he right?"

"It doesn't matter."

"It matters to me and everyone else associated with this case and the Proust case, Tommy. You betrayed your oath."

Tommy stood and reached behind his back. Sophia pulled her gun out and aimed it at him.

"Don't."

"I'm just pulling up my shirt." He brought his hands around slowly and showed them to Sophia.

"Get out."

"Please."

"Your retirement party in tomorrow night. You're going to go and act like you're having a great time. And then you're going to head to the precinct and turn yourself in. If you care about me, you'll do it. Don't make me be the one, Tommy."

Stinson stood and picked up his coat. "I'm pretty sure the writing's on the wall, Soph."

"You better hope so."

CHAPTER THIRTY-EIGHT

The next night, the squad celebrated Tommy's retirement, while he was still on the job. It was the only way he was guaranteed to show up. There was a huge party at Jules Maes Saloon in Georgetown, a place where he sewed many wild oats in his patrol days.

The bar was dark, with tall ceilings and a bank of pin ball machines along one wall. It smelled like forty years of hops and cigarettes.

He was late and Sophia was suddenly seized with panic that her ultimatum had led Tommy to do something rash.

The door swung open and Stinson walked in, his jacket over his shoulder and his weapon on his hip. He was missing his badge.

Jimmy toasted him first. "To the best detective I've ever worked with."

Stinson glanced at Sophia. "I've passed on all I know to Benedetti. She'll do me proud." He turned to her and held up his glass. "Although I just heard you're heading to homicide. Congratulations."

Sophia forced a smile.

"Hear, hear." There was a round of applause.

The room roared to life with music and the baritones of

mostly male officers.

Sophia finished her drink and went to the bar for a re-fill. Sitting on a barstool by himself, was the suit from her firearms review board.

"Coincidence or business?" Sophia said.

The man looked up, then stood and took out his phone. "Business."

Sophia looked out the front window. A caravan of black Suburbans screeched to a halt in front of the bar.

"What's going on?"

"Excuse me." The suit brushed past her and met two other similarly dressed agents as they walked into the bar. She followed them.

The men pushed through the crowd until they got to Tommy. One of the men took the drink out of Tommy's hand.

"Thomas Stinson, you're under arrest for the murder of David Montero."

Several cops surrounded the federal agents.

"Back up, fellas. Let 'em do their job," Tommy said. He looked at Sophia. "I'm sorry. He hurt you. I had to make it right."

The circle of friends and colleagues widened to let the men move Tommy to the waiting cars. Jess put her arm around Sophia and walked her out the front door.

Tommy never looked back.

A hand gently pressed her shoulder.

"Wake up."

Jess sat next to her on the bed and handed her a cup of coffee. Sophia sat up and propped a couple pillows behind her.

"Did you spend the night?"

"Yes. On the couch."

"I don't remember much about last night." Sophia pressed her temples. "How much did I drink?"

"I wasn't tracking but let's just say you must come from hardy stock."

"Just a lot of alcoholics."

Despite an aching hangover, Sophia weighed the option of telling Jess about her conversation with Tommy. Would she understand that Sophia had given Tommy the unprecedented courtesy of letting him turn himself in?

"Look for what it's worth, I made a call to a friend at the Bureau. They've been looking at Tommy for a while. The investigation was referred by the department to the public integrity squad at the FBI. They've been working this for months."

"But…"

"His prints were all over David's apartment, Sophia. His DNA was on David's skin, for chrissakes. That's why he wasn't around that day when you and I went to Queen Anne to meet with David. And he didn't come to the crime scene because a witness described him to the detectives."

"Why would he be so careless?"

"He wanted to get caught?"

Sophia sighed and closed her eyes.

"He was in love with you, wasn't he?"

Sophia stiffened. "How…?"

Jess laughed. "Some of the guys were even convinced you two…"

"Never."

"I know."

"And not because of that."

"That?"

"Never mind." Sophia laid back down. "So Taylor had a clue the whole time?"

Sophia's phone buzzed on the nightstand.

"Speak of the devil." Jess handed her the phone.

"Fuck. I don't want to talk to anyone, especially not him."

"Take the call." Jess stood and walked to the door. "I'll be in the other room if you need anything." She gently closed the door behind her.

"Benedetti, it's Taylor. You still half in the bag?"

Jesus, what a prick.

"I'm just having a cup of coffee."

"Good. Make sure you're sober or at least swallow a bottle of mouthwash. You're in my squad now. Grab your gear and meet me at the office in an hour."

"I…" Sophia swung her legs out of bed, glanced at the clock and stumbled toward the shower.

"Your mine now, Benedetti."

Sophia threw the phone on the bed and stripped off her sweats. She was really going to have to work on Taylor's attitude.

She didn't belong to anyone.

THE END

Made in the USA
San Bernardino, CA
07 May 2017